Bomb Boy

A Novel

Jay Grewal

Redemption
Publishing House

Redemption Publishing House

This book is a work of fiction. Names, characters, places and incidents are products of the author's imagination or are used fictitiously. Any resemblance to actual events or persons, living or dead, is entirely coincidental.

Copyright © 2018 Jay Grewal

Photograph taken by Niclas Hammarström

Cover designed by Jay Grewal

All rights reserved, including the rights to reproduce this book or portions thereof in any form whatsoever. For information please contact the author directly at JGrewal@AuthorJay.com

ISBN: 9781792181450

DEDICATION

To my nephew, Paras, and my niece, Sarah, dreams most definitely do come true. You just have to want them bad enough and understand that there is no victory without failure.

ALSO BY JAY GREWAL

A Slave to Want

The Sound of Sunrise

AKNOWLEDGMENTS

I have to start by thanking my incredible friends, Sanjeev Grewal and Anju Sohal, for reading this manuscript in its rawest form, and for giving me advice throughout the entire process. You were both just as important to this book's completion as I was. You are more than just my friends, you are my spiritual gurus, guiding me through this journey.

Thank you to my parents for always making sure I had everything I needed to chase after my dreams. Through all the judgements and the encouragements (both of which were needed to fuel me), you showed me what it means to be *better*.

I want to thank some special people like Mojan Motamedi, Aman Grewal, Prab Grewal, Raman Sekhon and my brother, Surinder Grewal, for believing that I might just have something special inside me to share with the world.

Thanks to Aliyah Khalil for the translations, and Nathan Tyson and Victoria Phillips for helping me with military protocol as it was very important and integral to the story.

PREFACE

After the US forces invaded Iraq, a kind of madness drifted on the wind. It became the four-way intersection where hysteria, panic, fear and remorse collided with such significant force that a part of you was instantly maimed in the collision. Right and wrong became these abstract things that I would debate about after the fact, in the silent recesses of my mind, where the only judge and juror was me.

I don't think anyone truly understood the tremendous scope of the operation. They thought Saddam would simply fold over and the rest of the country would follow. But resistance is a funny thing. We are programmed to resist. It's the single greatest quality that mankind possesses and also the most terrifying. Resistance came in droves, as various groups fought for power. Prophets exchanged their prayers for guns, politicians exchanged their ballots for bullets, and the real war had officially begun. Massive bombing raids commenced on cities where millions of people lived. Innocent people were left dead in their wake.

Some experts frequently referred to the invasion as a 'fatal mistake'. Iraq quickly became an illegitimate child that nobody wanted to be responsible for.

After Saddam was overthrown, a kind of fear lay about at the feet of that city and in the lap of every man, woman and child. Although some good was done, we still felt the pang of the conquered.

The very same eyes that held us, now avoided us, the same hands that welcomed us, now pushed us back, the same lips that praised us, now shouted obscenities in countless languages. It was all just too much. Too many women in widow's black, mourning not only their husbands, but sons and daughters as well—a sea of grief. Bodies lay on the ground, more bodies than hands to bury them. Iraqi women grieved over their husbands, their hands grimy and black with dirt as if they had buried themselves as well. I remember their cries as they saw us. They yelled with the full force of their voices, "Yalla imshi!" which meant go out from here.

Back home they spoke of our victory, yet slowly our victory faded and we became, not saviors, but death dealers in a ghost-ridden town. Three million internal refugees had been displaced without school, electricity, healthcare, clean water and food. Devastation was everywhere. Where families once gathered, corpses now lay; where homes once stood, the listless now slept; where crops once grew, barren fields now sat; where laughter once rang, fearful whispers now spread; and where children once played, men with guns now roamed. That's not a victory by anyone's standards, especially not mine. Then again, our opinions didn't really matter. We were just the fall guys.

CHAPTER 1

Sadr City, Iraq, 2005

"Santoli, burn that motherfucker!" I heard over my radio.
It didn't feel right to kill a man while he was praying.
"Take the shot, Santoli! What the hell are you waiting for?"
I guess I was waiting for it to feel right…or just less wrong. But sometimes your orders and your morals will collide. Unfortunately, orders carry more weight, and they win every time.
"Santoli!"
If a man thinks it so shall it be…and so I thought it. The word *kill* appeared in my cortex and my brain fired the motor neurons inside my spinal cord, which sent a chemical impulse down to my muscle, causing my finger to squeeze the trigger of my M16. I could feel the raw power surging through my arm. Split-second chaos. In that moment I was God, and I decided who lived and who died.

Pulling the trigger engaged the sear which released the hammer. The hammer struck the firing pin and pushed it into the primer. The powder combusted inside the case and sent the bullet down the barrel and out of the rifle. Once the 5.56 caliber round left the muzzle it became a projectile, capable of killing anything, everything. It was death, wrapped in a full metal jacket, travelling at a speed of 3,260 feet per second.

Suddenly I was reminded of Newton's first law of motion: Every object in a state of uniform motion tends to remain in that state unless an external force is applied to it—in this case, the head of an Iraqi insurgent.

Do you know what a round like that does to a person's head? It's like drilling a hole through a watermelon. There isn't much blood at first, then as they hit the ground, it oozes out like an oil spill out of a tanker. But I didn't flinch; I couldn't. This was now my life. I was a mailman, delivering bullets to bodies. No postage required, no overnight express, just a blink of an eye delivery system.

While searching for my next target, I heard a hissing sound near my position. *Hiss* meant the bullets were close. From the adjacent rooftop, black hoods descended upon me, while enemy Kalashnikovs rang from the distance. It was just another Monday morning. I hadn't even had my breakfast yet, just two cups of coffee to keep me wired.

The hissing soon became a snapping and the enemy was only a few yards away. Struggling, sweating, with my finger twitching, I pulled the trigger and emptied my magazine, turning brains into scrambled eggs.

I looked down at the city street, and in the midst of gunfire, an old Iraqi man sat on a bench reading the newspaper as if it was just another ordinary day. It took a car exploding for him to finally grab his shit and make a run for it.

The sounds escalated, growing increasingly more intense, until finally, the din of bullets stopped, and I heard the words, "All clear," through the radio.

When I got down off the roof, a bloody body lay before me. There was no stepping around the blood; it was everywhere, so I stepped through it and dragged his spirit across the dry Iraqi soil, back toward the Humvee. "Coming out!" I shouted.

The wind blew red dust in all directions, and through the grit, all I could see were pulverized buildings, threatening to give out, discarded shrapnel, pools of blood, and wasted banners ignorantly celebrating liberation, while the ones next to them were begging for God.

But that's war. And our sergeant used to say, "War doesn't determine who's right; war determines who's left, and I'm planning on living until the end." That was Rev, AKA Reverend Ernie Castor. He was one of those overachievers, who had a shelf filled with trophies and a wall covered with medals. He was even born two months premature. I guess he couldn't wait to get his life started. He probably even started walking at six months. But for all his achievements, he was a humble man. He spoke of God in a way as not to offend you, but to make you think about the deeper questions from a different perspective.

He was always ready to debate an atheist at the drop of a hat. "Every man has mentioned God's name at one point in his life, even if it's just to denounce Him," he would say. "Me? I'm trying to believe in something bigger than myself." It was no wonder he became the consciousness of the group. It's a comforting feeling when you have a leader who can make the right decisions, especially at times when even you don't know what those are. I suppose it was hard for him to lead a team like ours, we were a team of bastards, after all. There wasn't a single father among us—not one that mattered anyway.

Never before had you seen four men who had no purpose being together forced into each other's company. There was Corporal Arrigo Batali, who most would describe as a peaceful man. He was twenty-five-years-old and spoke Arabic and Farsi fluently. You could spot him from a hundred meters away. He walked with this distinctive hunch. A million years of evolution, yet Batali still couldn't walk upright. His shoulders were always slouched forward, and he had a slight curve in his spine. When I asked him if there was anything wrong with his back, he replied, "No. I just got used to walking this way. Walking upright is exhausting."

His chicken neck would always pitch forward anytime he spoke. Not exactly the kind of behavior you want when you're on recon. He couldn't look around a corner, without projecting his entire head forward. But at least he was harmless, which is more than I could say about our Grenadier, Aries Alvarez, a twenty-one-year-old brash punk. I honestly didn't know what he was doing in recon; he was clearly an infantry jarhead. A grunt. He was younger than me but built like a tank. A towering trunk of nonsense is what I used to call him. He was 6'4, 250 pounds, with big, battering ram arms and legs the size of Roman columns. He had a twelve-gallon head and a gash on the hollows of his cheekbones. A professional wrestler is what he reminded me of most. It was no wonder, since he wanted to become one as soon as he returned back home. But someone should've told him there were no cameras around. He spoke as if he was on Monday Night Raw, calling out an opponent.

As I returned to the Humvee, he slipped on a pair of Oakleys and said, "I am the Marine, which makes me a machine, well-oiled, programmed to follow orders, to seek out and destroy. My emotions are shut off, my adrenaline is pumped up, and I come guaranteed with a one year warranty—anything beyond that and the Marine Corps can't be held accountable!" The overwhelming pride came out through his loud, obnoxious voice. "I am the Marine!" he would say as if it was his professional wrestler name. "Ooooooooooooh-rrrrrraaaaaaaaaaah!" He always held his ooh-rahs for six seconds just in case someone missed it. Then he would kiss his dog tags and smile like he was sitting at Sunday dinner with his family.

His aim was shit, that's the other thing I remember about him. But with a full magazine, I guess it didn't really matter. Screaming at the top of his lungs, he let loose like some 1930's gangster in a low budget film: his fingers chattering, gut churning, legs pumping, heart racing, brow beating and pits sweating. Everything quickly became Swiss cheese: doors, buildings, cars, wagons, and yes, even his target. What he didn't hit from a direct shot was inevitably caught by a ricocheting bullet.

He stood, arms slung over the crossbars of the Humvee, with a cigarette between his greasy fingers. He blew a perfect smoke ring and watched it rise into the air.

I smirked at him and said, "It looks like you put a bullet in pretty much everything in a two-block radius."

He took his shades off and gave me the finger, while flicking his cigarette at my chest. "Let's get the hell out of here. Our work is done."

I looked up from the American eagle inked on his massive arm to the reflection of my own face in his giant pupils, "Whatever you say, buddy."

Suddenly, I saw a man lurking in an alleyway. It was my job to assess every threat, big or small. He was in traditional garb with a bandana covering one eye, a disdainful look in the other and a cheap Iraqi cigarette in his ailing fingers. He looked me in the eyes, fearless and yelled something in Arabic. It's funny how an unknown language can still make sense on the inside. I heard 'asshole'. I might have been wrong, but not by much, maybe not asshole, maybe devil, bastard, baby killer. What's the difference? I got the gist of it. It meant leave my country, leave us alone, stop killing. I said nothing in return. I did my job. I assessed the threat. He wasn't dangerous, just some store clerk, merchant, vagabond, hiding out, waiting for the bullets to stop.

From behind him, a little boy came running out and stumbled, landing on his knees, right on top of a ragged flyer shouting: FREEDOM! Out of his dirty, soiled hands, spilled out empty shell casings, which he was most likely trying to recycle.

He stood up and looked back at our war machines and foreign flags and trembled. His long black lashes and the intense flex of his brow brought my attention to his powerful brown eyes that seemed to have their own gravitational pull. Although he was just a boy, he looked as if he had lived an entire lifetime. He stared at me unblinkingly, and there, I remained, trapped in the corners of his eyes, unable to look away. His small, soft face—blackened from the dirt and debris—spoke in volume, the tortuous road that had shaped out his life: a labyrinth of love and hate, filled with crusades of hope.

After a minute, those young, innocent eyes finally blinked, releasing me from their hold, and I heard Alvarez yelling, "Let's get the hell out of here!"

When I looked back, the boy was gone, scurried back down the narrow alleyway I'm sure.

We all got into the Humvee and headed back to our Forward Operating Base, which was located on the outskirts of Baghdad, just north of Sadr city. As soon as we crossed the border, we saw exploded vehicles on the side of the highway, dead bodies and disintegrating buildings.

From the backseat, Alvarez slapped me on the shoulder and said, "I could go for a second round right now."

I smirked. "The pawns are done for today."

"I aint no pawn. I'm a King, you hear me!"

"You're a drone, Alvarez. We all are."

He grabbed his dog tags as if they were his resumé. "This is who I am," he said. "I'm a Marine, and Marines follow orders." He said it as if that's all we were, as if being a Marine was what would define us one day.

The comment didn't sit well with Batali. "Not me. I'm more than a piece of metal hanging around my neck. I'm more than just my blood type, my religion and my last name. My memories are not on this piece of tin, nor are my hopes or my dreams. A craftsman crafts and still he has his handiwork. What does a Marine have, but blood and tears?"

"We're the right hand of America," Alvarez fired back. He was just as clumsy with his words as he was with his rifle—both aims were off.

Batali's superior debating skills would, however, reign on this day. "That hand can be righteous or fatal depending on who's swinging it. Iraq is definitely a threat and I like to believe that we're here to stop that threat, but that's not all we're here for. After all, a war is not initiated by soldiers; it's paid and bought for by duplicitous men in suits who drive down the price of oil. Men who have never set foot in afflicted countries or bled for anything meaningful, yet watched from above on satellite streams, sipping coffee in their armchairs. If you really want to see chickens with their heads cut off, just tell the pencil-pushing geeks on capitol hill that the price of crude oil is rising."

"You don't know what the hell you're talking about," Alvarez said, flicking Batali's ear like a third grader.

But Batali finished his thought. "The greed of oil is what will lead to the downfall of man. Correction: *has* led to the downfall of man. This world should've been counted in dollars, not souls. The population is fifty trillion, and still the interest accumulates. Life is expendable, while dollars are invested, and sadly too many dollars have been invested in making life expendable."

"Be careful, Batali," Alvarez warned. "You're starting to sound like the locals."

He smirked. "You leave water in a plastic bottle long enough and it begins tasting like plastic."

I turned to Rev to see what he thought of Batali's words, but from the look of it, he didn't think anything at all. He sat in the passenger seat, calm as could be. And when we came across a shepherd on the road who was tending to his flock of a hundred or so, Rev said, "I will not be led astray, and no shepherd may lead me." I guess it was his way of saying, he had already made up his mind and was protected from all other ideologies.

We came to a stop and waited as the shepherd herded his sheep across the dusty terrain. Through the window, I watched in wonder, the colors of sunset: a tangerine, saffron sky, that looked like it was painted by Claude Monet. It floated over the landscape, which waited patiently to swallow up the setting sun. The nameless wind brought with it stories of summer times spent floating down Galena river, with my cousin, Kelly, in an old kayak our grandfather had left behind. We would go fishing using homemade rods that Kelly had whittled out of two old broomsticks in woodworking class. We'd stay out there by ourselves, talking about girls and random dreams, watching the world through the unadulterated sunlight. Only at that brief moment when we were wedged between night and day, would we finally head back home, running barefoot through the afterlight.

With all the disappointments and regrets in my life, those rare poignant moments—which passed all too soon—were all I had to keep any shred of imagination alive within me. I had consciously surrendered over to my memories when Alvarez's axe-like voice brought me crashing back down to reality. "Can this guy hurry the fuck up already!"

    The herd had cleared the road, and I put away my smile, somewhere deep down, to be resurrected later when I desperately needed to get away from this place.

CHAPTER 2

Every morning, the loudspeakers of a nearby mosque would wail *Adhan*: a call to prayer. The whole country was seeking out God. Even the most hardened fighters didn't fight during prayer. When prayer started, the fighting stopped; when the praying stopped, the fighting began immediately—one right after the other. Such a strange contrast, guns and God, I mean—creation and destruction, side by side. But they never stopped praying, not once, not even after the bombing raids. Maybe they thought if they did, the guns would take over entirely. Something tells me that in the end there will only be one: Guns or God.

As I splashed water in my face and looked up into the mirror, my mind skipped a beat and for a second, I didn't recognize my own reflection. He looked much older than what I remember, his eyes were hardened and creased with pain, his hair was thinning, falling out, due to the stress, and his lips were dry and cracked—a perfect portrait of sickness. I've aged ten years in only three. It all seemed so surreal. Not like a dream. As a matter of fact, I hadn't had a single dream since I had arrived in Iraq. It was clearly a bad sign. Maybe my brain thought *this* was the nightmare, so by the time I closed my eyes it was too exhausted to conjure up anything else.

I gave my head a shake. There was no time to waste in self-reflection. I had to be re-upped, regrouped, reassessed, reassembled, restarted and ready to go. That's war for you; it's a Band-Aid, not stitches. They want your body fully functional, even if your mind isn't. I thought to myself *I killed three people last night, but no one cares, there'll be more causalities today and again more tomorrow.* I had gotten used to driving into bullets and bombs, day after day, getting shot at, getting mortared, often with no idea what our objective was. I couldn't recall what happened yesterday, or the day before that, or the one before that, only that it happened. Time wasn't a thief as much as a kleptomaniac out here. It was all routine: wake up, shower, eat, shit, and suit up. I had become good at routine.

As I stepped outside, dust hung in the air, the kind of dust that never quite settles: soft, just waiting to escape the ground. It didn't matter if you had allergies or not, here, the dust inflamed everything: your throat, eyes and sinuses. It rose into the blistering hot air, which was shaping up to break the hundred-degree mark. Even this early, the heat was oppressive. The sun was so hot that it turned an M16 into a branding iron, which could only be handled with gloves.

As I reached for mine, I saw Rev over by the head shed, talking to Nadeel. She ran a local orphanage, taking care of children who had lost their families. I had seen her on the base before, collecting donated supplies and rations, but I never had the opportunity to talk to her.

I remember the first time I saw her, everything in my head went quiet. My inner voice took a seat and let me observe without judgment, her olive skin, earthy eyes, green and hazel, which reflected her pretty red hijab. She was beautiful. Not the kind of beauty you see on the cover of Cosmo, but the kind of beauty you see on the cover of National Geographic—a lost beauty, something not of this world. I could give you a million different literary tools to describe her, but she wasn't made up of metaphors or analogies, she was flesh and blood. I remember thinking if she was a woman then I had never seen a woman before, not one like her anyway. There was something so humble about her, like she was the first prototype in a line of better women, returning back to the nature of what women were supposed to be, what God intended them to be: loving, caring, strong, confident and powerful.

As I admired her beauty, I heard Alvarez's loud obnoxious voice rise up from behind me. "Damn that bitch is fine!" He was that hair you get in your eye that you just can't get out, that apple peel that gets stuck in your teeth. He was a blockhead, a stone-cold hick from some godforsaken, backwoods town in the middle of nowhere.

Just as Nadeel got into her old pickup truck, our eyes met for a moment, and I entertained the possibility that someone like her would ever go for someone like me.

"I'll definitely be thinking about her tonight." Alvarez said, ruining the moment.

I tried changing the subject. "You ready to roll out?"

"I'm always ready. I have to hold myself back at times."

"Can't wait to get shot at, huh?"

He smirked. "This is war, and I'm Aries, the *god* of war."

"Of course you are," I said, egging him on. "You're a beast, buddy."

He smiled as if it were a compliment. I could tell he wasn't the kind of man who had friends—clearly, since he couldn't distinguish between a sarcastic remark and a sincere one.

He nodded toward the head shed. "Here comes Baseball."

I turned around and saw Staff Sergeant Ryan Benson, AKA Baseball coming our way. He had skin like a baseball mitt, a wide stance, a lazy curve ball for an eye, and the way he smiled at the young recruits, you'd swear he was a switch-hitter.

Alvarez smirked. "This piece of shit's finally got the courtesy to get up off his ass, out of his air-conditioned office, and grace us with his presence."

As much as I disagreed with Alvarez on practically everything, he was right this time. Benson was a complete asshole; I couldn't stand his face. He had one of those faces you just don't like, but you can't explain why. Maybe his eyes reminded me of some two-bit bully from high school, perhaps his nose had a bump that subconsciously made me think of the crotchety old man down the street, or his mouth had the characteristics of a mean old teacher. Whatever it was, something about those features collectively put together just didn't sit well with me.

Benson shouted, "Attention!" and we all huddled around the Command Operations Center for a debrief.

Every time he opened his mouth, I remember thinking, *Go fuck yourself.*

"Listen up Marines…" he continued.

Go fuck yourself.

He got two inches from my face, saliva spewing from his upper lip. "After exploiting and assessing all the information at their disposal and analyzing possible sightings, Intel is confident that they have a possible trace on Abdul Razzaq. You're rolling out right now."

A drop of his saliva landed on my cheek, but I didn't flinch, I just thought *Go fuck yourself.*

He shouted, "Dismissed!"

Go fuck yourself. That one almost slipped out of my mouth.

We were heading on patrol through some of the most dangerous areas in Iraq. I strapped on my 782 Gear: sixty pounds of gear and ammunition, which weighed more heavily by the hour. My shoulders had gotten used to the weight, strapping it on and off, through three months, working eighteen to twenty-four hours, patrolling from one end of nowhere to the other. Not to mention through all the mortar fire, IEDs, barricades, poverty, starvation, displacement camps and violence. After witnessing all that, I felt more comfortable with my gear on than off. It had become my security blanket—one that I wouldn't dare venture off without.

As we rolled out of the base at zero-six-hundred, I was wired. I had to be. Here, if you're not awake, you'll most likely end up dead. I didn't dare yawn. I couldn't afford the distraction.

Within a matter of minutes, we were stuck in the eternal clots of traffic that filled the dusty Iraqi streets. Large diesel-fueled machines coughed thick, black smoke, while sitting side by side with cars and buses, rushing toward toppled-over buildings, trying desperately to make appointments that were never penciled in. Even with all the chaos within the city, I couldn't help but notice how interesting this place was. The first few days I saw Iraq one color at a time: the soft green glow through night-vision goggles, a city cast in red by the jutting flares, and yellow through my protective shades. But there was some color here, not much, but some. It was definitely a place where minds were led by stories of kings and biblical events, as described in the Bible or in history books. This was the cradle of civilization, Babylon, Mesopotamia, a place the world had long forgotten…until now. Sadly, it took these events to bring our attention back to this place, and I mean complete attention.

We trekked through Sadr city on high alert. Over a million people crammed into a several square block suburb of Baghdad. I remember how before I arrived in Iraq I was imagining a simple place, one filled with farmers, mud-brick buildings, and blissful ignorance. But that wasn't exactly the case. We were immediately taught that you can't underestimate your enemy. A crude bomb can kill just as many men as a sophisticated one can. Blood can be spilt, bones can be broken, and flesh can be torn with only a sharp stick. This mentality made everyone a threat, even women, even children.

I remember how the streets of Sadr city felt more like a sideshow circus than anything else, one made up of bulletproof horses and iron elephants. There was the world's most combustible man, the armless child, the never-ending line of widows, and lo and behold, the greatest freak show of them all. The single biggest oddity. The killing machine. The Marine.

We made our way through the narrow alleyways and torn, cobblestone streets, with children waving Iraqi flags at us and chanting, "America go home!"

I noticed one of the flags was faded blue with an off-color stripe. The kid had painted over the red, white and blue stripes of Old Glory and turned it into some abomination. He looked at me and shouted at the top of his lungs like a drill-sergeant, "America go home!"

To be proud of a country is an important thing, but what pride was there in a broken city, filled with poverty and devastation. It was just as useless as having a jacket in the summer or holding a candle in the sun. How could they be so cavalier when only a few feet from them was an orphan lying by the wayside, wrapped up in a representation of his country: a torn Iraqi flag, which he used as a blanket.

The sight of him brought my feet to a standstill and the weight on my back felt twice as heavy. This was the only way Iraq could comfort him now. There would be no warm, cherished memories of his home. It was a sobering reminder that the ones who have the least to gain, suffer the most.

Rev pushed me off my stiff pose and said, "Keep moving."

And so I did. Through the sight of my rifle, I saw a narrow view of the world—too narrow to have an opinion that counts.

We continued on, heading deeper into the maze of alleyways, when a sudden movement put us all on edge. All rifles rose quickly.

"What the hell is it?" I asked.

Batali's stare was intense. "Something shot behind that truck over there in the corner."

All rifles were ready. My heart was pounding and I could feel a sense of temporal tunnel vision (a sort of cognitive narrowing). All other thoughts evacuated my mind, leaving me to focus solely on the idea of survival. With the back of my hand, I wiped the sweat from my brow and prepared for what was most likely going to be a shootout. Training helps prepare you for situations like this, but truth be told, eighty percent of it is totally unpredictable and unorganized. *Here we go!* I thought. *Time to get some.*

As we took aim, from behind the vehicle, a dog came running out.

"God damn it!" shouted Alvarez. "Those fuckers are everywhere."

The entire city was filled with stray dogs; they were in every nook and cranny. They were like the ghosts of a dead city. Their heat signatures and quick movements had us on edge. The stray stopped and stared at me as if it knew something that I didn't yet know, some soul secret, which was beyond my comprehension. This war had gone to the dogs. The longer I stared at it, the more I felt heat exhaustion setting in. Under moments of extreme stress and exhaustion, your eyes begin to play tricks on you, which is a scary thing given the fact that this place was strange enough on its own without any other mental afflictions.

I got caught in the dog's gaze. It looked at me almost in recognition, its ears pricked high and tail still and flaccid. It had a scar on it that ran from belly to back, letting me know that it was indeed a survivor. Its eyes were vulnerable, yet fearless, reflecting my own. I could see its mouth opening, as if about to speak some important message, but before I could make it out, I heard that incessant sound of bullets again.

Rev shouted, "Contact right, fifty meters!" He was illuminated by bright, white flashes. It was mortar fire.

Alvarez and I looked at one another. We both knew what was going on: ambush.

Multiple blasts stunned us. We all sought cover from the direction of the enemy fire.

They dropped in a gas bomb, which limited our visibility. Stuck in that squalid alleyway, I heard something coming toward me. I quickly spun around and trained my rifle in the direction of the sound. The lingering smoke continued to obscure my sight. I scanned for a target. I heard it coming, getting closer. Whatever it was it sounded big.

In the distance, through the smoke, a large object appeared. It fanned toward me, quickly filling my line of sight. It came right at me, and I dived out the way. It was a donkey that was caught on fire, wailing as it ran past me.

Rev's voice cut through the din. "Return fire!"

We attempted to gain fire superiority through suppressing fire.

Bullets kept barking out from behind me.

Then suddenly, a young boy appeared in front of me as if he

materialized out of nowhere. In the crook of his arm was an Ak-47. I shot him a hostile look and he fired back with a look of contention. I couldn't tell if he was a friendly local or part of the militia. There are no ranks or uniforms out here, and guns don't always mean enemy. Good people were fighting for their survival as well.

If it were any other day or any other time, I wouldn't have hesitated to shoot, but it was as if I had reached my mental quota for the week, as to how many lives I could successfully take without breaking down. With my weapon trained on him, in broken Arabic, I said, "Ermee elmastara!" (Throw the ruler down!)

Wait. That's not right. The correct words escaped me. Who could remember in a moment like that?

Neither one of us blinked, neither one of us could afford to. I could hear his labored breathing over the gunfire. He was out of breath—perhaps from the attack, or simply out of fear. He looked scared, not like an insurgent who had taken countless lives, but like a boy who was just trying to make sense of it all. He stood before me, his shoelaces untied and tears pooling in the corners of his eyes. He still needed his mother to tell him to put his coat on before going out or tie his shoes before he tripped over his own feet.

A long silence passed, the first moments in what would be one of the most defining moments of my life.

I tried again to get him to stand down. "Ermee elmusadas." (Throw the gun down).

This time the words sounded right.

He must've got it that time.

A hint of recognition took over his face and he looked like he understood me. He looked like he was about to reply with some comforting words. He looked like he was about to put the gun down. But his true intentions, I suppose we'll never know. Because just as he opened his mouth, through the smoke, I heard Alvarez behind me, yelling, "I got him!"

My words emerged slowly. "Wait...wait." Too slow to matter. Too slow to help. Too little too late.

An empty shell casing flew through the gun's ejection port, and I wished with all my might his bullet would miss the boy, harder than I have ever wished anything in my life. Harder than I wished I never met my ex-girlfriend, Sophia, when she told me she was pregnant. Harder than I wished my father had stuck around for longer than a minute.

Harder than I wished my mother to stop drinking away her pain. But wishing is a pastime fit for fools, and it has no purpose in the real world.

The shell floated—still and harmless now—through the air and fell to the ground in a clink of horror. Even with Alvarez's shitty aim, the boy didn't stand a chance. A spray of blood floated just above his head like a light spring mist and his face twitched as if a fly had landed on his nose unexpectedly. His eyes rolled back into his head and his weapon slowly peeled out of his hands. Bullets are much faster than words, I'm afraid.

The words, "Don't shoot," fell softly from my lips, just as the boy fell forcefully to the ground, dust clouding from his shoes.

He was going to put the gun down. I know it. I know he was. I could see it in his eyes.

Alvarez remained unmoved by the act. "You're welcome," he boasted as if he had saved my life somehow.

I said nothing in return. There is no black or white in a warzone, only shades of grey. What one man sees another may not, what one man feels another may not. Sometimes that kind of thinking saves your life, and sometimes it breaks your heart. Today it was the latter. But Alvarez wasn't wrong to shoot, nor did I blame him. This was war, after all. You hesitate, you die. He saw a threat and assessed it. He didn't see what I saw: a scared and confused child, trembling. He didn't see the waterworks or the emotion on his face. Then again, he didn't have the time. Better to be riddled with guilt than bullets is how he saw it. I'm not sure the two are all that different.

Sadly, the day was just getting started. I'm sure they'll be a few more fatalities before it's done. You can count on it.

As I stepped over the body of the boy, I saw a chocolate bar in his shirt pocket, half melted, with smudges of it still on his cheek. He was just a stupid kid. It was a sad sight to see. Life taken in the midst of youth is no different than an abortion too late aborted. I should know.

The gate of one of the houses flew open and a woman emerged. Her screams pierced the air. With a shattered soul, she rushed to the boy's side, cradling his head, which contained a pencil-sized hole right through the center of his forehead.

I looked inside the home and saw two more children huddling underneath the kitchen table. The boy was an innocent. He was just protecting his family. The new man of the house. Clearly his father wasn't around—probably dead.

His mother cried aloud, her lap covered in blood. It was still pouring out of him, through the exit wound.

Alvarez stepped over her, trying not to look down or look back.

The woman was hysterical. She saw the boy's flaccid shoelaces and began tying them as if he was five-years-old and heading off to his first day of school...or clearly his last.

She looked up at me, slack-jawed and hopeless. Jabbering in Arabic, she called me, "Jinn," which were spiritual creatures who inhabited an unseen world. The Quran says they're apparitions made of a smokeless and scorching fire.

Alvarez had no remorse for her. "Move the fuck out the way!"

I knew I couldn't count on him to be there emotionally. Like a man convicted of a misdemeanor he would be the first to *bail*.

Machine guns barked, and I tried to push the woman back into her home, but she wouldn't leave her son's side. I tried lifting him up, but she wouldn't let me. She yelled, "La tlmsho!" (Don't touch him!)

Seriously? Now my Arabic comes back to me?

I told her it wasn't safe. There were more guns coming.

She ignored me and began dragging her son back into the house by his dead arm, painting a bloody streak on the cobble-stone in front of her home—the most unwelcoming of welcome mats.

As much as I didn't want the other children to see the body of their brother, there was nothing I could do. Tiny screams joined the woman's wails inside, filling the home with pain, while out in the alley, the bullets kept coming.

Alvarez took cover behind a nearby cart to maintain effective fire against the enemy.

For a moment, I was frozen in the alleyway, as if someone had just injected me with a suicidal virus. The attack was still going on. Bullets whizzed by me.

I heard Alvarez yelling, "Get down asshole!"

Out of the several rounds fired in my direction, not a single bullet hit me. *Perhaps I am Jinn. Unseen. Untouched. Invincible.* My body sought cover on the side of the house, while my spirit walked through the walls of the boy's home and saw him lying there on the floor, with his family huddled over him, inconsolable.

Before I knew it, I was back in my body, a place I never really left, but the heat will make you see and feel things that aren't possible—the same heat that had nearly dried the boy's blood on the street. Time had already forgotten him it would seem; yet at the same time, my hands were still wet with his blood. I wiped them on my pants, just as Alvarez ran out from behind the cart and joined me on the side of the house.

After a few minutes, Rev and Batali ran to our location. "We're gonna get fucked up staying here." Rev took one look at me and the blood on my hands. "Are you shot?"

I snapped out of my paralysis and shook my head. "It's not mine."

Rev quickly assessed the situation; he knew we were a greater force than our enemy. He pointed up ahead. "We're going into *that* house to establish a base of fire."

Not the easiest task, mind you. Every house in Iraq had a six to eight-foot wall encompassing it. And the closest one—the one Rev decided on—was no different. Just by eyeing it, I could tell it was a good eight feet high.

Rev gave me that look that said *you're up to bat*.

My survival mode kicked back in and I slowly got ready to run.

Rev, Batali and Alvarez laid down effective fire, while I bolted for the wall. It was one of the most vulnerable positions to find yourself in: gun down, back to the enemy. In a situation like that, if you're lucky you'll get one, maybe two tries at scaling that wall, before the enemy catches you in the back.

I took in a deep breath and shot out like a bullet. Three steps before the wall, I prepared myself for the leap of my life. I slammed into the wall with the full force of my body. I didn't get very high. I heard a bullet ricochet off the brick wall near my head. With a final burst of energy, I pulled myself up and over, landing on the other side. I quickly negotiated through the entry gate and opened it up for the rest of the team.

Alvarez came in first, then Batali, and Rev—who was always the hero—trailed a couple meters behind, making sure the rest of us were safe.

The house gave us an increased advantage in terms of firing position to be effective against our enemy, not to mention greater cover to reorganize and communicate for air support.

"I only got one mag left," Alvarez said.

"I'm running low as well," Batali added.

"Conserve your ammo," Rev ordered, "we're going to need every bullet. Who knows how long we'll be held up in this place waiting for reinforcements." He began calling into headquarters. "We need close air support." Unfortunately for us, the messages weren't getting through to the base. "We'll have to secure the roof, to get better reception."

"I'll check it out," I told Rev.

Before I could move, he grabbed me by the shoulder. "Now's not the time to get caught up in your head. We need you."

I pushed the thought of the young boy to the back of my mind. "Yes Sergeant."

"I'll go with him," Alvarez said, taking the lead.

We walked through the abandoned house, which still had family portraits on the wall and a trail of clothes lying on the ground. Another family that had left everything they knew behind, hoping to escape the war.

Alvarez picked up a framed picture of a teenage girl and leered over it like a dirty uncle. "Too bad this place is empty. I wouldn't mind being locked up in here with this chick."

I was too exhausted to even role my eyes. "Let's get this over with."

We were headed toward the stairs, when I noticed a sawed-off shotgun in an open metal safe box under the stairs. Hoping to find some ammunition, I dumped the box on the ground and started sifting through it. The only items that were of any use were a box of flares and a single incendiary round. Grabbing the shotgun and pocketing the round, we ascended up the stairs to the roof, which made for a perfect stronghold.

Thank God for the stuffy, muggy nights in Iraq, for which people built five-foot walls around their rooftop to sleep within. It was our best bet to win the fight.

However, just as I opened the door to the roof, enemy bullets punched shafts of light right through the door. POP-POP-POP.

"Sniper on the adjacent roof!" Alvarez yelled.

"No shit!"

The rooftop was too vulnerable. The enemy had a greater height over us. It was only by a couple of feet, but in a firefight even an inch counts for everything.

"We can't expose ourselves," Alvarez said. "We're gonna have to use the second story windows."

"Wait," I replied. "I think we can get him."

"What are you smoking? No way we got a clear shot from here.

They're shooting out of draining holes in the wall. We have to suppress the enemy, and quick, the sun is going down. We don't wanna be stuck here the night."

"Both you and I know that seizing that roof is the quickest way out of here." I cracked the door a tiny bit. "Now you see that small wall by the cot?"

Alvarez took a quick glance. "Yeah, I see it."

"One of us gets behind that, while the other uses that oil drum to cover him."

Alvarez raised a brow. "So, who's it gonna be?"

"I'll do it," I said. "I'm a better shot."

"What makes you think you're a better shot than me?"

"Trust me, I don't wanna put my neck on the line, but the truth of the matter is, my shot's more accurate. Not to mention you only have one mag left."

Alvarez had no choice but to concede. "Alright. It's your show. You provide the lightening, I'll provide the thunder. Just make sure you don't fuck this up."

Suddenly, the firing stopped, and I knew that somewhere the sniper was either reloading or exhaling a long breath to steady his aim. I looked to Alvarez. "Cover your ears!"

I wound up and tossed a flashbang fifty yards out onto the next roof, in hopes of disorienting the enemy.

"Now," Alvarez said to me.

We were off like two horses bolting out the paddock at the Kentucky Derby. I quickly sought cover behind the small wall, while Alvarez used a large oil drum as his shield and watched my back.

The shots kept coming toward the door. The enemy didn't see me. I lay prone, psyching myself up, before taking two deep breaths and putting my eye to the scope. Aligning it with an area in the wall pocked by shell marks, my crosshairs tracked across rooftops, following blown trash, swaying fronds and ragged curtains flapping in the wind— anything that had the slightest movement.

"Where the hell are you?" I whispered to myself.

Then by accident, I landed on the shooter—or rather the arm of his jacket, which quickly moved back behind a barrier. He was a hundred meters away, situated in a nest, with nothing exposed. He was clearly well trained. I had no clear shot, even from my new position. And to make matters worse, the sun was nearly gone. It's funny how time lapses like a movie scene when you're watching the world through a scope. You're the only one standing still, while everyone moves on without you.

Alvarez gave me a nod and mouthed the words, "Do you have a shot?"

I was about to shake my head, when I suddenly noticed a pile of firewood just behind the enemy's position.

An idea shot through my mind: I still had the incendiary round in my pocket. I quickly loaded it up into the sawed-off shotgun and trained my sights on the enemy. Compensating for windage, I steadied my arms and took in a breath. Just as the enemy raised his rifle and took a quick aim at Alvarez, I took aim at the large pile of firewood. I only had one shot at this before exposing my position. I took in another breath, and my finger pressed down on the trigger. BANG! In the blink of an eye, the incendiary round lodged itself in the wood.

I watched carefully through my scope, hoping to see some smoke, but there was nothing. *Hell, it was a one in a million shot anyway.* Suddenly my arm twitched and my scope wobbled off-target by a whole city block. As I moved back to the enemy's position and looked for another opportunity, I saw a hint of smoke rising from the wood.

It can't be.

The round had done its job. It was one of those *holy shit* moments. It's funny where the brain goes in moments like that. I guess we really don't have too many victories in life. I remember thinking how I had never made such an accurate shot like that in my life—not in sports, not at the carnival, not even at home with my dirty socks in the hamper.

The wood slowly ignited, without the enemy's knowledge. I watched and waited until the entire pile lit up, putting the fire to the enemy's back. He began kicking it, hoping to knock it over or just get it away from him. The lit pieces of wood began dropping down on him one by one.

Trying to escape being burned alive, he exposed himself, running right into my scope. As he reached center, he was met with a bullet POP. I saw the red mist floating above his head, just before he laid out flat.

Alvarez looked almost upset that it wasn't him who had made the shot. With an expressionless face, he radioed into Rev. "We got the roof."

Just when we thought we were in the clear, a semi down on the street, filled with barrels of gasoline, ignited, setting ablaze everything around it. Palm trees, like Roman candles, burned in the twilight—a scene right out of Dante's Inferno.

"These Hajjis are crazy!" Alvarez shouted.

I carefully looked over the walled-roof, and was met with a shower of dust, fragments of brick, and burning leaves from a long row of burnt palms. I could see people fleeing down alleys, trying to get away from the warzone.

Since the area was too hot for air support, the QRF (quick reaction force) was dispatched to retrieve us. Rev took out a flare gun and shot a flare to direct them to our position. His flare arced across the distant sky like some man-made constellation. It momentarily aligned itself with the bright blue star of Bethlehem—one, a sign of peace, and the other a sign of distress. It floated above the city, painting the buildings red, and bathing us all in its fiery light. It was as if we had descended into hell.

We were quickly evacuated back to the base, where I dropped my battle gear and instantly shed a hundred pounds. Most of it was equipment, but I felt myself losing mass. My eyes were sunken, my cheeks were concave. I looked like a corpse. I had sweated off at least fifteen pounds since I had arrived in Iraq.

I immediately went to the showers, across from the barracks. Stepping into the crammed shower stall, I turned on the water and stood beneath the stream, cleansing myself of a day that began a very long time ago. I could feel blood dripping off of me. I was covered in it. It wasn't mine. It belonged to the boy in the alley. I could almost see his face reflected in my wash basin. He was barely fifteen. Why couldn't he have stayed inside, hidden under the table with his family? Their entire life was now changed forever. Without any negligence or intention found on Alvarez's part, their son would most likely be written off as a casualty of war, a death fee paid on his behalf, and life simply goes on.

Back home, the challenges children face seemed simple in comparison. School shootings, as devastating and overwhelming as they are, are still rare. Here, a boy gets shot in front of his home with an M16 in broad daylight, and it's just another day. Every time I see something like that, I lose a bit of myself. My morality shrinks to the size of a mustard seed, and I find myself desperately searching for a glimmer of hope. By the end there'll be nothing left of me but a sullen uniform and a pint of blood—both of which will do me no good if I don't have hope.

As I stepped out of the shower, Batali came into the latrines to take a piss. He stared at me in the mirror, a cold look on his marble face, as if he could read my mind. "You alright?" he asked.

"Yeah, I'm good."

"You sure? I've seen that look before. I've had that look before."

I let out a breath. "Just thinking about that kid in the alley."

Batali paused a moment. "What came first, war or peace?" he asked, changing the subject...or so I thought.

"Peace?" I replied, not fully understanding where he was going with the question.

He shook his head. "War, of course. What is peace without war? Not even a word. War came first. War is inevitable, and only human beings are capable of it. We're the only animal capable of savagery. Animals only know how to hunt and eat, man, on the other hand, makes a conscious decision to kill. He plans and plots a demise." His eyes slowly drifted away from mine. "It's in our nature to destroy ourselves," he continued. "As long as men have built things to protect themselves, others have built things to kill them. Someone made the bulletproof vest, the next day, someone made an armor piercing bullet. Someone created bullet resistant glass, and the next day, someone made a rocket propelled grenade. The oldest skulls in the world have blunt force trauma. That means if someone took away all the weapons in the world, we would find a way to kill each other with sticks. Take away the sticks and we would cut each other with our words and kill each other with false promises of peace. That's just who we are." He stared straight at me, hiding nothing. "So who cares if some die in our war for peace, there's no crime in killing the already dead. It's just humans being human...right?"

I glared at him and shook my head. "I know you don't believe that."

"It's not about what I believe, it's about reality, or rather the reality of *this* place and *this* war." Batali simply turned around and walked out, leaving me alone.

I found no comfort in his words, mostly because there was a level of truth to them.

CHAPTER 3

At zero-seven-hundred the next morning, an entourage of black Suburbans approached the Forward Operating Base. At the first initial checkpoint, guards carefully examined the contents of the SUVs and took the occupants' weapons before allowing them to enter.

Through the dark tinted windows of the middle vehicle, the light from a lit cigar illuminated the silhouette of a man. I could see the figure fading in and out as he sucked on the cigar—the lit embers breathing life to his face. The window rolled down and a pair of black Ray-Bans appeared. Suddenly, the front doors opened and through the trail of smoke, two men exited, dressed in expensive three-piece suits. They opened the rear door and out stepped Mr. Ray-Bans, otherwise known as Abrehem Abbas Muhammad Al-Mahdi. Now there's a mouthful for you. He was in his mid-sixties with salt and pepper hair, and a pair of broad shoulders that had held up over time. He had a quiet focus about him, which added to his all-commanding mannerism. His suit was a finely tailored three-button Armani, his cigar, only the finest Cuban stogie, and on his wrist was a gold Rolex that could've paid for my college tuition, if I ever got accepted to one that is.

A four-man security detail surrounded him, nearly blurring him from view. He pulled the Ray-Bans down to the bridge of his nose, revealing the intense look in his eyes, which were alert, cunning and smart.

Ryan Benson, with his mannequin-like charisma, flashed a dopey grin and greeted Al-Mahdi by the gate, shaking his hand. Even some suits from Langley had shown up to praise Al-Mahdi and personally thank him for his support. As they stood there, negotiating, what I can only presume was Al-Mahdi's intel fee, Benson patted him on the back and nodded, accepting the terms of their agreement. They exchanged pleasantries and cigars—two bullshitters trying to bullshit each other about bullshit. Al-Mahdi looked uncomfortably over at his aide, Samir, who looked down at his watch and then gently nodded, as if to say *everything is on schedule.*

Benson escorted Al-Mahdi and his entourage across the base, toward the communication's tent, where the rest of us waited for the meeting to begin. Benson walked right past us, a folder in one hand and a plastic evidence bag in the other. He stepped to the podium and opened his folder, while forty officers—seated lecture hall-style—waited for him to speak.

"Intelligence sources believe that the recent attacks in Sadr city are being carried out by *one*, very skilled Terror Cell. He pulled out a bloody shirt, still dripping wet, from the plastic bag: a pale blue button-down, something a manager of a Walmart would wear. Benson nodded to the young boot standing below the television and he inserted a tape into the VCR. It was a grainy video showing the latest beheading of an American journalist. With all the resources at these terrorist's disposal you'd think they could afford better recording equipment.

A man in a head wrap, yammered propaganda, while another stood ready with a machete in his hand, ready to cut the poor son of a bitch's head off. The man looked up into the camera, revealing the fear in his eyes—the kind of fear the western world could never imagine. The biggest concern back home is hoping you don't get mugged. But these men don't care to mug you. The only thing they want from you is blood. There is no negotiating with them. We have nothing they want. Only our immediate evacuation from their country could stop them. Wait. *Stop* is the wrong word, *redirect* is more appropriate. Because men with power never surrender it, they only redirect it.

In this case, however; it was too late. There was nothing we could do. Down came the blade and washed the spider out. The journalist's body fell over, and the floor became wet with blood. If you've never seen a beheading before, it's quite surreal. We've seen so many fake beheadings in movies that there is a part of us that is jaded by it, but the other part that knows the difference between real and fake is suddenly reminded how much a man's head being cut off, looks a lot like a tree being chopped down. It's not a single clean motion. They have to hack at it, through the bone and cartilage. Meanwhile, the victim is feeling every blow, slowly bleeding out. It's very disturbing to say the least.

As the video concluded, Benson recapped by saying, "Now for those of you who don't speak Arabic, let me translate for you. He said, 'Blood of the infidels will pour—enough to drown everyone standing in our way'. The insurgency is getting stronger. They have men everywhere, even in the upper echelons of the government. We have to fight fire with fire. To that end, let me introduce you to our fire: Abrehem Abbas Muhammed Al-Mahdi, who has emphatically endorsed America, even during Saddam's reign."

He said it like Al-Mahdi was a saint who had blessed America. The same man, who only minutes ago, was compensated for his intel. Still, they introduced him as if he were doing this out of the goodness of his heart.

Al-Mahdi, who at this point, had just been standing in the back of the room, observing, took the podium like a Baptist preacher taking the pulpit. He cleared his throat, and in accented English, addressed the men. "Iraq is currently infected by an ideal, which is hatred disguised in a mask of nationalism to fool the people. It is an ideal that is being spread by a very dangerous man. They call him Abdul-Razzaq: The Provider. He has been accused by the United States government of providing financial and material support to Al-Qaeda in Iraq."

Al-Mahdi's aide took notes as he spoke.

"Make no mistake about it," Al-Mahdi continued, "like all important leaders, he is not seeking martyrdom. He's the kind of man who wants to be alive long enough to see the fruits of his labor. Hopefully by working together we can put an end to this man and his campaign." Al-Mahdi lingered on the mic for a second, making sure to look every Marine in their eyes.

Benson then once again took the podium and reiterated his thoughts. "As the days go on, Mr. Al-Mahdi will be meeting with our team and sharing his intel. Thank you, gentlemen, you're excused."

As the meeting concluded, Benson introduced Al-Mahdi to our team.

He reached out his hand and said, "Asalaam Alaykum" (Peace be upon you). His hands were like sandpaper. Not the hands of a business man, but the hands of a man who had worked his way up the ladder, built himself up from nothing, out of ruins. You can tell a lot about a man from his hands. I don't trust soft hands anymore. They seem conceited, judgmental, too delicate to have done anything meaningful in this life. I'm afraid I might crush them even in my most softest of grips.

Benson told Al-Mahdi about the latest attacks and his aide, Samir, began reverse engineering the entire attack, tracing out the path of the insurgents.

Samir was a smart man. If I didn't know any better, I'd swear he was brought in for his expertise in forensic ballistics. Just by looking at the pictures, he knew what kind of bullets the insurgents used, what gun they came from, what angle they were shot from, and the distance they covered. He turned to the map pinned to the bulletin board and pointed to a building two blocks away from the explosions. "Here!" he said. "This is where they were standing." He immediately knew. "This is all consistent with what we have learned about Razzaq. He is within the city." He drew a line across from the attack zone to two obscure locations. "These are the safe houses that they operate out of."

"Well what are we waiting for?" Rev said. "I can get a live-Op going right now. In two hours' time, we'll have a team in place ready to move on the target."

Al-Mahdi humbly put up his hands and said, "Rabbana afrigh 'alayna sabran."

"Excuse me?" Rev said, looking at Al-Mahdi

"It's from the Qur'an," Mahdi replied. "It means 'Our Lord! Pour upon us patience'. It was chanted by the army of David when they went forth to meet the army of Goliath. We have to be patient now, things are not that easy. This area houses many insurgent sympathizers. My sources tell us that Razzaq will be meeting with his generals this week. Better we get them all with one stone."

Alvarez shook his giant melon of a head, "Why would these people help him out?"

Al-Mahdi took off his Ray-bans and handed them to his security guard, who cleaned them and handed them back. "Where you see the enemy, they see a revolutionary," he said. "Every villain walks a fine line. There is not a single one born who looks in the mirror and sees a villain; he only sees his own version of the truth."

"Truth has no versions," Alvarez fired back.

"Oh, I'm sure you have a few back home who don't see the difference either."

Alvarez snorted. "Regardless, these aren't Bond villains; they're second rate henchmen. They'll never see us coming."

"They're a lot smarter than you think, with a lot more firepower than you can handle alone." Al-Mahdi was right. The scariest thing about humanity is that even the most inept man can start a fire that even the best of us can't put out.

Alvarez went to open his big mouth again, and Rev instantly shot him a definite *stand the fuck down* hard eye.

Alvarez had no choice but to bite his tongue. I could tell he was ready to explode, however; he wasn't exactly the kind of man who took criticism well. Then again, what's a grunt like him know about building nations anyway? Politics were not exactly his strong suit. The only business suit he had ever worn were his cammies, the closest thing he had to a tie were his dog tags, and the only thing resembling a briefcase that he ever held was his M16. He was trained to kill, and that's all he was good for. So, he did the only thing he could do: he walked off by himself, shaking off the comment.

The briefing ended and Al-Mahdi exited, his assistant right behind him, looking nervously at his watch. Al-Mahdi was about to step into the Suburban when he looked up and our eyes met for a moment. He gave me a courtesy nod to confirm we were on the same side, but I hadn't yet decided if that was the case. Not that it would've mattered even if I had. If they ordered me to protect him, I would. If they ordered me to take him out, I would. My allegiance lay with my country; my own views of the man were irrelevant.

Benson had assigned a squad of two Humvees to escort Al-Mahdi's security detail. Although he preferred to avoid arousing the insurgency of our newly found alliance, Benson insisted that he was a high-priority and we had to assure his safety.

Al-Mahdi reluctantly agreed, and our convoy rolled out in a plume of dust. The security detail blasted along a desert highway, with one Humvee in the middle, carrying Bravo Company, and ours tailing the last Suburban, which contained Al-Mahdi, his aide, Samir, and two security guards.

Alvarez was behind the wheel, driving like a man possessed. Rev sat in the passenger seat, while Batali and I sat in the back, bracing ourselves for certain death—if not from the enemy then surely from Alvarez's driving.

"What the hell are these jerk-offs doing?" Alvarez shouted.

"They're all over the road!"

"Stay calm," Rev said, "that's standard procedure. At this speed, they'd be able to tell if someone were tailing them."

"Someone would need a Ferrari to keep up with these guys." Alvarez amused.

Suddenly, something appeared ahead on the highway. The voice of Sullivan from Bravo Company came over the radio, "We got movement on the road."

A mud-caked truck sat in the middle of the road, broken down and abandoned.

The lead Suburban came to a stop a hundred yards from the unoccupied vehicle.

"What the hell is this?" Alvarez squawked.

Rev turned to me. "What do you think it is?"

I shook my head. "Could just be a broken-down truck, or it could be an IED. Your call, Rev."

Alvarez kept checking his rearview mirror. "Something doesn't feel right."

"Pull up to the Suburban's window," Rev commanded.

Alvarez pulled up side-by-side with Al-Mahdi's SUV.

He rolled down his window and Rev said, "It could be a trap. We should take an alternate route."

Al-Mahdi looked to his aide, who nodded. "I agree."

"You have the lead," Al-Mahdi said to Rev.

Rev slapped Alvarez on the shoulder. "Let's move out."

In the middle of reversing the Humvee, a rocket-propelled grenade flew out from the back of the cargo truck, and detonated into the first SUV, causing a huge explosion. Shrapnel and debris were everywhere.

"What the fuck!" Alvarez shouted.

Together, we sat on the edge of our seats, caught somewhere between fear and rage.

Al-Mahdi's security began shouting on their walkie-talkies. As they prepared to reverse their SUV, rogue shots were fired from both sides and the driver of Al-Mahdi's Suburban was shot in the head.

Camouflaged in the sand, two insurgent members began shooting at the first Humvee. Sullivan and his team aimed their weapons and returned fire, killing the men immediately.

The remaining Suburbans were now sitting ducks.

"Wait…what's that?" Rev said, pointing off into the desert.

The barren range came to life as something moved. The heat waves and the light refraction off the desert-scape made the object undulate rhythmically.

"What the hell is that?" Batali said, his voice cracking in fear.

It was a huge off-road vehicle, barreling straight toward us.

Alvarez leaned on the horn, yelling, "There's another one!"

It was another vehicle coming from the opposite side, impossibly fast.

Rev shouted, "Weapons ready!"

With the help of Bravo Company, we began firing at them.

But the off-road vehicles stayed on course.

One of them hammered the lead Suburban's driver side, causing it to barrel roll. The passenger was launched out his window, head-first. Blood and dust heaved into the air as wild shots rang out from all directions.

"We got rapid-fire left and right!" Rev shouted.

Batali got into the turret and began firing the .50 cal machine gun.

Bullets snapped into our windshield, starring the glass.

The enemy fired on Al-Mahdi's Suburban from the side windows. The clean, showroom-grade truck quickly became a block of Swiss-cheese. The window of the Humvee beside the seat where I was sitting was cracked, but still in one piece. *Thank god for bulletproof glass.*

Rev shouted, "Open fire!" and we fired back with everything we had.

Alvarez barked out a full magazine into the land cruiser. "Get some!"

The bullets kept coming, tearing the Suburban in half. *Surely nobody could've survived this absolute cluster-fuck.*

Rev looked over his shoulder at me. "We gotta get Al-Mahdi out!"

I gave him a nod. "I'm on it."

Sullivan, along with Rev, made sure I was covered.

Staying low, I stalked to the rear, right side of the Suburban. All its vital fluids were leaking; the bulletproof windows—having met their breaking point—finally shattered, and all four wheels were now giant deflated soufflés.

Rev continued to provide supporting fire from the Humvee.

A bullet snapped past my face and I stumbled back.

Rev emptied his magazine, taking out the two insurgents, who were firing at me. One of them, he shot in the shoulder, the other, square in the jaw.

He threw me a nod and I threw him one back, letting him know I was alright.

By this time, Batali had completely decimated one of the land cruisers with the machine gun.

It's easy to lose yourself in moments like this, but we're trained to keep our composure. I had a job to do and I was going to do it. I quickly got to my feet and wrestled open the back door of the Suburban. To my surprise, Al-Mahdi was still alive. Not a single bullet hit him. The security guards had taken the full brunt of the attack.

His aide, Samir, reached out a bloody hand from the front seat; he was still alive as well.

"Can you walk?" I asked Al-Mahdi.

He nodded.

I peeled open the passenger side door, extracting Samir, which wasn't an easy task. He had taken a bullet in the arm and was losing blood fast. He began screaming something indecipherable—delirium most likely.

Another bullet just barely missed us, and we bolted sideways trying to get the enemy out of our line of sight.

I dragged a barely conscious Samir awkwardly through the chaos, back toward the Humvee. Opening up the back door, I helped him inside.

Al-Mahdi, who hadn't even given Samir a second look, quickly jumped into the backseat and slammed the door shut.

Rev messaged Sullivan to turn around. He then turned to Alvarez, shouted, "Get us out of here!" and hopped back into the passenger side.

Alvarez quickly got behind the wheel, reversed a hundred meters, completed a one-hundred-eighty-degree turn, and roared back down the highway, followed by Bravo Company.

Our eyes flickered over, just in time to see another truck, blocking off our path.

Rev shouted, "Push past it!"

Alvarez stepped on the gas. "Alright boys, hold onto your balls!"

We hammered the truck head on, while Rev took one clean shot at the driver, who was still fidgeting with his rifle. A surgeon couldn't have done a better job of removing the man's eye than Rev's M16 did.

Alvarez jumped on the gas and we raced off, back down the

highway. "I think we're clear."

Even after we got past the chaos, my finger remained hovering over the trigger of my rifle. I couldn't seem to let it go. My heart was pumping at an incredible pace.

All five of us sat without speaking for what seemed like an hour, but I'm sure was only twenty minutes—the longest twenty minutes ever. It took Alvarez's garbage mouth to finally acknowledge that we had in fact survived. "I think I shit my pants."

"I think we all did," I replied, finally taking a regular sized breath.

I wrapped an SOF tourniquet around Samir's arm. "The bullet went clear out the other side," I told him. "You'll be fine."

He sighed and then looked to Al-Mahdi, who was nearly catatonic, his face held tight between his hands. Samir patted him on the back as if to say *everything was going to be alright*. The gesture was an interesting one, seeing as how Al-Mahdi didn't think about Samir for even a second, while the attack was going on.

As we drove, and the sun slowly descended into the landscape, I sat there thinking about my life. I guess death defying moments like that really make you think about the beginning. I looked up into the fading sky and the millions of sparkling lights that slowly emerged. It's amazing how many stars you could see out there. *How funny is it*, I thought, *that there's a universal order to things, governing something as large as a star and as tiny as an atom, yet there is no universal order to man.* Our bodies obey the laws of physics and time, but our behavior contradicts order with every turn we make.

The stars reminded me of the endless days of summer and the Fourth of July, watching the look on people's faces and how they grew bright by the symphony of fireworks. I remember climbing my favorite tree in my grandmother's backyard, trying to see the thunderous skies, while feeling the wind sweep past my face, and recite its poetry through the red, white and blue, which hung on the roof of my grandmother's house. I hadn't really appreciated a night sky like that for a long time. But as I mentioned, being that close to the end makes you think about the beginning.

Back on base, Alvarez recounted our ordeal for the platoon. He went on and on as if it were the greatest battle of all time, exaggerating all the while. Instead of six shooters, there were now ten. As if six weren't enough. As if even one wasn't enough to kill everybody.

"Thank God the enemy was a bad shot," Alvarez proclaimed. "These Hajjis can't hit anything without an RPG, I swear."

I looked to Rev, and he gave me a little shrug, which was his way of saying *let the baby have his bottle.*

"They haven't made a body bag big enough to hold me!" Alvarez continued. "I'm a bad, bad man! You remember that you towel heads!" He shouted into the air. Then out came the wrestler's callout. "These assholes still aint impressed by my power. Well I said it before and I'll say it again, I am unbreakable! My bones might as well be made out of Adamantium. I bleed liquid nitrogen and spit battery acid. I am a 6'4, 250 pound runaway freight train. I am big, I am bad, and I am unstoppable. They're all choirboys compared to me! *They* are not the ones to fear. *I am* the one to fear! Alexander was not a conqueror, he was 5'6 and 150 pounds; I am a conqueror! Genghis Khan was not a barbarian, he was 5'10 and 180 pounds; I am a barbarian! I'm the one you don't want standing across from you. I'm the one you don't wanna find in a dark alley. I am the monster under your bed. I am the Marine! Ooooooooh-rrrrrraaaaaaaaaah!"

It was a sad display. Men like Alvarez, who wanted war, the very definition of it, and nothing less, were glad to listen to his stories. I remember when I first met him, he bit down his lawless tongue and yelled, "Let loose the dogs of war!"

Ironically, that's exactly what they were, with their dog tags dangling around their necks, a bark in their throat, shouting, 'Get Some!' They were here with a bone to pick—that much was clear.

Just as Alvarez concluded his over-exaggerated account of the details, I saw Sullivan from Bravo Company off by the corner of the base. He was perched on a slab of torn concrete, sitting there with one hand under his chin and the other resting on his knee—a true reflection of Rodin's Thinker.

When I approached him, he slowly looked up and gave me a solemn nod. "Another close one, huh?"

I smirked. "Too close for comfort."

A smile escaped his lips, but his eyes fell victim to the sad, little voice in his head. His facial expression soon followed. He shut his eyes, and there was a moment before he reopened them, where I thought he was going to laugh, but instead, he became quiet as could be.

I asked him if everything was alright, but then instantly thought how remedial the question sounded. *Why would anything be alright?*

He shrugged his shoulders like I expected him to do. The response that followed, however, wasn't something I expected at all.

"Dying in combat, that's the only way out isn't it?" There was a kind of deadness in his eyes. It was obvious he had been here way too long. Longer than most. And definitely longer than me.

"Maybe it'll be me next time," he continued. "A messenger will come knocking on my parents' door, saying, 'We regret to inform you that your son has died in combat'. They'll put my name on a memorial wall next to a thousand others and remember me on Veterans Day then forget about me for another year." His head dropped. "Fuck this place. I wanna go home."

When I first met Sullivan, he was about a buck eighty, filled with piss and vinegar. But now as he sat there, his head hanging low and the life draining away from his eyes, barely a hundred and fifty pounds, he looked like an in-patient at Bellevue, in serious need of some anti-depressants.

He got up, grabbed his rifle and said, "Make sure your soul doesn't get evicted from your body. There's no coming back from that."

I looked into his eyes and believed it. I had only ever seen that look once before: in my father's eyes. He was also a military man: rough, stern, stubborn and chaotic. He knew a thing or two about war. Growing up, everyone tells you to be original, but I think imitating others is how we learn what we want and don't want in our lives. I remember how I wanted to be just like my father when I was a kid, until I saw those qualities in him that made me want to be anyone else. Every kid thinks their dad is Superman, but I remember the day I found out that Superman's kryptonite was heroine. I found him shooting up in the bathroom and he kicked the door in my face so hard that he broke my nose.

That's the other thing I remember about him; he had a lot of rage inside him. He stored it in the back of his mind and hoarded it in every corner of his heart, as if it defined him somehow. He had that poor man's mentality, where nothing was ever enough, and nothing was ever *good* enough. It was the same attitude that drove everybody out of his life, I'm sure.

My most memorable moment with him was when I fell off my bike and scraped my knee. He stood me up, slapped me across my face and said, "Men don't cry." He told a six-year-old kid that men don't cry,

and all I wanted to ask him was, what about boys? But nothing ever came out. I never told him how I really felt. He died before I could ever show him the real me. We never met, the two us; we just grazed each other and kept on going like the same poles of two magnets repelled by each other. As a matter of fact, 'Repel' is the perfect word:
/rə'pel/
Verb
1. drive or force (an attack or attacker) back or away.
2. be repulsive or distasteful to.

That's exactly what we were to each other. He would put these limitations on me of what I can and cannot do. Even your worst enemy doesn't do that to you. They think you're capable of anything, that's why they prepare themselves for your attack. Not my father though; he thought I was wasting my time, hoping and wishing for a better life. "This is all there is," he would say, "and all there'll ever be: this shitty house, this shitty marriage and this shitty existence." That's all he knew.

294 people died in the Gulf War, but my father wasn't one of them. He came home safely. He didn't die between the crosshairs of the enemy; he died completely alone, on a cold bathroom floor with a heroine syringe stuck in his arm. That was my father. They say that the steps of a good man are ordered by the Lord. Well, I can't help but wonder who ordered his steps. Then again, I'm still trying to figure out who ordered mine.

If Sullivan was in the same state of mind as my father, then the worst was yet to come. He gave me a sad little nod and walked away from me. I wanted to stop him. I wanted to talk to him and help him out, but it'd be like the blind leading the blind. After all, there's a reason why they tell you to put on your oxygen mask first before assisting others on a plane. You can't help anybody if you're on the verge of dying yourself.

CHAPTER 4

There it was again, over the speakers, heavy with static, the prayer call. It was always on time, every morning, followed by the other thing that was always on time: the sun. It was relentless that morning as we crossed over into Yarmouk, Baghdad. We arrived at an iron gate, which was well fortified and protected by at least half a dozen guards, bristling with automatic weapons. A guard waved us in, and we drove up the circular driveway of a massive, walled compound. It was a sight to see: splendor and squalor sitting side-by-side. But that was Iraq. As a matter of fact, that was the entire Middle East. That's what happens when the line between rich and poor is so far apart, yet the space around them is limited.

Alvarez stepped out of the Humvee and hawked out a loogie. "How much do you think this place would cost back home?"

"More than you'll ever make in your lifetime," I said.

He snorted with derision. "Who needs all this anyway. Just give me a farm and some cows and I'm good."

"Don't forget the sheep," Batali added. "I know how you farm boys get when you haven't fucked in a while."

Alvarez sneered and Batali quickly moved to the other side of the Humvee.

"Focus," Rev interjected. "It's time to move out."

As Alvarez pushed past me, Rev whispered. "Keep an eye on him. Make sure he doesn't cause an international incident."

"Keeping an eye on him has become a full-time job."

"Well, there are men who raise the bar, and then there are men who limbo under it. If Alvarez is the latter, then I need you to be the former."

"That's not what I signed up for."

Rev smirked. "It's what we *both* signed up for. We just didn't know it."

As we walked into the compound, a camera lens zoomed in on us. The whole place was under surveillance. Four security men waited to escort us up to see Al-Mahdi. I could see the telltale bulge under their jackets: a 9mm Luger, maybe a .357 Magnum, either way, it was unnerving.

We entered a huge foyer, which contained a giant granite fountain. The entire place wreaked of impersonal wealth: gold fixtures, diamond chandeliers, platinum art pieces, silver tea sets, ivory inlay, and marble everything. And I mean everything: floors, a spiral staircase, pillars, banisters, and tabletops. Every kind of marble you could imagine: Italian, Indian, Chinese, German, and Spanish. Enough marble to empty out a quarry.

Alvarez let out a whistle. "Well la-di-da, would you look at this place."

"This way please," a guard directed.

We made our way up the extravagant steps, where only thirty minutes away, a mere hop, skip and a jump across the Tigris River, children were battling hunger. With two silver platters of half-eaten French hors d'oeuvre being brought down from the top floor by servants, it was plain to see that hunger was clearly not an issue here.

I remember how cold it was in the compound. The air conditioning was cranked so high, you'd swear you were in a Canadian city in the dead of winter.

The guard escorted us down a long hallway—where the air was thick with cigar smoke—toward a large office located at the end. There were at least half a dozen men surrounding it. Some were ex-Iraqi police, some were ex-military, and some were just plain civilians with enough firepower to level the place. But I guess good help is hard to find; I should know. I looked over at Alvarez and he winked an eye at me as if affirming my thoughts. *Idiot.*

We entered the office, unnoticed by Al-Mahdi, who was kneeling on a prayer rug in the middle of the room, reciting the Islamic daily prayer. I scanned the faces in the room. The only one I recognized was Al-Mahdi's aide, Samir, who sat in the corner, wearing a sling to protect his gunshot wound. *I guess there's no sick leave here.*

He glanced at me briefly and gave me a little nod; his way of saying thanks for saving my life.

Al-Mahdi finished reciting his prayers and pressed his forehead to the rug. As he struggled back up to his feet, Samir ran to his side and handed him his cane. He was dressed down for the first time, wearing a white thawb (a traditional ankle length dress shirt). It was as if he was trying to look like a man of the people, when I got the feeling he was anything but.

Al-Mahdi gave Rev a simple nod and there it was: the quid pro quo, a green duffle bag, which Rev put on the floor—the contents of which none of us were privy to. I assumed it contained money, more than we made in six months. We earned ours the hard way, through blood, sweat and tears; Al-Mahdi earned his shaking hands, and eavesdropping on high-ranking officials. The only thing that was clear was that neither one of us was happy with our positions.

Al-Mahdi's men looked at us dead-eyed, but not Al-Mahdi. His eyes were calculating, moving with a sense of purpose, studying us, dissecting us, assessing our capabilities, while questions were pooling in his mind. He was careful with his steps, making sure to never position his back to the door.

Without a word, he went and sat behind his desk, pushing aside an ashtray overflowing with burnt-out cigars, beneath which, skewed about, were snapshots of the shattered Suburban. From the bullet holes in the back door, and the crunched passenger side, it was obvious that Al-Mahdi had made it out by the skin of his teeth. You wouldn't know it however, from the look on his peaceful, airbrushed, Time Magazine face. He was safe and serene in his fortress, surrounded by his personal army and his material things.

As my eyes swept across the room, past the prominently displayed taxidermic game hanging on the wall (a lion's head, a boar, a ram), I noticed a collection of jazz albums on the shelf. Some of the greats, like Charlie Parker, Charles Mingus, Louis Armstrong and the list went on and on. He had an enormous portrait of the album Head Hunters by Herbie Hancock looming over his desk—clearly a man with taste.

If you were wondering what a bastard like me knows about good music, you'd be surprised. My grandmother had the biggest collection of jazz albums anyone had ever seen. Not to mention, a saxophone reed from The Prince of Darkness himself: Miles Davis. She would tell me about how he handed it to her offstage, right after a concert in a small little dive in Louisiana.

We'd listen to her stories and play those albums every Sunday afternoon, immediately after church. It was some of the most inspiring music I had ever heard. The kind of music, that without, music itself would not exist. Albums like Charlie Parker: The Essential, Miles Davis: Miles Smiles, and Ornette Coleman: The Shape of Jazz to Come. The sound of Jazz always brought back some good memories. As I stared at the collection and thought about those soulful Sunday afternoons, a brief smile came over me, which Al-Mahdi noticed.

"Are you a fan?" he asked, pointing at his records.

Rev looked to me trying to decipher our private conversation.

I gave him a quick nod. "You have an impressive collection."

"I'm glad you approve. Men your age don't care much for jazz."

"It takes a delicate ear to appreciate it."

"Yes! I agree. My two biggest loves in life are Jazz and cigars." He nudged a cigar humidor toward us. "Please help yourself."

"No thanks, I don't smoke."

"Don't mind if I do," Alvarez said, reaching for one.

Rev slapped his hand like a child reaching for a cookie before dinner. Speaking on behalf of all of us, he said, "Thank you, but no."

Al-Mahdi got the message. He took in a deep drag. "Of course, just business then."

"Yes...please."

Just then, Samir silently excused himself from the room, making sure to grab the duffle bag on his way out.

Al-Mahdi pointed to a giant bulletin board, covered with maps marked with terrorist hot-spots, blueprints of buildings along with utility schematics. But even with all his paperwork and planning we were still no closer to defeating our enemy, and Rev let him know it.

"This information is useless. They're moving their locations constantly, and more importantly, they know that we know this."

"Yes, Sergeant, but as my father would always say, 'Even the hardest game to hunt, follow patterns'."

Even though Al-Mahdi was able to weave words with his silver tongue, Rev was not impressed. "All these old Arabic proverbs don't account for anything."

The blatant attempt to play on Al-Mahdi's beliefs didn't bother him the slightest. He lit a new cigar, from the remaining embers of the last one, leaned back in his leather armchair and exhaled a cloud of smoke. "We are close to figuring out the pattern, and where Razzaq will be."

Rev took in a deep breath. I could tell he was exhausted by Al-Mahdi and men like him, who thought they were experts, when we were the ones putting our lives on the line. "Why are we having this meeting here and not on the base?"

Smoke curled from Al-Mahdi's lips. "After the last attack, the enemy clearly knows I am working with the military. Conspirators are everywhere. Here at least I am safe. There are guards patrolling the entire neighborhood." He stood up and stepped toward a large bay window. It was the first time he had positioned his back to us. "I no longer care to hide behind a veil. We must send a message to the insurgency that we are not afraid, that our numbers are just as strong as theirs. And the longer we remain quiet, the longer the game will continue. We have to show the people that we are working together to bring peace to Iraq and help create a stable democratic government."

"And how are you going to do that?" Rev asked.

Al-Mahdi turned from the window. "By showing them that America has no vested interest in Iraqi oil."

I was taken aback.

Batali, on the other hand, remained unmoved. He had been preaching the same gospel for quite some time now.

Rev, who had no comment when Batali brought up the subject, now all of a sudden, spoke up. "What are you talking about?"

"Come now, Sergeant, you know exactly what I'm talking about. After all, the devil is in the details."

Rev remained quiet.

"Slaughterhouses build corrals in circles, so the animals can't see the blood and will continue moving forward, unaware of their demise. The people can't see where you're herding them; they can't see that it's all for your benefit and not theirs."

Al-Mahdi was the kind of man who liked to hear the sound of his own voice, and Rev was a patient listener, who would let men talk, hoping they would slip up and reveal a hidden side to their psyche.

"Now we both know that Saddam would've been overthrown eventually," Al-Mahdi continued, "by his own people or another country. So maybe you're here to keep more than just the peace…perhaps the oil as well?"

Rev raised a brow and sharpened his eyes.

Al-Mahdi didn't back down. "So, once you have set up your pipelines, what's next, Iran perhaps? We both know that the Saudi's and the Kuwaiti's are already in bed with you. Then you will control the world's oil supply. And Iraq will become the dog under the table, eating scraps, while you feast on filet mignon. You'll give us just enough to keep us satisfied. Isn't that the plan?"

Rev looked Al-Mahdi in the eyes. "You've got your information wrong; we came here to find WMD."

"A denial common to soldiers. Let me ask you, Sergeant, did you find these weapons of mass destruction?"

Rev said nothing, because there was nothing to say.

"Of course you haven't found them. It was just the reason to bring you over here, was it not?"

I could tell Rev was reaching his boiling point with Al-Mahdi's rhetorical questions, but he controlled his anger, which was starting to show through the bulging vein on his neck.

"Now, if we knew your next move," Al-Mahdi continued, "we could not only co-ordinate a more effective strike, but also put the people's minds at rest. Then you would have their trust."

He was baiting us to talk about our strategy. Rev looked at him with the best poker face I've ever seen. The same face that had taken many of the boots for all they had, including myself for a cool grand when I first arrived on base. "You supply the intel," he replied, "We'll devise the plan. You don't need to know the specifics."

Al-Mahdi scoffed. "This is a partnership, is it not?"

"No. This is not a partnership, this is a one-night stand, and we got our dick wrapped twice for safety."

Suddenly, diplomacy was out the window.

The response was clearly not sitting well with Al-Mahdi. He looked about the room at his guards, as if Rev's words were blasphemous. "You talk with this much disrespect after all the information I have provided." He sneered at Rev. "Must I remind you that the same water which supports a boat can also sink it."

"That sounded like a threat," Rev said, taking a step back. "For your sake, I hope it wasn't, because you need us a lot more than we need you. Without us, all your handshaking and promises aren't worth shit."

Al-Mahdi was insulted—a man in his position being treated like a busboy on his first day. "You think just because Saddam is gone and that you have your feet on Iraqi soil that you are in control here? You are nothing without the information I have. I know these streets, and more importantly I know what is under them. America thinks itself to be the world's police, but this is far more than a domestic disturbance."

I could feel the tension in the room; you could've cut it with a butter knife.

Samir once again entered the office, slowly, as if he had been eavesdropping from the hallway.

Rev took a breath and calmed himself. He knew that his superiors relied on him to speak on their behalf, and he couldn't simply go flying off the handle. "The Iraqi police and army liaise with us, then they just as immediately go straight to the insurgents and tell them we're coming. We can't afford to trust anyone with our plans, even you."

The room was dead silent, all eyes on Al-Mahdi.

Rev leaned over his desk, and guards watched with cold eyes, their hands roving over their guns.

Al-Mahdi put up a hand as if to say *everyone stand down*. And they all did.

As the meeting settled back to a comfortable level, Rev said, "We both want the same outcome. The enemy is highly organized. If there are no overtures of peace between us, then we will fail indefinitely."

Al-Mahdi moved with a cold confidence. He took another puff of his cigar and glared at Samir, who stared back confidently. "When you are ready," he said, "I will be here to advise you."

As I studied both Rev and Al-Mahdi, my imagination took over and I could see Earth in its entirety from deep space. Suddenly, everything became just one thing. Just one blue blip. So small and fragile, yet alive and breathing. Floating in the abyss, I could hear the concerning messages transmitted into space from all the countless voices, the duplicitous doctrines being force-fed to the masses. Was any of it the truth? Then, a small crack appeared in my helmet and my suit began decompressing. I could feel my eye sockets being pulled out of my scull. I could feel eternity crumbling away, pulling me back down toward Earth. Or at least that's what it felt like in that moment. But I'm afraid my imagination couldn't take me far enough away from that conversation or the emotions in that room.

Rev stepped back and gave Al-Mahdi a simple nod. I think both men knew how close they had just come to complete and utter destruction.

CHAPTER 5

Rev and I sat with the hot Iraqi sun on our backs, playing chess on an old antique board that his old man had given him before heading off on his first tour. The sweat creased his brow and ran down the sides of his temples. The look in his eyes was intense. This was more than just a game to him; this was war on a microscopic scale.

He moved his knight forward like a sniper on a rooftop, able to take any piece he wanted from the corner of the board.

As I moved my pawn, I couldn't help but see myself in the piece. Pawns are, after all, the frontline, the sacrificial lambs, sent out to clear the path and set up perimeters.

Rev remained fearless; soon came out his rook, charging horizontally, and just like America, it captured pieces by *occupying* the same square.

Battle started. Bloodshed everywhere. Rev took out piece after piece, making his way toward my base. His Queen came out and shot across the board like a drone dropping bombs along the way.

Just like war, both sides had a vested interest. Both sides believed they were in the right. Both sides were willing to die for victory, all the while, the King watched from his throne, like a president, waving his flag for church and state. 'Die for us,' he shouted. 'Die for us!'

Unlike the real thing, this war only took a matter of minutes. Even though I had him on the run at one point, Rev put me in check. I was cornered from all sides. Again and again, I moved and he followed. He was relentless. He looked up at me, winked an eye and said, "Get some!" Then swooping in like a gunship, he annihilated everything.

"Check mate."

"I almost had you that time," I said, trying to hold onto a shred of dignity.

Rev smirked. "Pride goeth before the fall, my friend. Remember that."

Just as Rev stood up from the table, Ryan Benson belted out, "Saddle up, boys. We've confirmed Razzaq's whereabouts. You're rolling out!"

Our entire platoon had been assembled: two trucks with five personnel each, with an assault element and a base of fire. Just enough firepower to do the job without incurring a lot of unnecessary risk.

Rev, Batali and I, along with Alvarez and Sullivan from Bravo Company, were on the weapons team. The basic tactic was for us to provide cover, while the attack team dashed forward.

We rolled through the city, strapped in a Cougar HE (an MRAP vehicle, structured to be resistant to landmines and improvised munitions). A beast of a vehicle.

Inside, Rev and I sat across from each other. "You think Razzaq's going to be there?" I asked him.

"I don't know. We have no choice but to trust Al-Mahdi's intel."

I was nervous. "You know I dread the moments before a firefight, more than the actual bullets."

Rev smirked. "Not me. This is the calm before the storm."

"But the storm is still coming," I reminded him.

"Let it come," he said fearlessly. He then patted his forearm where the number 515 was tattooed.

"What's that?"

Rev smiled. "That there is my saving grace. Let's just hope it keeps us safe today." He turned on his two-way radio so everyone could hear him and shouted a verse from Tennyson's poem: Charge of the Light Brigade.

"Theirs not to make reply,
Theirs not to reason why,
Theirs but to do and die:
Into the valley of Death
Rode the six hundred."

The men all cheered with a thunderous, "Oooorraaah!"

I looked at Rev and he looked back at me courageous, fearless, his brow raised as if to say *let's take this asshole down!*

Within twenty minutes our squad had reached the gated safe house in the Shiite slums of Sadr city.

Alvarez studied the compound through his binoculars. "I thought Intel said the building was white?"

"So?" I replied.

"Well, that there is off-white."

"Are you kidding me? That's white."

"In what world is that white? You fuckin' color blind?"

"You know what, you're right, Alvarez. Maybe we should ask the neighbors, 'excuse me, but we're looking for the terrorist on the block, would you happen to know where he lives?'"

"Focus men," Rev said. "We got movement by the South entrance." He then pointed at me. "You, Sullivan and Alvarez take the roof of the adjacent building and give us the bird's-eye view."

The three of us did as Rev ordered, quickly and swiftly moving into place, while the attack-team covered us. We seized the unoccupied house, using it as a post to conduct surveillance, and to observe down the two main streets from the target house.

"Roof's all clear," said Sullivan. "We got the house in our sights." His concentration was intense, his focus was mesmerizing.

"What do you see?" I asked him.

"Everything...."

He was perched high on the ledge, staring down his scope at the smog-bound cityscape, training it on the heads of random people, waiting to pick off anyone he wanted. He could see everything. He was omniscient. He was death. In his hands was a Barret, a large .50 caliber sniper rifle: a specialty weapon with an extremely long range. How long? Let's just say it's got a max effective range of 1,830 meters. In other words, *too* long for any human being to feel safe. This thing could snipe you in the middle of Thanksgiving dinner through an open window from a mile down the road, and everyone at the table would think you just passed out due to the tryptophan in the turkey. That's one scary, badass weapon, if you ask me.

"What do you see up there?" Rev radioed in.

Sullivan squinted his left eye. "A sea of hijabs. The streets are crawling with people."

A group of Arabs were heeding the call to prayer.

"Anyone look suspicious?" Rev asked.

"This is Iraq," Alvarez squawked, "everyone looks suspicious."

"That wasn't *too* racist," I said looking at him.

"Everyone is wearing the same god damn thing; it's the perfect camo."

As I turned away from Alvarez, a feather suddenly flew by on a pillowing breeze, peaceful as could be, and I fell into the lull: the calm that Rev spoke of. I let out the breath I was unknowingly holding, and the world went silent for a moment. It was as if I was looking outside myself, in the silent space between feeling too much and feeling nothing at all, right between sensory overload and deprivation. Somewhere within that space, I found two parts calm and one part storm, with one knee rooted on the ground, surrendering to the lull, and the other raised up, ready for the battle to begin. It's a strange place to find yourself.

The feather flew out of sight, and suddenly, my perfect concoction of calm was diluted with an uneven amount of storm. "Everyone hold your position, I think I see something." I studied the compound through my binoculars. "I think we got something under the awning on the far side of the road."

"I see it," Sullivan said, dialing in the range on his rifle.

"Do you see the high value target anywhere?" Rev asked.

I focused in on his face. "No. I think it might be a front man though."

"Well, it's not what I wanted for Christmas," Rev remarked, "but I suppose it'll have to do."

Suddenly the man disappeared behind the house. "Wait. I lost him. He's on the right side of the house."

"Does anyone have eyes on the enemy?" Rev asked. "I need eyes on the target."

"Negative!" Sullivan replied.

"No visual," Alvarez confirmed.

"This might be our only opportunity to get this guy." There was a strain of anger in Rev's voice.

As I surveyed the target house, another man appeared, one with a pair of binoculars. "Wait," I said, "I got signs of surveillance."

"Where?" Rev eagerly asked.

"By the western wall."

The man caught a glimpse of Rev and the fire-team. He raised his hand in the air, all five fingers coiling into a fist. He was clearly signaling somebody. "You're exposed!" I shouted. "Fall back!"

I locked eyes with the militiaman. He looked right at me, and then suddenly, it was pandemonium. Armed Iraqis in civilian clothes appeared from the side of the house. Bullets reigned, as a firefight broke out with the insurgency.

"We're exchanging fire!" Rev shouted.

The insurgents scattered, and civilians rushed to their homes, desperately trying to escape the kill zone. It was like watching colliding particles, pushing off of each other, sending some hurdling into space.

Another shape materialized on the balcony. "There's another one."

"I got him in my sights," Sullivan said, taking aim at the target. He had meticulous precision, which came from years of being a sniper. He pulled the trigger and clipped the assailant from what felt like a mile away. The bullet hit the insurgent in the neck, leaving him immobile.

Three more men came out from the side entrance. "Be advised," I warned, "enemies approaching from all sides."

The men started back toward Rev.

Dropping my mag, I loaded a fresh one and proceeded to empty it on the insurgents' position, taking out two of the three men. As I trained my rifle on the last man, an explosion rocked my ribcage. The shockwave rippled through my skin like a carnival act taking a cannonball to the stomach in slow motion.

"Where the hell did that come from?" Alvarez shouted.

I followed the tracer's trajectory to find a rocket man on the roof. "RPG on the roof of the target house!"

"Let him have it!" Sullivan commanded.

A lightning-quick reload and I was ready for a second round. I took the shot, which penetrated the rocket man's chest. He spun around, dropped to his knees and prematurely launched the rocket in the opposite direction, toward civilian homes.

Fuck!

The rocket-propelled grenade flew over the house and through the window of an adjacent home. In the downstairs' window, I could see a frightened woman scooping up her little daughter and quickly closing the curtains.

My mind was racing, screaming, *Get out!*

Seeing women and children in imminent peril and being unable to help them is the most terrifying thing. But it was too late. The walls of the house detonated from the inside. The roof gave way and the house imploded.

God no! My body tensed up and I bit down hard, nearly cutting off the tip of my tongue. The air was quickly filling up with dust and ash, making it impossible to see. My mind was slipping away into a panic. I felt that suffocating weight again, causing me to drown to my knees. My throat closed up and my eyes filled up with tears. I felt like a hurricane, unapologetically sweeping up homes and families in my endless cycle of chaos.

I could hear Rev on the radio. "Cease fire, we got them all."

But just like the alleyway earlier, I couldn't move.

Alvarez slapped me on the back and said, "One more for the good guys."

Sullivan remained perched on the edge of the building, refusing to move until everyone was clear of the kill zone.

The fire finally ceased; I wiped my face and assessed the situation.

"Someone give me accountability of all personnel," Rev asked.

I was paralyzed, my eyes glued to the leveled home.

"We got one dead and four wounded," Alvarez said. "The enemy's been neutralized, five dead. High value target not accounted for."

"Sacrificial lambs," Rev remarked. "Razzaq was never even here. It was all a ploy. They knew we were coming. Come on down, boys; let's get out of this place."

On the ground floor, Rev stood solemnly staring down at the body of a young boot. "We don't know our enemy at all. We expect one thing and get another, every single time."

At least the boot came here voluntarily, but what about the mother and daughter in the exploding house? How did they deserve any of this? I remember the look on the woman's face as she rushed her daughter inside. I don't think I've ever seen anyone so terrified, and that's saying a lot.

Looking for survivors, we continued on through the debris and devastation, through the dust, smoke and an entire city block of concrete and rebar. I quickly dropped my rifle and grabbed a shovel. We reach for things that can protect us in moments of despair. In that moment, I knew that a shovel could help my guilt a lot more than my rifle could. Even though my mind was telling me that everyone was already dead. I had to see for myself, I had to see a body, a limb, something.

Just as I thought it, there it was: a woman's hand. I turned to a young boot and shouted, "Marine, help me with this!"

Together, we removed a big chunk of rubble, and found a man and woman, laying side by side, their faces splattered with blood. A little boy was wrapped up in a sheet, curled up next to his father, and a little girl no older than six was crushed beneath a slab of concrete. The room was filled with the sweet, coppery scent of blood. It stained the cotton sheets a deep burgundy and mixed together with the dust to create a deathly paste.

I was momentarily overwhelmed by the enormity of the crime. It was one of those *what have I done* moments.

I checked the vital signs of the father. He was dead. As was the mother. I took a knee between the bodies and brushed my hand over the white sheet and suddenly felt a weak pulse from the boy's wrist. Then, a silent heartbeat from underneath the sheet. I stared into the father's lifeless eyes as I removed his arms from around his son. Suddenly the body of the little boy moved. It was a miracle that anyone had survived at all, let alone him, with his fragile body, laying in the most awkward position.

The boy opened his eyes and stared into mine, and I stared back, vacantly. The child looked at his father and his face changed color instantly, like a thermometer being dropped into a scolding cup of water.

I recognized him; it was the little boy from the streets: the one with the powerful eyes. He slowly lost consciousness. His lids collapsed and his neck went limp.

I looked up at Rev. "He needs medical attention quick."

As I pulled him out, a crowd shifted nervously, unsure of how to proceed. Their fists were angry, yet their feet were scared, unable to move. Across the street was another home left in ruins. No survivors whatsoever.

Women placed their hands over the eyes of their children like little blinders, so they couldn't see the horror. They shouted curses in Arabic.

"Alshaitan yrkabk!" (Satan be upon you!)

"Ebin alsharmota!" (Son of a bitch!)

"Kol khara!" (Eat Shit!)

The vindictive threats kept coming, and the roar of the crowd increased.

Rev looked around calculatingly. "Take the boy," he said. "Let's go."

I cradled him in my arms, back to the Humvee, where I sat in the backseat, checking his vital signs. Dust was caked in the lines of his face. As I wiped away the blood, which was clouding his eyes, suddenly, they opened once again.

"Keef Halk?" (How are you?) I asked him.

"Hal anta b khayr?" (Are you alright?)

He didn't speak. He slowly slipped back into unconsciousness.

I told him everything was going to be OK. Thankfully he wasn't awake to hear it, because it felt like the biggest lie I had ever told anyone. It reminded me of all the lies I used to tell my ex-girlfriend, Sophia. As a matter of fact, looking down at the boy, he reminded me of another child who didn't stand a chance in this world.

I was only fifteen when Sophia broke the news to me that she was pregnant. My first reaction was anger, "You're not keeping that baby," I told her, "and that's final!"

"Why not?" she shouted at the top of her lungs, holding a home pregnancy test in one hand and her belly in the other.

It was one of those moments where you couldn't hold back the truth no matter how hard you tried. "Because I don't love you!"

She fell to the floor, her arms oozing off in either direction. Her heart broke; I could hear it. Liquid meteors rained from the orbs of her eyes and entered the atmosphere of her cheeks. The black hole of her mouth opened up and sucked in every molecule of oxygen in her vicinity, and the empty space between her nose and lips became wet with emotion. Her face was a microcosm unto itself. She got up off the floor and took a run at me, beating her small, fragile hands over and over on my chest. "I hate you!" she shouted. "I hate you!"

But in that moment, I didn't care about her feelings. Her suffering was irrelevant to my own selfish needs. My whole life I've been guilty of that: putting myself before others. I treated Sophia like garbage when all she wanted to do was love me.

What I remember most about her is how passionate she was about astronomy. She would tell me about stars, supernovas, galaxies and about the universe and how miracles unfold. She once compared me to a dying star: light incarnate, rearranging the building-blocks of her universe and creating a new beginning for us. But sadly, there was no *us*. There was only me. I remember everything she told me about stars, but for the life of me, I can't remember her last name. It's funny what we choose to remember in life.

Other than my mother, a woman who held down two jobs just so she could hold me up, Sophia was the only other girl who truly understood me. When the time came, I took her to the abortion hospital myself. I owed her that much at least. I owed her a lot more, but in that moment that was all I was willing to acknowledge. As soon as we walked in, my eyes drifted to the small clock on the wall. The time was 11:34—one of those numbers that had been following me around my whole life. It didn't matter if it was AM or PM my eyes always seemed to find the clock at 11:34.

As we sat there in the examination room, Sophia beside me, her face in her hands, and her eyes filled with regret, I stared blankly at a packed garbage bag in the back room, wondering if somewhere there was a garbage dump littered with abandoned fetuses. Children that nobody wanted, children that weren't fit for the world, quietly ripped from a soundproof womb where no one could hear them scream.

The doctor ran us down the procedure and called it elective pregnancy termination, but it was more like forced in Sophia's case. They gave her a sonogram to determine if the pregnancy was viable, that is to say she was still in her first trimester. And there it was, a tiny blip on the screen: our baby.

At five weeks old, though the embryo is only about the size of a grain of sand, the heart is pumping blood. That's where we start off: as a grain of sand. Yet somewhere, somehow, we grow up with a sense of entitlement, as if the world owes us something. As if hightide couldn't just as simply wash us away, back to the ocean of nothingness from which we came.

Forgetting where she was, Sophia saw the sonogram, smiled, and maternally reached for my hand. It reminded me of the first day I met her. It was junior year. She was a wallflower with a quiet demeanor, big bubble gum lips and beautiful hazel eyes, which reminded me of the red and green Aspen leaves that I had only ever seen in Sierra Nevada, near South Lake. The poor girl never knew what hit her. I was her first boyfriend. All she knew about love is what she learned from me. And all I taught her was bullshit that I got from watching my parents hurt each other. You could've called her an optimist or just plain naive; both words were interchangeable as far as I was concerned.

Sophia's mother had passed away early on, so she never had a chance to build that bond with her. All she ever wanted was to be a mother herself. Now she sat there, with a seed inside her, planted, but never watered, forced to abandon it. But what choice did I have? I wasn't a father; I was a sperm donor. What could I offer a child? I had no guidance of my own. I was just a stupid kid, stumbling along the way, trying to avoid my father's shoes, which unfortunately for me, were always the perfect size.

Maybe being a fuck-up was in my DNA. As far back as I can remember, the cards were always stacked against me. I've never held four kings, let alone two. I was dealt the lowest number of the lowest suit and forced to bluff my way through the game of life. Sophia just happened to be on the other end of the table, trying to win without so much as a pair.

I paid the price of an abortion, yet it cost me much more than I could've imagined. There's interest that you have to pay on an abortion. You pay it every time you think, dream, or hope for a child. You pay for the rest of your life with all the possibilities of what that child could've been. No one tells you that. In the moment you're so scared that you just want it over and done with. You realize the gravity of the situation much later.

After everything was said and done, I told Sophia to avoid me at all costs, that being around me would bring her absolutely no comfort, that she'd get stuck in a net that she couldn't escape. But that didn't stop her. She came back around after the pain settled. And around and around we went like some painful carousel. *Will someone please stop this ride*, I remember thinking. *Please God, I have to get off before I lose my mind.*

She went from blonde, to jet black, to auburn, to brunette, and all the way back, hoping, wishing desperately to become someone else, someone more interesting, someone I could possibly love. Near the end it was obvious that the sweet little wallflower had now dried up on the vine. The pain was more than just internal. She would cut herself, secretly, but I knew. You don't miss signs like that, not unless you're blind, or you do it intentionally. *Let her kill herself* you think. At least you'll be rid of her for good.

She was a glutton for punishment. So was I, I suppose. She ended up taking a piece of me every single time we had it out. If we were smarter, we would've called it quits the first time and saved ourselves a world of hurt. But then again, I've seen smarter people go through the exact same thing, the exact same way. It's in our nature to hurt each other. Maybe love and hate are more intertwined than we think. Maybe that's the real relationship, the one true balance in the universe, with forgiveness being the scale in between, teetering left and right, depending on the weight of either soul.

    Sophia always said I was a hard man to get to know. *Difficult*, I believe is the word she would use. I'm not entirely sure she was wrong. I tried being honest with her and with myself. I tried to turn my life around, but like trying to sail a boat, while building it at the same time, I got over ambitious. Now, all I'm left with is the product of my ambition: nothing. It couldn't have been more evident than in that moment. As I sat there with this little boy in my arms, all my memories failed and my hope faded. I began to feel an ache in my soul. It was clear that neither of our lives would ever be the same again.

CHAPTER 6

That night in the infirmary, I could hear the little boy muttering in his sleep. His thin, whispery voice spoke softly, and his eyelids flickered in a dream. From the ether of his subconscious, he whispered, "Omee." The word meant mother. That's who he was crying for.

I was faced with the reality that when his family tree came tumbling down and his seeds of longevity died in the dirt, my hands were the ones wrapped around the axe, my voice was the one crying, *timber*. The boy didn't know this, and I didn't have the courage to tell him. Perhaps I could sew his broken branch to my barren tree. Maybe we could adopt each other, that way we'd both have a family. Standing there, pregnant with guilt, I reached out and touched his hand. The contact brought the sleeping appendage to life and he wrapped his fingers around mine.

Get it together, I remember thinking; *you're here to do a job.*

I refuted myself. *But this is the job. We're here to protect these people, or at least that's what I was told, and that's the mission I'm going to fulfill.*

Protect them? We can't even protect ourselves.

The boy's eyes sprung to life and he pulled away from me, taking a seat at the edge of the bed. He put up a wall, endless and impenetrable.

"My name is Will," I told him, "but everyone calls me Santoli."

He saw the American flag pin on my chest and moved away from me. Like a suppressed people in the face of a dictator, he drew his eyes to the floor and submissively put his hands in his lap.

"Can you understand me?"

He silently nodded.

"What's your name?"

He didn't answer.

His eyes reflected the light coming in from the hallway like nothing I had seen before. I remember thinking *why are the things that reflect the most amount of light also the sharpest?* It's no wonder most of us fear the light. In that moment, he could've cut me in half with those beams of light, leaving me only half a man, which is exactly what I felt like.

"Where's my mother?" he asked, desperately looking around the infirmary.

I looked at him with bloodshot eyes, which were well overdue for some sleep. "There's been an accident," I told him. "You're going to be alright."

"Where's Omee, Abbi, Selima?"

Hearing their names only made the news harder to repeat. "I'm sorry." I shook my head.

He saw the look in my eyes and instantly knew. As the words sunk in, his face slowly imploded: his eyes squeezed together, his bottom lip collided into his top, and his cheeks retreated up toward his eye sockets. A veil of tears streamed down his face. His hands began shaking so fast they became a blur, phasing in and out of reality. From the way his eyes dropped away, I could tell he didn't want to be here anymore. If only he could've shook his body at the same frequency and fazed right out of existence.

"I'm sorry," I said again, putting a hand on his shoulder.

He put up his five-fingered shield and covered his face, but his tears went on forever, seeping out through his little hands.

It was zero-three-hundred before he finally cried himself to sleep.

I left him with the nurse and slunk back to the barracks, where I laid in bed for two hours, thinking about what his life was going to be like with a vision of a future now marred. The loss pressed down on me like a crushing weight. I thought about my own family, unconventional as it was. I thought about the first winter after my mother passed, and the ardor that had cooled and solidified, forming the biggest chip on my shoulder. I remember how the cold held me down and seemed to seep down to my bones—a bruising cold that felt like it was going to last forever. It took me a long time to piece myself back together. It hurt me to think about how this boy's deconstruction had only begun. It's nothing a child should ever have to go through.

As tired as my body was, there was no sleeping that night. The second the sun rose, I got up and went to the head shed hoping to find some answers.

Benson was sitting at his desk, blowing on a hot cup of coffee.

"Staff Sergeant?" I said, standing in the doorway of his office.

He waved me in. "Come in. Sit down."

I took a seat as Benson sipped his coffee, calmly like it was just another day at the office. I patiently waited for him to finish reading the latest intel report.

"Jesus! What these savages are capable of scares me." He dropped the report on his desk. "Now the Bible says, 'love your enemies and pray for those who persecute you'. Well, I'm not sure if I can do that. Not this time."

I gave him a nod as if I cared at all about what he was yammering on about.

"You believe in heaven, son?" he asked, forcing me back into his conversation.

I glimpsed a weathered Bible sitting on his desk and I shook my head. "I've never seen heaven, but I can account for hell, sir. I believe I'm there right now."

He looked at me cold-eyed. "Well, I can see why you feel that way. But I still believe in heaven. I believe in God and burning bushes." He had that kind of insipid personality that made you want to come up with any excuse to walk away.

"With all due respect, sir, lighting a fire isn't so hard; it's putting it out that's difficult. I've seen more than just bushes burning out here. But I have yet to see anyone put them out."

He sat back in his chair. "So I take it you're an atheist?"

Again, I shook my head. "I've prayed to God, sometimes out of fear, sometimes out of habit, but something tells me that if there is a God: a being capable of creating the universe, He doesn't care one way or another if I believe in Him or not."

Benson put a hand under his chin and looked me up and down. "Kids your age aren't too concerned with being saved."

"Saved?"

"Yeah saved?"

I smirked.

Benson changed the tone of his voice. "I say something funny?"

I wiped the smirk off my face. "My father once told me that the only thing that can truly save a man is two clenched fists, an iron will and a bucket of hero's blood. If that's the case, then I'm not sure I got it in me to be saved at all, sir."

Benson gave me a long, drawn-out, "Uh huh," as if I had just trampled on his beliefs.

"Well, anyway, what are you doing here, Santoli?"

"I came to ask about the boy, sir."

Benson took another long, slow sip from his cup. "His name is Ali Hassan. He speaks pretty good English, as a matter of fact. It turns out his father was a teacher."

"How is he?"

"Physically speaking, he's going to be fine. It's amazing he survived a blast like that. He has no other family, however; both his grandparents are deceased, and his uncle was killed by insurgents."

I tried to hold back my emotions. "What's going to happen to him now?"

"We've ran a few humanitarian missions to a nearby orphanage. I've called them. They said they have room for him."

"That's it?"

Benson looked up from his cup, confused. "I don't quite follow."

"In a world where everything is compartmentalized and put into tables and categories and classified as something, Ali's simply miscellaneous?"

Benson took in a deep breath. "It's a harsh reality we've been forced to live in. I know how you feel, son, but there's only so much we can do. It's a good orphanage run by good people, trying to make a difference. It's the best place for him."

I tried, without success, to make some sort of sense out of that. "Can I see him?"

Benson got up from his table. "Of course. He's in the other room right now."

Ali sat in a neighboring interrogation room. He seemed uncomfortable. Perhaps it was all the uniforms, or the weapons in the room, or the situation at hand, or the hard-straight-backed chair he was sitting in—most likely it was all of them.

Benson and I entered silently and watched as a Navy Corpsmen asked him about his family. Ali began talking about his father, a Sunni Muslim, who was a teacher and a scholar of many languages and religions. He talked about his younger sister, Selima, who loved to sing and dance. And he talked about his mother, a strong, able woman, who fought for women's rights in Iraq. He spoke about them all in the present tense, as if they were in the next room, waiting to take him back home, back to his life. I suppose denial made it easier for the time being. But the moment the Corpsmen used the word *was*, when referring to his sister, Ali let out a long breath as if someone had knocked the wind right out of him. His hands sat depressed in his lap, and he stared weakly at the table in front of him. He had the kind of face that provoked pity.

Benson leaned into the boy's ear, uncomfortably close, and said, "We're all sorry for your loss, son." But Benson had used that line one too many times in his life, and it sounded insincere. Even at his young age, Ali knew that an apology contaminated by insincerity, was completely worthless. He looked up with disgust. He didn't speak. He couldn't. He was obviously in great pain.

Benson followed it up with, "You're going to be OK." He then opened the door, paused for a second, glanced at me and said, "You can leave now, Santoli, the facilitators will handle this."

I took a look at Ali and our surroundings dissolved away. I was thirteen-years-old again, standing by my father's grave, staring at the inscription my grandmother had written herself. *'We can only pray that God condemn this inherent trait bequeathed by our forefathers. Let it die here with us, and let it be kept out the ears of our sons. Let no more generations go off to war. It's an all too scary thing with the power to take away your innocence and change you forever'.*

Yet here I was, on foreign soil, following in my father's ill-guided footsteps. When I looked at Ali, I saw a part of myself. I saw *my* story, and there isn't a man alive who can walk out on his own life story. The ones who try end up destroying more than just themselves in the process.

I asked Benson if I could take the boy to the orphanage personally.

Although he allowed it, he raised a brow like I was getting too close and making things harder on myself. He was right. I was standing at an event horizon: a boundary in space-time in which the gravitational pull becomes so great that escape is impossible. I couldn't turn my back on Ali even if I wanted to. Walking away from him in that moment would've sealed his fate. I know from personal experience that having hate inside your heart is a lot like having a bomb strapped to your chest: activating it will destroy *you* as well, and that's the last thing I wanted for him.

"Come on, Ali," I said. "Let's go."

He slowly crawled out of his chair and followed after me, not sure what to expect. I put an arm around his shoulder and kept it there until we got into the Humvee.

While on route to the orphanage, Ali sat in the back, near the window. He slowly moved toward the door into a beam of sunlight and closed his eyes, bathing his face in it. I could tell it brought to mind some comforting memory for Ali. From the looks of it, the sun was the only thing that had not yet abandoned him. In a country where it's eighty-six degrees in the shade, I guess you could always count on the sun to be there.

Ali looked like he was replaying every day of his life, every feverish memory he had ever accumulated. Although his face remained in the light, he broke the silence and began talking about his mother and how she would cradle him in the heat of the sun, and how his father would take him down to the sun-dabbled river to tow little wooden boats, and how he would race the sunsets with his sister, trying to get home, before the sun went down. "My mother would pinch our cheeks and make us Bamia with lamb," he said.

I had tried the dish before, it was a sort of lamb stew with okra. Very delicious. According to Ali, his mother's was the best. He reminisced on the softness of her voice and the words that she used to describe her love, words like 'rouhi' (You are one with my soul.) He talked about how he felt the first time his father took him to see the golden-domed al-Askari Shrine in the city of Samarra. He said he felt small standing in its shadow. And when we drove by some wind-blown tents, he pointed and told us about the nomadic tribes that lived in the desert and the stories that his father would tell him before going to bed. His words teleported me to his early childhood, and for a moment, I could feel the love that Ali had felt.

After a few minutes, he moved out of the sun, folding up his memories from long ago, of things he once believed or wanted to believe were possible. He looked at me—his sun-lit eyes now half-open—and said one simple word. "Home." He wanted to see for himself. He wanted to know for sure that it was all gone.

I looked to Rev. "Sergeant?"

He looked at the boy with sincerity. "It's not exactly a safe place right now."

Ali said, "Please." his little voice cracking with every vowel.

"I suppose we have time," Rev replied. He had a heart, after all. I'm sure that had to be a requirement to be a reverend. As he looked at Ali, I could tell he was thinking of his own son, back home. As a father, the idea of an abandoned child most likely broke his heart.

We turned the corner and Ali's eyes lit up in recognition of his street. But as he saw his block, now disfigured by war, his head slowly dropped away. RPGs had hit the whole neighborhood. It was a miracle that Ali had survived. But some miracles are hard to understand in the beginning, if at all.

Ali got out and stared at the sunbaked blood on the torn chunks of concrete. The place where he slept was now rubble and the balcony where he would sneak out to watch the stars was now a mangled heap of iron. He turned his attention across the street at a ruined home.

Ali pointed and said, "That's my friend, Jamail's house."

In the ruins, I saw a crippled teddy bear staring back at me. Jamail and his family were gone. No doubt making their way out of the city, pushing a wheelbarrow filled with their earthly possessions, possibly trying to cross over into Syria or Jordan, whichever country would have them.

Ali let his thoughts roam, telling me how the two of them used to play soccer and pick figs from the tree that stood in Jamail's courtyard. He told me about the adventures they would have and the memories left behind in footprints, etched in dusty fields, fighting invisible monsters. A time when the wind whispered their names and their imagination had no equal. Back when bicycles were horses and sticks were swords and the two of them were princes of kingdoms that could only be seen through the eyes of a child.

I watched as his thoughts soared high into the air, yet they couldn't land safely. With each word that left this mouth, he lost more and more of his innocence, until finally, his thoughts crashed in the middle of a sentence and I could tell he wanted to cry. Although he didn't want me to see, I noticed his thumb digging into the palm of his hand to keep his mind off his emotions. I felt wrong for even noticing. I felt like I was prying on his hurt.

"I'll be in the truck," I said, giving him a moment alone.

From the back of the Humvee, I saw Ali sitting on the ground, cross-legged, his body convulsing and his hands supporting his ailing face. There can be no more of a desolate place then one's own broken home.

I wanted to comfort him, but he didn't want my sympathy. I clenched my hand into a fist and hit myself in the thigh over and over until I had painted it black and blue. In the process of beating myself up, Alvarez looked back at me and said, "Need a hand?"

When I finally stopped, I was suddenly reminded of Benson's questions about God and being saved. Desperate times call for desperate measures, so I turned to the stooge behind the wheel and asked, "Hey, Alvarez?"

"Yeah?" he said, picking his nose with his giant, sausage finger.

"You believe in God?"

He let out a chuckle. "Well, none of the promises that God made me ever came true, but the deal I made with the devil is doing just fine."

I should've known that his answer wasn't going to be helpful at all.

Outside, Ali sat on the ground still crying into his hands.

"It's time to go," Rev said to the boy.

Ali stood up and dusted himself off. Within the rubble, he noticed a small potted plant (as frail as himself), and one random family picture that had survived the devastation. He broke the frame on the ground, pocketed the picture, and picked up the plant, cradling it protectively under his arm. He carefully stepped through the place where he grew up and held his secrets—a place which was now gravel under his shoe—and got back into the Humvee, trying unsuccessfully to hide his sadness.

CHAPTER 7

The orphanage sat on a street lined with shelled buildings. It was slightly dilapidated, with thick walls, high arches, and light spilling in from its mission windows. There were hundreds of these independent, unofficial orphanages in Iraq, sheltering the countless souls scattered here, whose pain had become someone else's currency, and whose war had become someone else's peace. There were so many children: Sunni, Shia, Kurdish and Turkish, all living in this one small confined space.

Here, the boys ate, slept, studied and attempted to continue on with their lives. But in reality, this was a barbershop where boys went to get their dreams trimmed down, their expectations cut, and their hopes shaved and thinned out. They walked out into the world with a bad attitude and a bad haircut to match. It was the last thing I wanted for Ali.

Alvarez looked at the children as if they were just an old, beat-up fruit stand on the side of a country road that you stop at, pick, taste, and then go about your way. In other words the last person you want visiting an orphanage. I discretely asked Rev if I could take Ali inside on my own, to which he agreed.

As we entered the orphanage, a man stood in the entryway. He introduced himself as Yusuf, one of the caretakers. Just like Benson, he had one of those faces that I immediately didn't like. That squint, that crease, that nose that subconsciously reminded me of something untrustworthy, like a rat. He had a contemptuous look on his face, or was it the look of impotent rage? I couldn't tell anymore. They both looked the same to me.

As he eyed Ali, standing there with a backpack filled with all his earthly possessions, a smile appeared on his face and he said, "This way."

Yusuf led us up to the sleeping quarters where the boys slept. There were thirty of them, all crammed in one studio sized room, filled with bunk beds, strewn with fragments of childhood artifacts, excavated from the ruins of a hundred family homes. There was a ratty old soccer ball, half a dozen teddy bears, countless figurines lining the windowsill, a figure airplane hanging from the ceiling, a bucket full of small, plastic animals, and a stack of worn Superman comic books that looked like they had passed through the hands of every child there.

The boys all stopped and took notice of us. Thirty pairs of eyes turned toward us all at once. These children of a motherless tribe, who had no amendments to call upon, bricked up behind stone walls, in this fortress of solitude, where even Superman couldn't save them. Their painted-on smiles easily washed away at the sight of a Marine in the doorway: the bearer of bad news.

Standing there, potted plant in hand, Ali's eyes strayed about the room and slowly entered it as if he was entering a hostage situation. He looked at the boys and their silent demands. They had all lost someone in their life. You'd think it would have helped them bond, but it was quite the opposite effect. They were on guard, ready to battle anyone who walked through the door. They held Ali's peace, tightly clenched in their little hands. But Ali had lost family as well and he was just as guarded. He stood there, unwavering, with the discipline of a soldier.

"Go on," Yusuf said in Arabic, "that bunk is free." He pointed to the last bunk at the end, where a young boy was flipping through TV channels: Al Jazeera, BBC, each one showing some terrorist act, suicide bombings, American attacks, drone attacks that killed innocent people.

Then from behind me, I heard a female voice proclaim, "Eghlek altelfaz w eaamal wajebatk." (Turn off the TV and finish your homework.)

The little boy in front of the TV, quickly flicked it off and jumped into his bed. The rest of the boys scattered.

From the darkness, *she* entered. It was Nadeel, looking beautiful as ever. The first time I had seen her on the base I remember thinking she was femininity wrapped in true-grit. The most breathtaking woman

I had ever seen. That was my first impression of her. However, my impression of her on that day, left me spiraling.

She turned to Yusuf and said something in Arabic. I could understand some of it, something about leaving the door unlocked, and putting the children's life in danger.

Yusuf apologized looking rather insincere.

Then she pointed at me as if to ask who I was, and Yusuf shook his head and replied, "Eben alkalb," a curse I understood. It meant son of a dog. I had been called it too many times already.

I scrounged together the only little bit of Arabic I knew, or at least enough to tell her I barely knew any at all. "Ana ma fehempt." (I don't understand.) "Tet Kalam Ingleezi?" (Do you speak English?)

She stopped and raised an eyebrow. "Yes…very well, in fact. Along with Farsi, French and Turkish."

I was taken aback; I didn't expect her English to be so perfect. "I'm Santoli." I put out my hand for her to shake.

She looked down at it then back at me, replying, "You should go now."

I was confused. Her face was a hieroglyph, completely indecipherable. "Did I do something wrong?"

"I would explain it to you, Mr. Santoli, but you don't have the right eyes to see this place."

"Brown?" I replied.

She shook her head, unamused. "I don't mean their color; I mean their persuasion. They only see what the military wants them to see. They don't see what's really going on here."

"And what's that?" I asked, a little fearful of her response.

She put her hand in a random stream of light, which was cutting through the room. "Those are more than just cracks in the wall."

I followed the stream of light to find a wall marred by shell-holes.

"Look around you," she said pointing to the children. "These are the inheritors of the kingdom, the kingdom that you have left in ruins. 800,000 orphans in all. I would say your occupation could be compared to that of a bull in a china shop, but then again, I've seen a bull in a China shop and they are as nimble as can be. The military, on the other hand, is stomping about, trying to kill a rabbit with an elephant gun. And when they miss, many get hurt, yet no apologies are made—none that count for anything. I guess atrocities are easier to handle when they're part of the job description."

I opened my mouth, but she cut me off before I could respond.

"You take no responsibility on your part. You dirty your hands with the crimes of your superiors, with the blood of the innocent. Then you go rest your head on your pillow, knowing it wasn't your call, and use your orders as soap to clean away your guilt. You were just doing your job, you tell yourself. On any other job, you'd be fired if you performed with that much incompetence."

I took a step back. "You're making a lot of bold conjectures, don't you think?"

She looked at me and smirked. "A conjecture is an opinion formed on the basis of incomplete information. I know what I have seen, and I'm not stating that because war kills, therefore that makes you a killer; I'm saying you're a killer, because you have killed…have you not?"

The directness of her question caught me off guard. Even though she was right, I didn't answer.

She shook her head like I was a stupid kid, who would never learn or be good for anything. "You Americans have made Iraq out to be a monster, as if a child was never born here, played here, dreamed here, as if beautiful things are incapable of growing in its soil. How could you be so cavalier with people's lives?"

I finally mustered up the courage to speak. "We came here to stop Saddam."

"Saddam wasn't Iraq. These boys are Iraq, their mothers, their fathers, their brothers, their sisters. They *were* Iraq. No different than you or I—just a family trying to live and stay together."

"Look, we're here to help."

Nadeel drew her eyes away from me. "And that may be true, but you have to keep in mind that seeing tanks rumbling down the streets is just as scary as low flying planes in New York City. You have taken this country more like conquering heroes and less like peacemakers. We are scared. *We*, the people, not the insurgents, they don't fear you, but *we* are scared. Men, women and children, who have no idea what they are supposed to do now, displaced with no homes to run to, no doors to close, no beds to hide under. *We* are scared."

I looked about the room, into the eyes of the children and they spoke without words, their little faces reiterating everything Nadeel just said.

"Will you be the one to tell a mother that you're sorry for her loss," she continued, "and then tell her son that you're sorry you broke his mother's heart? Will you comfort them? Or will you pack up your bags and get back on your mechanical horses and leave, while the people are left shivering, peeking through curtains, scared out of their wits?"

I just stood there, listening.

"From Saddam to America, in their minds they've just exchanged one evil for another. You are an occupation, and there has never been a good occupation. House raids, death squads, check points, curfews, detentions, blood in the streets, constant violence, destruction and no growth. That is what you have left here. That is what people will remember you for: not liberators, but destroyers."

She approached a window that overlooked the courtyard. "Look at those children out there, those hungry souls. They have lost their families. They never even got a chance to bury them. They never got to bathe their bodies or enshroud them in a white linen cloth. They never heard the Janazah prayer, or saw the burial of the dead, making sure that their head was facing toward Mecca. Look, look down there!"

Down in the courtyard was a vast field of white roses, countless, thousands of roses.

"Each rose down there is a tombstone for a child, lost or dead."

It was a cemetery made from living things. Amidst the roses, on the outer edge of the field were scores and scores of candles, and a large stone with an epitaph that read: *Amal*, which meant Hope.

"They're gone," Nadeel continued, "but their names are here, along with who they were and why they were killed. Maybe that will make people think twice about war."

I immediately thought about the poem that my grandmother had engraved on my father's tombstone. The fact that I was standing in Iraq, confirmed that no amount of words could change anything.

Ali looked up at Nadeel, his eyes full of questions.

She gently touched his face, trying to reach through his pain. "We can't replace your family, and we won't try, but we will help you find your peace. I promise." The devotion she had toward these children was beyond question. No wonder the riot of emotion toward individuals like me (tourists, who were just visiting), while she was here for the long haul, left to pick up the broken pieces.

She called over a little boy named Hakim, who was sweeping the floor. He dropped his broom and came running over. He had a charming little cherub smile and humble brown eyes.

"Hakim will show you around, and help you settle in."

Hakim, who had been through this drill too many times, smiled and said, "Come with me."

Ali moved slowly around the room, feeling things: the smoothness of the cabinet glass, the warm base of a desk lamp and the softness of the bed sheets. He put his plant down on a table by his bed and laid his head down on the pillow, like he hadn't slept in days.

I turned to Nadeel and she didn't hide her disdain at all. Once she was done casting her verbal stones at me, she chased me out with her tongue—her words rushing me out the door. "It's time for you to go."

I looked at her a final time with a sense of deep and profound loss in my eyes.

Again, her eyes shouted *Leave!*

And so I did.

On my way back to the Humvee, I heard a voice call out from the field. "I see you met Nadeel." It was another caretaker, a tall, skinny, middle-aged man. Just having finished his prayer, he was getting off his knees. In his hand was a copy of the Quran. "Salaah is a sacred meeting with Allah five times a day," he said. "There is nothing between a servant and his lord during prayer. I try and remind myself that the Holy Quran cannot be left in the hands of the unqualified and those with pretensions to its interpretation. The fact is clear: God never entrusts the path of guidance to the unworthy, however knowledgeable." He reached out his hand. "My name is Raheem."

I solemnly shook it. "Santoli."

Raheem was a veteran of this place, a man who had seen it all. He looked cool and brisk in his white, linen garbs despite the heat. There was an innocence in his eyes and a kind of softness in his smile.

"I hope we'll see you again, Santoli," he said.

I shrugged my shoulders. "I don't know if that's a good idea. No one really seems to want me here."

"Don't mind Nadeel, she's protective of these children. Also, the uniform doesn't help. She hates uniforms. They remind her too much of Saddam's army."

My eyes lingered on the countless roses and the nameless children they represented. "I should go," I said to Raheem.

He gave me a nod. "Of course. Asalaam Alaykum." (Peace be upon you.)

Upon me? Why would it be upon me?

I turned around and headed beyond the walls, where my team

waited impatiently.

Alvarez laid down the horn. "You took long enough. You know how hot it is in this tin can?"

I sat in the backseat, blankly looking out the window, facing a true struggle with my soul.

Rev turned toward me. "You alright?"

I looked up and finally asked him the one question that was weighing on my mind, the question I wanted to ask him on so many occasions, but could never bring myself to ask. "Are you confident about what we're doing here?"

Rev was taken aback. "I'm only confident of one thing in life and that's my family. I'm here for them. I'm here to make sure they're safe. Why do you ask?"

I shook my head. "You ever seen a room full of recycled children? It'll make you think twice about every decision you ever made in your life."

"You did what you had to do. That's life. We can't stop it."

"I wish I could, just for a second to catch my breath."

Rev reached into his bag and threw me his camera. "Here…"

"What's this for?"

"That there is the only thing that can stop time. That's as close as we're allowed to get. Time is not something you stop or control, it's something you endure."

I looked down at the camera and realized that I didn't have a single picture of my parents or even of myself. Not a single snapshot of me and my old man playing ball, or cutting a cake, just empty photo albums and frames with fake families laminated in them. The only memories I had were the faded ones in my head, where my perception of the truth was the only truth I knew. I took the camera and put it in my bag, hoping to see Ali again. To stop time for a second, to catch my breath and to remember him the way he was now: completely innocent, before reality truly set in and he became as cold and hard as some of those older children.

After forty-eight hours of no sleep and being emotionally exhausted, I was ready to shut down. It was late-afternoon going into evening and the sun was sinking fast. We got back to the base, and as I went to put my gear away, Sullivan's locker, locker 239, was open and empty, its door swinging gently in the wind.

I turned to Aikman in Bravo Company and asked, "Where's

Sullivan?"

It was so silent you could hear a pin drop. Everybody was staring at everybody, saying without saying, knowing without knowing. I had once again made the mistake of asking a remedial question. There are only two responses when you see a man's empty locker: he either left the easy way or the hard way.

Aikman's eyes fell away. "He took a shot in the head." He then pointed to a Mortuary Affairs convoy that was heading off the base. In it, were half a dozen bodies. Sullivan was finally heading home, just as he predicted.

CHAPTER 8

The next morning, we picked up an informant from a small village just north of Sha'ab called A'saliyah. The man's name was Zaid. He was a shepherd, the occupation of a man-child, descended from a long line of shepherds, dating back nearly a thousand years. He was barely twenty-years-old, yet he was already a father of three. Here you had no choice but to grow up and grow up fast. There was no heading off to college or living in your parents' basement. This was a dose of reality early on. I'm not sure if I could've even handled it, but for Zaid, this was all he knew.

He was a good man, and his mask, he wore exceptionally well. Although he hated us with every fiber of his being, he hated the enemy even more. He would smile every time we drove by—this fake smile safety-pinned to his cheeks. Damn, that boy was good. He would've made a great CIA agent. 'Yes sir, no sir,' he would say politely, while secretly screaming profanities in his mind. He would put out his hand, eagerly for us to shake, while his eyes searched for any source of water to wipe away our filth. He was like a dog in a kennel, praising the dog catcher—a poor slave in his own kingdom.

I wanted to tell him it was OK to hate me, but he never said anything of the sort. It was yes sir or no sir, and that's all. If you asked, he would give you his opinion on the best goat paths to take, or the quickest route to his village, and if you indulged him, he would tell you how hard it was to grow any kind of crop out in the dead soil near his home. Corn was the easiest. That's why he always had bags full of the stuff: corn for breakfast, lunch and dinner, corn for holidays and special occasions. Man cannot live on bread alone, but Zaid ate corn every day like it was a blessing. And perhaps it was. But blessings are hard to see with spoiled eyes, which is what I had—spoiled by years of half-eaten plates, and buffets as far as the eye could see. I thought Zaid was strong of mind. Much stronger than me. This twenty-year-old kid, who back home would've probably been flipping burgers at McDonald's, was more a man than I was.

Anytime he heard or saw anything suspicious, he would inform us. One could say it was for the cash, but no. Zaid was the first man I had ever met who wasn't driven by money, and the only man I had ever met who didn't need it or want it. Everything his family had they shared and traded with their neighbors, and beyond the needs of his family, there was nothing else he wanted. A healthy child, a loving wife and a strong herd is all Zaid needed. I admired him for that.

As soon as we arrived at his small, modest home (a quaint mud-brick building on the outskirts of town), he began directing us in Arabic, leading us toward what Zaid referred to as 'a suspicious truck'. Our interpreter, Batali, translated his words to our team.

Zaid packed a bag of food for the orphans in the village. The streets were filled with them. A pack of boys, thirty or more, living in squalor, all peddling labors with their dusty clothes and faces. It's amazing how brave little children can be. You tell them a scary story and they'll crawl into bed with you, afraid to go to sleep, yet real things like war, guns and machines don't frighten them as much. Some ran up to us slapping the windows of our Humvee, while others threw rocks and yelled curses.

Zaid indulged them; he patted them on the head, handed them food, and then told them to stop. Surprisingly, they listened. It was a good thing, because Alvarez was getting ready to throw something back.

"They keep throwing those rocks and I'll give them something to be frightened of," he said.

Rev got a good laugh out of it.

In all the confusion, Zaid got ahead of himself and I had to pull him back and remind him that this was no scavenger hunt. "Be careful," I said, making an obvious hand sign for an exploding bomb.

He smiled, saying, "Allah will save me."

Alvarez smirked. "If He was able to do that, we wouldn't be here. I don't think there's much your God can do."

Zaid was offended by the comment and made the mistake of debating Alvarez—a pointless attempt. There was no getting through to a man like him. Hell, he should've wiped his mouth with toilet paper, for the amount of shit he talked.

Still, Zaid demanded to be heard. He began in English, "You say my god is…is…." and when his tongue got twisted up in our words, he turned to Batali and finished the rest in Arabic.

Batali was taken aback by his comment.

"What did he say?" Alvarez retorted.

"I don't think you want to know."

Just like you would expect a bully to do, Alvarez squatted down to Batali's height. "Either way, I'm gonna get it out of you, so save yourself a world of hurt and just tell me."

Batali let the intimidation tactic get to him. He was never comfortable with his 5'6 height, and having a beast like Alvarez mocking him, didn't sit well with him. He shrugged his shoulders. "He said, 'Do you honestly believe you and I have a different God? That the painter used a separate brush on you than He did on me?'"

Alvarez smirked at the comment, and for the first time, the young man who kept to yes sir and no sir, finally let loose with his opinion. As he spoke, Batali translated. "Should I take the word Allah out of my mouth? Should I change it into something that doesn't offend you so much? Should I call him Jesus? Then perhaps, you'll understand me. What if I change the cover of the Quran and write Bible on it, then maybe you'll see that words, regardless of what language they're written in, can still be as beautiful as your beliefs. That a search for God is a search for God, for good, for righteousness."

Alvarez looked away. It was the first time he had no rebuttal. How do you rebut a comment like that anyway?

"Come on boys, concentrate," Rev said, alleviating the tension between Zaid and Alvarez.

Zaid resurrected his modest tone and replied, "Yes, sir." He then quietly led us three clicks from his house, where he claimed insurgents had planted mortars in an abandoned truck. He led the way and our company followed with Batali, translating every word that came to his dry lips.

A blast of dust swept past us and Zaid became very anxious. He pointed north and said, "Habūb! Habūb!"

Batali quickly translated. "He said a sand storm is coming."

"Sand storm?" Alvarez interjected. "What the hell's he talking about? There's no storm."

Rev turned to us and said, "There won't be any air support during a sandstorm, so don't get yourselves shot."

Alvarez smirked. "I don't know what this clown's talking about, Rev. There's no storm."

Suddenly, the storm appeared out of nowhere. Zaid knew it was coming, just from a few grains blowing in the wind. He had learned to listen to the whispers of this place. It was a skill that had helped him greatly.

As the brewing storm came in, red sand blew mercilessly from every direction. Iraq was suddenly terraformed into Mars. The storm consumed everything. Funnels of wind erased buildings, cars, limbs, people and even Iraq itself. Completely darkened by the sandstorm, we moved on, breathing through our scarfs. Through the void, I could only make out the vague impression of a village.

Voices emerged from the gloom, as Martians ran for safety, breathing through the crude masks of their fingers, straining to see through the flurries, which grew thicker by the second. Ghostly bodies lingered in the distance like apparitions. I was sure this is what Hell looked like on a Monday morning.

We continued on and Zaid yelled, "Lif yassar!"

Batali turned back to us and said, "Turn nine o'clock!"

We moved through the sand and grit, squinting, playing follow the leader.

"Ala Tool," Zaid said.

Batali shouted, "Straight ahead!"

I looked to my left and Rev was gone. "Does anyone have eyes on Rev?"

"Negative," replied Batali. "I can't see anything in front of me."

We heard a low snapping sound, and Alvarez yelled, "Shots fired three o'clock, two-hundred meters!"

We all raised our rifles.

A man appeared on the road, holding something in the crook of his arm.

"We got a possible target," Alvarez shouted.

Sand was swirling everywhere, enough to make visibility impossible.

The man moved through the flurry and Alvarez said, "I'm gonna put this Hajji down!"

"No...wait!"

The storm cleared just enough to see that it was a civilian with a donkey cart, holding a shovel. "Negative! Negative!" This time I tried to beat Alvarez's trigger finger.

"Didn't copy that!" Alvarez shouted.

"I said negative! It's just a shovel. Lower your rifle."

The man waved his hand, unaware of how close he had come to being executed.

All weapons lowered fast. All except Alvarez that is. His rifle was now aimed right at Zaid's head.

Batali and I exchanged a glance: *what the hell?*

"What are you doing?" Batali asked him carefully.

"Fuck this Iraqi piece of shit. He's a front man. He's been setting us up this whole time!"

Voices stepped over one another, trying to take control of the situation. "Lower your rifle!"

"Relax!"

"Take it easy, Alvarez!"

Alvarez's finger floated above the trigger. In his eyes was the strain of a hedonist.

Zaid took a step back.

Alvarez shouted, "You move again and I'll take the pulp out of you, boy, I swear to God."

"Marine, did you hear me?" I said. "Lower your rifle!"

Alvarez's face quickly became a mask of sweat. He wasn't bluffing. "This piece of shit is a wolf in disguise. Look at him."

Zaid began to shake.

Alvarez was losing it. His eyes were peeled back, exposing a career-ending violence, and his finger was itching to pull the trigger. "Grandma, what big eyes you have, better to see us with, I suppose."

"What the hell are you doing?"

He shoved the muzzle of his rifle in Zaid's face. "Grandma, what big teeth you have got, better to eat us up with."

I drew my rifle and pointed it right into Alvarez's shocked, red face—point blank range. He was a powder keg, and I was one step away from being the fuse. The last thing I wanted to do was put Zaid's life in danger.

Alvarez's tone changed immediately. Although his rifle remained fixed on Zaid, he focused his attention onto me. "You just opened up a-whole-nother can of beans, Santoli!" In that moment it didn't matter that we were on the same team.

Zaid shared his glare between Alvarez and me, two men as different from each other as lions and hyenas, yet made from the same things: uniforms, a code of honor, and American ideals.

Alvarez had this look in his eyes as if he loved it when someone stood up to him. He thrived on confrontation—a true bully through and through.

I pricked up my courage and stabbed him in the chest with my rifle. "Put it down, Alvarez! I'm not gonna say it again."

Then, through the grit and grime, came the voice of reason. "What's going on here?" It was Rev. His voice immediately forced composure from Alvarez.

I waited for him to lower his rifle first. If Rev hadn't forced his hand, he would've cut Zaid down right in the middle of the street without any remorse. The second he lowered his weapon, I lowered mine, but I knew that this was far from over. Alvarez wasn't the kind of man to let things go.

After an hour, there was a lull in the storm, taking with it some of the ego—only some. As we continued on, I could feel Alvarez's eyes burning into the back of my head, untangling the wrinkles in my brain. He was the least of my concerns. All around us, death was waiting for us to slip up, or make one bad move, just waiting in the shadows to take us home. I would not give it the satisfaction. I took in slow measured breaths and concentrated on the task at hand.

We followed the pulse of the village toward the ticker, except *this* heart was designed to blow. Each person became a palpitation and our eyes, two trained fingertips, compressing against its carotid artery.

"We're close," Batali said, translating Zaid's now shaky voice.

"Are you sure?" Rev asked him.

Zaid nodded. "There," he said, "that truck."

The pigeon-shit covered truck was parked in front of a building on a block, populated by storefronts.

"We have to cordon off the streets," Rev said, "then evacuate these people."

The Military Police were called in to clear civilian onlookers from nearby stores, allowing us to dispatch an explosive ordinance disposal unit to neutralize the threat. The city center was abuzz with Marines and military vehicles as they frantically cordoned off the street.

In the back of the truck, the EOD unit found a cache of improvised explosive devices—enough to do some serious damage.

The truck was parked in front of a building, which looked abandoned. Rev wanted to check it out to make sure it was all clear.

There was a Buick-sized hole in the front of the building, through which we entered. On the wall, in the foyer, perforated by bullets, was a huge mural. It was a scene from the Quran: the Angel Gabriel in the ear of the Prophet Muhammed. It was beautiful to say the least.

"I thought it was considered sacrilegious to draw the Prophet Muhammed?" I said to Batali.

"It is," he replied. "But something tells me, whoever did this is not concerned with blasphemy." Batali, who was a theology major, was captivated by the mural. Like some museum curator, he pointed to it and said, "This is Muhammad's first revelation. On a day toward the end of the month of Ramadan, he left the city and walked into the hills of Hira on the mountain of Jabal an-Nour, near Mecca, to fast and pray. Just before the dawn, of the next day, he heard a voice. The voice grew louder and louder, it seemed to come from all directions, and even from inside Muhammad himself. Then suddenly, he was visited by the Archangel Gabriel, who was holding a cloth of green brocade.

'Read,' said the Angel.

Muhammad was stunned. 'I cannot read!'

The Angel squeezed Muhammad, and then released him. 'Read' he commanded.

'I cannot read,' Muhammad said, a little louder this time.

The Angel squeezed him again, tighter than before. 'Read.'

'I cannot read?' Muhammad said, even louder. He was now afraid of being squeezed again.

'Read,' said the Angel.

Muhammad recited with perfect accuracy. 'Proclaim! In the name of thy Lord who created man from a drop of blood. Proclaim! In the name of the Almighty God who taught man the use of the pen and taught him what he knew not before.'"

Alvarez, who had only hours earlier reprimanded Zaid for his beliefs, was now rapt in attention like a child hearing a bedtime story for the first time. It was as if he didn't want Batali to finish. As he admired the painting, we heard a soft moan coming from the second floor of the building.

All heads turned in synchrony and Rev gave me that look which meant *be ready for anything.*

We slowly made our way up the stairs. I could feel my heart pounding as Rev led us blindly up the darkened steps.

Batali hugged the wall, petrified. Alvarez, on the other hand, had to hold himself back, in fear of letting out all his previous bottled up rage.

I wiped the sweat from my brow and prepared myself for a firefight. My brain communicated the message: fingers ready, eyes focused and ears pricked. I was fighting every instinct I had to run away, going deeper and deeper into the fear. Our boots made little nocking sounds on the hard, concrete floor. I remember trying to pick up my heels to limit the sound as much as I could.

There it was again, the moan. Someone on the next floor was struggling. The sound was coming from the first room, which was lit with that soft, sanitized light that you find in morgues. We moved swiftly, covering either side of the door. With a nod from Rev, in we went, to whatever awaited us.

The room was filled with ammunition boxes, assault rifles, grenades and counterfeit US currency, at least three-hundred thousand dollars' worth.

In the darkest corner of the room, was a man in a chair, flex-cuffed with his hands behind his back, and the riddled body of a teenager on the floor. On a random table in front of him, a kilo of heroin sat on a sheet of butcher paper. It was clear that he was being drugged and forced to cooperate.

"You speak English?" Alvarez said, squeezing the man by the back of his neck.

He shook his head, scared.

"Who is he?" Rev asked me.

It wasn't a face I recognized. "He's nobody," I said looking into his eyes.

My words must have transcended all language barriers, because he looked at me, angry at my comment, as if his pain was worth nothing.

"Ask him why he was kidnapped, and by who," Rev said to Batali.

Batali asked, and the man answered in a low, breathless voice. "He's a watchmaker," Batali said, translating his words. "He was being forced to help his kidnappers put together IEDs."

I noticed a camcorder aimed in the window. As I looked through the lens, it auto-focused down to the city street, bringing a Marine's distorted face into view. They were trying to catch footage of us, being blown to bits, to be used in their next propaganda video.

Rev backed away from the man in the chair and pointed to me, "Santoli, you're up to bat."

I spread a series of playing cards of Al Qaeda personnel across the table, each one displaying an ugly mugshot. I swear they've never had a pretty boy in power. From the pictures it looked as if even smiling was illegal here. Then again, what's there to smile about? I looked to Batali and told him to ask the man if he recognized any of the faces.

His anxiety was evident. He was shaking.

"It's OK," I said, "take your time."

He shook his head, like he had never seen any of the men before.

Alvarez was impatient and steaming. He slammed his hands on the table. "You're wasting your breath, he doesn't know shit!"

The man shifted in his chair uncomfortably: a telltale sign that there was something he wasn't telling us.

"He *does* know," I said. "He's just afraid to talk." I told him to take another look, and this time, I watched his eyes. I followed his gaze across the row of mugshots. His eyes rested on *one* longer than the rest. It was only a fraction of a second, but that's all it took to break him. He looked up and shook his head, his eyelids blinking quickly. Too quickly. He was lying. But there was no point in calling him out on it, he had inadvertently told me everything I wanted to know.

Rev eyed me. "You got it?"

"Yup." I picked up the picture of Sayyid Al-Zerjawi. "This is our guy." He was a lean, gangly man with a raggedy face, swirled with scars, and a beard that had never been touched by a trimmer. "Intel says he works for Abdul-Razzaq."

"You sure?" Rev confirmed.

"I'd bet my life on it."

Alvarez took a squat and spat a loogie from across the room, which landed by my feet. "You might just have to."

The man in the chair began mumbling Arabic prayers under his lip.

"What's he going on about?" Rev asked Batali.

"He's praying for his wife and children."

I grabbed the picture of Al-Zerjawi and put it in his face. "Where is this man?"

He turned to me, pleading in Arabic, which Batali translated as, "You have to protect my family."

He was just a puppet, so I knew that everything he said came with strings attached. "Tell him his family's dead if we don't get to this man."

Alvarez decided to throw in his two cents as well. "They'll know we have you, and the first thing they'll do is step across your threshold and light up your home like it's Hanukkah."

I shook my head. *Hanukkah? Wrong religion idiot.*

"If you want them safe," I continued on with the man, "tell me what you know."

As Batali translated, the man's face changed, and he slowly and meticulously told us everything: how he was forced to make IEDs, and where they were all located: outside of town, on highways and on dirt roads. He told us how to deactivate them as well. But the one thing he couldn't tell us, was where to find Zerjawi. He had only seen the man once, and that was over a week ago. He could've been anywhere by now.

As soon as he was done spilling the beans, Rev said, "Get him out of here!"

"Should we detain him?" I asked.

"No. From the sounds of it, he doesn't know anything else. He's just a poor son of a bitch who got caught up in something he couldn't control."

Just as we cut his flex-cuffs, he wrapped himself around my legs, begging and shouting in Arabic. "Wa kaif aalaty?"

"He said, what about my family?" Batali translated.

Alvarez looked hard at the man for a second, then he headed back downstairs. He wanted nothing to do with him. For the first time, I wish I could've done the same, and been as closed off and emotionally unavailable as him. But that just wasn't me. I looked down at the man with sympathy. He was just one of the countless examples of innocent people being kidnapped or used by the insurgency to carry out their plans. There wasn't much we could do for him. We cut him loose, handed him some money and told him to take his family and quickly leave town. Hopefully he got out before it was too late.

The drive back to the base was quiet. Most rides were. We had expended our emotions until there was nothing left to say and barely anything left to feel.

As soon as we got back to the barracks, I dropped my gear and collapsed onto my cot. I must've been out for about an hour when I heard the sharp sound of a chain cord being pulled in the dark, followed by the relentless humming of energy, eking its way through an old lightbulb.

A sudden surge of light cut through the darkness and I saw a 9mm between my eyes with Alvarez's massive frame swooning over me, naked. He was sweating profusely, raining drops onto my face. "Watch ye therefore," he said, "for ye know not when the master of the house cometh." He had finally lost his mind—if he had one to begin with that is.

"What the hell are you doing?"

"I'm an assassin. You're a fool to sleep so soundly with an assassin in the room."

"You're all talk, Alvarez. Now get the fuck off me."

"You don't know me," he said applying more pressure, "you just think you do."

I tried to push him off me. "This isn't some game you're playing in your head; this is real!"

"Oh, I know," he said with a cold smirk. "Boy, I was born at Quantico. I can do the Quigley in my sleep. My grandfather was in World War II, my father was in Vietnam, I was born with a uniform!" He pulled the hammer of his gun back. "You ready?"

I didn't know if he was planning on killing me or fucking me. I have never hoped for a bullet so badly before.

Then he clarified and said, "It's time to die."

The bulb swung back and forth, casting long shadows across the room. The barracks became one giant pendulum, ticking down the final seconds of my life. Alvarez's face went in and out of light and shadow. I looked into his eyes, the eyes of a wild man. He looked like he could kill, because he had. I had witnessed it firsthand. He was one of those country boys who loved hunting. To him, I was just a deer in the crosshairs of his gun. He could kill me right now with no remorse.

"You sick fuck. Do it already."

He took out a red marker from his pocket and began drawing a bullseye on my forehead. "Just wanna make it perfect. You see if I avoid the brain stem and the thalamus, it won't affect your consciousness, so you'll remember every last second of it. You might even survive this. Now won't that be a sight to see. That's right, I aint as country as you thought I was."

My forehead was slick with sweat, and the red marker turned to paint, dripping down the sides of my face. I remember thinking he's an animal, but then again, animals are keener at killing than humans, so perhaps he had the leg up on me.

"You're sweating off the ink," he said, applying a fresh coat. "So now tell me, are you ready to die?"

I thought about the question. It had been posed to me many times, in moments of danger, when the odds of survival were fifty-fifty, but never when the inevitable result of death was a hundred percent. *Am I really ready to die?* Finally, after what seemed like an eternity, my lips uttered, "No...."

"Well, that's a crying shame, boy, because it's time to meet your maker."

The bare metal lips of the 9mm touched my skin, sending a cold shiver down my spine.

"Wait...I..."

"Too late!"

He pulled the trigger.

Click.

It was empty.

Alvarez burst out laughing, tears rolling down his cheeks. "Welcome to the suck, motherfucker!"

"What the hell?"

"I had you, boy. Oh, I had you shitting in your pants."

I finally let out a breath. I was sick to my stomach.

"Now we're even!" he said. "I want you to remember this moment the next time you get the idea to put a rifle in my face."

He lent me his hand, to help sit me up.

"Fuck you," I said, swatting it away.

"Come on, don't be a bitch about it. I promise your breakfast will taste that much better tomorrow."

There is no insubordination out here, not in the dog-pit, not for a threat. For a bullet wound maybe, but not a threat. This isn't high school. This is the real world. So, I sucked it up and gave him my hand. Strangely enough, I felt alive. Perhaps it was a good reminder. Perhaps I should thank him. Then again, the hell with him. I get enough

BOMB BOY

reminders here on a daily basis.

CHAPTER 9

When Rev said we were returning to the orphanage, to deliver food rations, I found myself feeling excited, yet nervous at the same time. Ali had never left my mind, not for a minute. As I walked down the narrow hallways of the orphanage, I saw children who were too young to walk, and ones who had lost both legs and couldn't walk at all. The sight of them made me feel weak. There are men who have never been to war, and there are children who can recount every moment of it. Children remember everything. They remember colors like military green, blood red and intestinal pink. They remember smells akin to burning flesh, decomposing bodies and gun powder. And they recall sounds such as screams, gunfire and mortars. It becomes a part of their subconscious, and they grow up fearing things, not fully knowing why.

Standing there, staring at them, I could feel my face cracking and anger spewing out. But for the sake of the children, I faked a smile and continued up the stairs, hoping that the sight of Ali would help me cope with the reality of this place.

The room, however, was empty. The plant that he had picked out of the ruins now sat by his bedside, healing, growing, hopefully just like him.

I returned downstairs where a young woman was chalking out a math lesson on the blackboard, while the children meticulously transcribed it out on their little ledgers. All but one that is: Ali. His hands were trembling slightly, and his paper was blank. There was a noticeable lack of rhythm in his eyes and a cold silence on his lips. School was the last thing on his mind.

Nadeel saw me spying in the hallway. "You're back."

I stepped back, choosing my words very carefully this time. "I wanted to see if the boy was alright. If there's anything I can do please let me know."

She gave me a once over. "Why do you care?"

I thought about telling her the truth, about the accident that claimed Ali's family, how I felt responsible, how it was my fault. But the truth only existed between the hundred milliseconds from when I thought it until the three-hundred milliseconds it took to reach my lips. Sadly, it didn't survive the journey. It was one of those moments where I knew what the right thing to do was, but I just couldn't bring myself to do it. The wrong thing seemed much easier.

I told her about everything, except the accident. "I wake up every day around boys who are not even old enough to shave, and yet have witnessed more bloodshed than a young doctor in his second year of residency in the trauma ward. Those boys signed up for it. They can take it. But Ali, on the other hand, he didn't sign up for any of this. He simply inherited a war. He doesn't deserve this life."

Nadeel gave me a nod, but there was nothing sweet or sensitive about it, she was only acknowledging the facts. "Why are men animals?" She said, hoping to be rid of us all.

Even though her question was meant to be rhetorical, an answer popped into my head and I blurted it out. "Maybe because it's simpler to be an animal than a human at times."

She raised an eyebrow.

"I've been a sheep in my life, even a wolf in sheep's clothing. I've been a fish out of water and the elephant in the room. I've been curious as a cat, cunning as a fox, and brave as a lion. I've been a dog, a pig, a chicken and even an ass, but a human was by far the hardest. Being human means being *humane*—something animals don't have to worry about."

"Perhaps you're right. But Ali needs more humanity than ever now. He just lost his family. He's not looking for a surrogate who's going to leave him as well." Her mood didn't lighten, not the slightest bit. She took my sincerity and threw it in a bucket of kerosene.

"You got one hell of a cold shoulder," I told her.

She cocked her head and retorted, "Cold shoulders are hard to thaw in a freezer."

"I get that you don't like me or what I represent, but I'm not saying this as a Marine, I'm saying this as someone who wants what's best for the boy."

She fired back without a pause. "But *you* are not what's best for the boy." Her words weren't the slightest bit watered-down; they were the equivalent of moonshine, hard and strong. "I've come across many men in uniforms fighting for false ideals. My father was kidnapped and killed by men in uniforms. At the age of twelve me and my mother were given the task of finding his murdered body in a morgue, after looking through a hundred others."

I felt nothing but empathy after hearing her story. "I lost my parents early on as well," I told her. "Not as tragically as you or Ali, but I know what it feels like to lose someone you love. I know what it feels like to stand there with questions and walk away without answers. I know how frightening it can be. I can relate to the boy."

My words hung between us like a fog.

"Do you want to know why I take care of these children? Because the majority of the people in Iraq who were suffering from the horrible conditions were poor and had no way of getting out. Without this place, these boys would become victims of the killings and the chaos, or without other means of survival, they would become perpetrators of crime or join the occupation's police force or army, which causes them to become targets themselves."

The gravity of her words made me feel so small and obsolete.

"You say you want what's best for the boy, well, I've heard enough words. Here, only actions prevail." She waited patiently for her words to adhere to my thick scull and then walked away from me.

As soon as the lesson concluded, the doors opened and the children poured out into the courtyard. All the children were running and laughing, all except Ali. He was quiet as could be—a lone planet on the outer edge of the galaxy. Although most of his bruises had faded away, one remained, pressed up against his heart. It had become more than just a bruise now; it was a part of him, like his last name. And just like his last name, he was the only one left to carry it.

I stood there watching him for a minute, trying to build up the courage and assemble the correct words.

As he sat there, a soccer ball rolled in between his legs, and an older boy shouted, "Ateny eyah!" (Pass it over!)

Ali didn't move.

The boy shouted again, and still, Ali remained silent.

BOMB BOY

The boy came, grabbed the ball then bounced it off of Ali's head and shouted, "Bomb boy! Bomb boy!" He recited it over and over, pointing and laughing at Ali.

Ali immediately said something to them in Arabic, which suddenly created an atmosphere of resentment among the group of boys.

They shouted back, "Bomb boy!"

I waited a moment to see what Ali would do.

They circled him, their little hostile hands clenched into fists. One boy shoved him, but Ali never backed down. He waded through them like water, unable to be drowned, his brow burning from the heat of their insults.

I saw the caretaker, Yusuf, quietly standing in the doorway. He was watching them, looking amused, like he couldn't care less if they tore each other apart.

The boy punched Ali in the stomach, knocking the wind out of him.

Before I could put a stop to it, a man's voice interrupted, scaling up into a shout, "Twaqafo an hatha kolkm ekhwa!" (Stop it. You're all brothers!) It was Raheem. He stopped them, separated the two and sent the other boys off in an opposite direction. Putting an arm around Ali—who remained unbroken by the storm of hatred—he leaned over and whispered something in his ear.

I approached the two, slowly. Raheem told Ali, "La tadahom yeselo elik." (Don't let them get to you.)

His voice reminded me of Stallone: deep and raspy, like an old lion that could no longer roar. It was heavy, somber and calming, the worst voice for lullabies, but the perfect voice for telling stories, which he loved to do.

"I've seen too much hate already," he said, patting his shirt pocket, where he kept a photo of his wife and young son—both now buried and gone. "These are my children now," he said, pointing them out individually, telling the story of their life. "That is Hosni," he said, taking note of Ali's attacker. "He is the youngest, asthmatic son of a chicken farmer. The two other boys with him are Ammar and Jawahirat, two brothers, who came here after their mother could no longer take care of them. A year ago, she promised she would return for them. Maybe one day she will, until then, they are searching for something to hold onto. Anger is just easier. They're not bad boys; they've just seen a lot of bad things. I don't blame them for not knowing the difference, but I try my best to teach them."

Raheem was a part of that long-gone generation of men who knew what it meant to be a man, to have integrity, to be a protector, to be responsible. Things I knew very little about.

I smiled at Ali, and he looked away as if it were all an act to get some emotion out of him. I knew it was going to take time to get through to him—time I was willing to invest. Anytime a humanitarian mission to the orphanage came up, I made sure I was on it. I would always catch Ali looking at me, studying me. His eyes were like a meat-tenderizer, and he took it to my heart, softening up every last stiff fiber that remained. Children usually imprint themselves onto their parents. I was the first face he had seen after his parents death. Maybe he took some solace in that, without knowing the truth.

As the days went by, Ali slowly began to open up to me. He told me about his father and how he was there in Firdos Square, watching Americans and Iraqis, side-by-side, as they pulled the rope, which took down the towering statue of Saddam. He told me how he used to avoid the statue, fearing the monster it was molded after. He told me all about his life, both the good moments and the bad. There were even days when he would make peace with his predicament and play and laugh and shout at the top of his lungs, which made me think that children had the ability to heal faster than adults. But then there were days, when the reality of his situation would sink in, and I would catch him sitting in a far-off corner of the courtyard, sobbing to himself. Sometimes he was caught somewhere in between the joy and pain, and a smile would make its way across his lips, but he would quickly rush it away, as if his face were freshly poured concrete that he was afraid would set forever in a smile, when smiling was the last thing he wanted to do.

He loved sitting on the roof of the orphanage, while bringing to mind old memories from his life, back when time and other matters had no meaning. He would tell me about star gazing on his roof with his father. He told me how awestruck he was by their beauty and the way they danced in the sky and worked in harmony. He wanted to travel beneath the stars, across every great shore. From one end of the earth to the other. He told me how he would even make wishes on shooting stars, while secretly being afraid of traveling so far away from home and losing himself in the journey. It was as if he was afraid of shining bright, yet never being seen—just like the stars he admired. He would then yawn and stretch his graceful arms into the air, as if to grasp the moon, and then fall into my arms, half-asleep and tired of dreaming his dreams aloud.

I tried to relate to him the best way I could. After all, the mutual connection between our two battered souls was undeniable. I don't know where I would've been without him. His courage made me reflect on my own life. Even with all the insurgency members we had stopped, the only time I felt like I was making a difference in Iraq was when I was at that orphanage. I could feel myself veering away from the military's template and sticking to the random acts of kindness that awakened parts of me previously repressed.

By the time summer rolled back around, the plant by Ali's bed was thriving, hopefully reflecting, on some level, Ali's own emotions. He was beginning to settle into this new life of his. Although he hadn't yet done it, I knew he had put down a preliminary plan on paper, of how he was going to take down all the walls he had built up in his life—a plan that I like to believe included me as well.

CHAPTER 10

One afternoon, out in front of the barracks, Alvarez had turned an empty shell into a crude barbecue, which Marines had gathered around. He was flipping some chicken he had gotten from a nearby vendor, which smelled amazing.

"Check out this idiot," Alvarez said, jabbing his index finger into Manning's chest, a young boot, who had no idea what he was getting himself into.

His loud, annoying voice cut through everyone. "He's got a tattoo of his girlfriend's name on his shoulder. Only a moron gets a tattoo of a chick he's just fucking. You're over here, while Jody's back home pounding your girlfriend in the ass."

"Fuck you!" Manning interjected, as he shoved Alvarez. A big mistake.

Alvarez stiffened at the insult and glared at him like a pit bull off the chain, his massive arms flexing. "You must be stupid, kid." It was funny how he called him a kid, even though he was only a year younger than him.

Manning immediately began to squirm.

Alvarez grabbed him by the neck and slammed him into the dirt. He put a boot on his neck and began shouting, "Come on bitch! Get up and give me a fight."

Manning squirmed, trying to get out from under his size thirteen boot. But it was no use, and no one else moved to help him either.

"Come on, Alvarez," I said, coming to Manning's rescue. "Let him up."

"The fuck's it to you?" he shouted, with frightening force.

I had had the misfortune of getting on his bad side before, which I was now convinced was his only side. "You proved your point. Now let the kid up!"

Alvarez smiled and winked an eye. "Be careful," he said, goading me on over our little incident. "You know what happens when someone crosses me."

I ignored his comment and focused on defusing the situation. "He's had enough, Alvarez."

He laced his fingers together and cracked all his knuckles at once, like a row of firecrackers. "I'll let you know when he's had enough, and right now, I think I'll get him to lick my boots clean and then wash my underwear. What do you think about that princess?" he said, looking down at Manning.

I walked up to him, face to face—an intimidation tactic that didn't work. Suddenly he looked twice my size. He looked big and I looked shriveled.

He shoved me—not even as hard as he could—and I went soaring back at least two meters.

I stepped up again and shoved him right back. Granted he didn't move back as far as I did, but at least he knew there would be consequences when picking a fight with me. "Let the kid up!"

Alvarez grinned a big country boy grin and removed his giant boot off the young recruit's neck. He winked an eye at me. Life was one big joke to him, and everyone was a punchline. He draped his big arm around my shoulders and said, "You got some balls, Santoli." He grabbed a Styrofoam plate, slapped down a big piece of chicken on it and handed it to me. "You've earned this. Not too many men have stood up to me. You've now done it twice."

For whatever crazy reason that actually meant something to him. Like I said, he was a true bully.

"I hear you've been spending a lot of time at that orphanage, charming that sweet little Iraqi bitch." As if his words weren't vile enough, tobacco flew out of his mouth as he spoke—specs of tar splattering across my face. "Oh I'd love a couple of hours alone with her."

A part of me wanted to say, 'Watch your mouth', but I knew it wasn't worth getting into a fight over. If anything, it only affirmed that my feelings for Nadeel were growing.

"You're wasting your time if you ask me," he continued. "You expend your emotions around these sad kids and you leave yourself vulnerable on the battlefield. I've seen it. Like when that kid got shot in the alleyway and you froze up. That shit'll get you killed."

"I wouldn't expect you to understand," I told him, "you need a heart first."

He smirked. "There's a reason why the words sympathetic and empathetic contain 'pathetic'. It makes for a sad, miserable version of a man."

"I'll keep that in mind," I said, trying to end the conversation as quickly as possible.

As he yammered on, I saw Raheem on the base, filling up his truck with donated supplies, and Nadeel off by the head shed talking to Rev.

All the boys' eyes widened at the sight of her. I couldn't blame them. After all, she was a woman of strength and undeniable grace.

Alvarez poked me in the ribs and said, "I was right, she is one sweet piece of ass. I'd like to get her into one of those belly dancing outfits and do a dance for me."

I shook my head. "Keep dreaming, grunt. You two aren't even the same species."

"Who needs to be the same species? As long as a snake can eat a rabbit, we'll do just fine." He struck a match, lit his cigarette and then pinched the flame out with his thumb and index finger, which he left on the smoldering tip of the match for a couple of seconds to show us how much of a badass he really was.

Rev saw me, along with the rest of the men, ogling Nadeel from afar and waved me over.

I tried not to look too eager as I made my way toward them. I put on a smile, which was easy to do around Nadeel. She was one of those women who were beautiful without trying. Not a shred of makeup on her, yet still she stood out in a crowd—so attractively rough. The first thought to cross my mind was *Sophia*. She had that same quality. I remember waking up to her soft, innocent face in the mornings, thinking the light must have been her best friend, the way it shined on her, and followed the lines of her face. It was obvious the light loved Nadeel just as much, if not more.

She adjusted her hijab, allowing her sea of dark brown hair to pour over her shoulders. "The children at the orphanage have put together a recital for the Marines," she said.

"Your presence has been formally requested," Rev said, finishing what she started.

I nodded. "Yes Sergeant."

Benson stepped out of the head shed and patted Rev on the shoulder. "Come join me Sergeant."

Rev excused himself, leaving me alone with Nadeel.

"Wait right here," I told her, running back to the barracks. I quickly grabbed an envelope that I had put aside and ran back, handing it over to her. "I want you to have this."

"What is it?" she said, taking it from me.

"It's my entire savings; it's not much, I know, but I want you to have it."

"I can't accept this," she said, trying to hand it back to me.

I shook my head. "The boys need food and supplies, so please take it."

She reluctantly took the envelope. "Thank you. It's very generous of you."

"How's Ali doing?" I asked.

The words hung in the air a moment. She searched my eyes to see if the question came from a sincere place or from a selfish one. "He's quiet," she replied. "Most of them are when they first arrive, but they get stronger."

"How?"

"Children are like roots. If given enough time, even roots can break through concrete."

"I hope so. I know he's hurting right now. I see it in his eyes. I know that hurt is like a broken window, you can't fix it; you can only replace the *pane*."

She gave me an ear and listened, but what I really wanted was her spine. She was brave, braver than any Marine I had ever met, because her bravery had nothing to do with a bulletproof vest or an M16.

"Families are reminders that we are not alone in the world," she said. "When we lose them, we realize that there is a certain loneliness that can never be filled. Ultimately the condition of life is one of being alone before God, but there is also nothing harder and scarier than being before God, when there's no one holding your hand."

"These boys won't have to be alone," I said. "You're giving them hope."

"Even I won't always be here. I will soon have to leave this place."

I was confused. "I thought this was home?"

"When living conditions in Baghdad became unbearable, my family had to leave our home and seek refuge in Amman, Jordan, with my uncle. That is where they are now. That is where I will have to go soon. They have already arranged my marriage to a man from Jordan."

Arranged? Shit! Why did I have to come across you now, here, in this place, under these circumstances? Feeling disheartened by the news, I covered it with a joke. "Someone actually wants to marry you?"

Her eyes looked slightly amused. She cocked an eyebrow. "Inshalla!"

"What's that mean?"

"If Allah wills it."

I smiled, as if there was any doubt. "Inshalla."

I could tell my affirmation hadn't convinced her. She glanced around, unsure of what to make of me. I then called her beautiful, and immediately she began painting a picture of a younger version of herself that was even more beautiful than the one standing before me.

"That can't be possible," I said to her.

She smiled, and her cheeks became stained with blush. Suddenly there was a hum of interest, and a hint of admiration in her eyes. "You should know that you're making a difference in Ali's life."

"I hope so," I said, "I hope I can honor his father and show him how to be a good man."

"Like you?" She had a theatricality about her, where I could never tell if she was being sarcastic or just cruel.

"Not like me at all," I said, giving into the cruelty, but also the truth. "I want Ali to be better than me."

"Don't be so hard on yourself," she said, easing up on me. "You have some good qualities in you as well."

"And bad ones of course?"

"Well, boys will be boys," she said, as if the world were out of men, as if all we'd ever be is boys. Maybe she was right. Maybe there were no more men left in the world. Come to think of it I'd never seen one. Just boys pretending to be men, denouncing their titles and exchanging them for heavier ones, like moving out of our boyhood home with our posters of heroes and table-top models of life, and into an unfamiliar neighborhood. I barely had a father. I was raised by a boy to be a boy.

Nadeel could tell; she knew it the second she met me. She was a great judge of character. Even without knowing my life story, she knew

I was holding back, afraid to relive certain moments, while unable to forget others. In an effort to get it out of me, she slowly began to open up about her life, hoping that I would reciprocate. She told me about the sunsets from her childhood and I told her about the fireworks on New Year's Eve. She told me about her mother and I told her about mine. She told me about her father and I told her about my mother again. She stopped me and said, "No. Tell me about your father."

"What's there to tell? I don't remember his face, but I can describe the back of his hand in great detail if you'd like."

The line made her think. Perhaps having an insight into my past would make her more sympathetic to my situation. But before we could finish our conversation, a voice got in the way.

It was Radner, a private from Bravo Company. "Santoli, come quick!" he said, with tense excitement. "They found a body hanging in the city square. They think it might be your shepherd boy."

"Zaid?" I asked.

"Whatever his name is, they found him dead."

It felt like somebody had punched me in the breadbasket as hard as they could. "What makes you think it's him?"

"He's bloodied up pretty bad, but we think it's him."

I turned to Nadeel, who quickly said, "Go...and be safe." It wasn't exactly how I wanted to finish our conversation, but nonetheless it was over.

Rev—who was only a few meters away—heard Radner shouting, and told Alvarez and me to get to the Humvee.

As we sped through the dirt roads of A'saliyah to ID the dead body, I kept on hoping they had somehow made a mistake. Out here, it could've been just about anybody. There were many people who were helping the military, which the insurgency was making examples of. As much as I wouldn't wish death upon anybody, on that day, I wished it had been anyone other than Zaid: the poor shepherd boy who never hurt a soul, the father of three kids, the polite little corn farmer, who believed that Allah would save him.

We arrived at the location and Rev and I jumped out before the Humvee even came to a complete stop. I had to see for myself. I had to know for sure. The truth didn't bring me any solace, however.

There it was, just like Radner said, a dead body, hanging, spinning like a top in the breeze. There was no mistaking it; it was him. The tongue that he used for his customary yes sir, no sir, had now been cut out of his mouth—a warning for anyone who dared to speak to us about the insurgency. They had used his body as target practice, staining his white linen garbs with swirls of blood, all of which reminded me of the barber's pole that hung outside the Lebanese hairdresser down the street from my house. There really is nothing that can prepare you for something like that.

The second I saw him, I could feel my biceps contracting like a prize-fighter before a championship bout. Then my entire arm went stiff and my hands became two small sledgehammers ready to destroy anyone who seemed even the slightest bit suspicious: the man across the street with a small package in his hands, the woman on the roof with a cellphone, the teenager in the back of the pickup truck with a backpack strapped over his shoulder. Everyone looked like they had a motive.

But those were all just visceral responses. I honestly can't tell you what I truly *felt* the second I saw him. I don't know if I blocked it out, or if I just felt every emotion all at once to the point I couldn't distinguish one from the other. I do, however, remember reverting inside, pulling all my senses away from reality and focusing them on just keeping my mind stable, my legs sturdy, my eyes level and my fingers ready to let loose.

Radner turned toward me; I could see his lips moving just beyond the current reach of my senses.

I had to ask him to repeat himself.

"Is that your guy?" he asked again, "Is that Hamed?"

"Zaid," I said correcting him.

"What's that?"

I turned around, grabbed him by the collar and yelled right in his face, "Zaid! His name is Zaid! Get it right asshole!"

"Woah…Relax!"

Rev grabbed me and pulled me away. "Get a hold of yourself."

I kept on shouting, unable to articulate my anger. "Fuck these motherfuckers, Rev! Fuck them all!"

"Hey! Take it easy! Getting angry is not going to do you any good right now."

Rev was right. I took in a deep breath and tried to calm myself the best I could, but stopping a racehorse in mid stride is a dangerous thing; my heart was racing just as fast. It felt like it was going to rip right out of my chest.

"Take a look at this," Rev said pointing at the ground, which was littered with surveillance pictures of us and Zaid. "They've been watching us for quite a while."

I looked over at Alvarez, who had put a gun in Zaid's face the last time we all saw him alive. He had this strange gleam in his eyes and an expression on his face that was hard to decipher. It was either satisfaction or surprise. I remember hoping for anything but satisfaction. He had gotten the drop on me before with his bullshit prank, but a man who takes satisfaction in the death of innocent people, isn't too far off turning a prank into a real-life event. And definitely not a man you want to share a room with. I never asked Alvarez what the look was. Perhaps I didn't want to hear the truth. He finally took his eyes off of Zaid's body and headed back to the Humvee.

But for me, moving a leg seemed impossible. I just stood there, staring at Zaid. Even after the last spectators had wandered off, I still couldn't move.

"We gotta get out of here," Rev said. "There's probably some Hajjis watching us right now, waiting to pick us off. Even worse, insurgents have had ample time to place and camouflage roadside bombs all around this place."

Rev's words floated over me. I was too busy looking across the street, at two boys who were playing soccer with an old patched-up soccer ball. Even with a body hanging only a few meters away from them, they went about playing their game. Their expressions never changed; they remained unmoved by the violence. It is said that when you make abnormal things seem normal you have officially succeeded at repressing a people. Well, abnormal was now their reality. We had made these children comfortable with the idea of death. There is no bigger sin in the world if you ask me.

"If only they knew," I said, turning to Rev."

He looked at me confused. "Knew what?"

"They push and push so hard trying to scare us, but if only they knew that we don't want to be here anymore than they want us here." It was as if the noose was now around *my* neck—getting tighter and tighter—and Rev could tell. "We promised Zaid he would be safe. We promised his family that they would always have him. But we lied. That's what we do. We lie to people. We're liars. There isn't enough ink housed in the New York Times to write down all the lies that we have told these people."

Even though Rev looked concerned for me, I could tell he was feeling the same thing. He never said it though. Not Rev. Not in a uniform. It wouldn't be appropriate.

I turned back toward the children, who were still playing. It's unfathomable what you find at times in the creases between reality and truth. The solidarity of hidden dunes brought with them dust devils fifty meters in diameter. The children played in them, burning to dust in the endless void. Their laughter rode the funnel all the way to the top. I closed my eyes and counted the octaves between their moments of rapture, hoping to find their frequency of vibration to help me leave that place behind—if even for a moment.

CHAPTER 11

On Tuesday of the following week, we returned to the orphanage, where the boys performed their recital: a song they had written themselves. I watched Ali put aside his stage fright and muster up the courage to sing a few words. He sang about his family, dedicating a verse to each of them. The first line was about his mother, who he called his angel, her hands like wings and eyes like the ocean. He then sang about his sister and her angelic voice that could be heard drifting on the wind, and from every corner of the house. Lastly, he sang about his father, or 'the hero' as he called him, how he would drop everything to help him and his sister—and he had, more times than Ali could count. As soon as he was done, he became noticeably aware of all the eyes on him, and he turned around and ran off the stage as fast as he could.

    I had that urge that I'm sure parents get to check up on their kids. I wanted to go back there and tell him how proud of him I was, and how well he sang, but the recital went on for another hour. I could see Alvarez dozing off in his chair. If it wasn't for Rev's elbow, he would have most likely fell asleep.

    After the last song, Raheem handed us a plate of Baytinijan Maqli (fried eggplant with tahini sauce), fatuous (a salad dish), and hummus with olive oil and pine nuts.

    Alvarez scoffed at the food. It was like handing caviar to a dog. He just wanted his dog food: hamburgers, hotdogs and chili fries.

    Rev called him a xenophobe, a fancy word which meant he had a fear of other cultures. But in reality, I think he just hated anything he didn't understand.

We finished our plate just as a noisy crowd of little children in colorful shirts, shorts, and old, torn sneakers surrounded us. Their open smiles cheered rays of sunshine, and their little hands pawed at us, reaching out for treats.

Yusuf came by and shewed them all away as if their powers had no effect on him. He had seen them all too often, I guess. When they dispersed I felt the happiness disperse with them.

I thought nothing of Yusuf, at first, but soon I found that I was unable to take my eyes off of him. He was always sniffing around like a rabid dog you couldn't trust. At the time I couldn't figure out if his anger was targeted at me or just the situation at hand. I couldn't figure out what he was doing at the orphanage. He reminded me of that one teacher that clearly hated children yet chose to teach. Why? What satisfaction did he take from being here? At least teachers get paid, he was doing it all for room and board. Maybe that was enough for him. Either way, I didn't like him.

Raheem, a man who was his complete opposite, saw me and made his way toward me. "Mr. Santoli, how are you with engines?"

"I can hold my own," I said.

"I hope that means you're good, because I could use some help with the school bus."

"Sure."

He handed me a bucket of greasy, assorted tools and said, "Follow me."

He led me out to a detached building, where the old bird's nest and rathole that he called a bus sat. It had been donated to the orphanage a decade ago by a farmer from the East.

"It used to work," Raheem said, like it was an old legend that he had heard about but couldn't confirm. "I believe we can get it working again. It would be nice to take the children out when the war simmers down. And God forbid it doesn't, then we can evacuate all of them to a safer place."

"Let's hope it doesn't come down to that," I said putting Raheem's mind at ease. I grabbed the tools and quickly got to work, while Raheem went off to find some spare parts.

I was sprawled on the floor, working beneath the bus, when I heard something and slid out to find Ali observing me. He seemed intrigued and curious, standing on his thin bird legs and slim ankles. Even through the shadows you could see his powerful eyes, which cut through the room, straight into mine. He saw my greasy hands and picked up a rag and handed it to me.

I wiped them off and invited him to take a seat and watch. "Can you do me a favor?" I asked him.

He nodded.

"Can you read the paper to me?" I pointed to a table. "My Arabic's not so good."

He took a hold of the paper and read it aloud in Arabic, forgetting that I couldn't understand the words. I didn't stop him, though. I wanted him to feel comfortable enough to speak his mother tongue in front of me, like he would have with his family. When he was finished, I asked him, "Can you translate something for me?"

He nodded again.

I opened the newspaper down the middle and pointed to a column. "Can you translate this for me?"

Before reading anything, he directed a brief but intense glance at me, and when he did finally speak, it was with great sincerity. He read about Iraqis who were turning out in great numbers, defying death threats and suicide bombers, all to vote in the country's first free election in fifty years. He then turned a few pages and stopped, reading as if for himself. His little hands slowly and deliberately traced out the lines of the words: over seven thousand Iraqis killed. His eyes drifted away from the page and in his soft, fragile voice, he asked, "What happens when we die?"

I stopped and looked at him. Within his eyes waged the perfect storm, filled with shipwrecks and regrets. "No one knows for sure," I said, dreading the question, which was better left in the hands of philosophers and poets. "But my grandfather once told me that during open heart surgery, he remembered a feeling of bliss. He said it was like a balloon being filled up with helium and let go. The next thing he remembers is the sounds of life-giving machines pumping and beeping, and the voices of panicked doctors saying, 'We got him back'. He said it was a peaceful feeling more than anything, like returning home after a long journey. Later he would come to find out that his heart had stopped during the surgery and he was pronounced clinically dead for two whole minutes. Now I don't know if it was just the ramblings of an old man, or if he really did feel something happening on the operating table. I like to think that it was true, that there is something waiting for us after we leave this place. Not a heaven or a hell, but perhaps bliss of some kind."

I'm not sure it was the answer Ali wanted to hear, or the one that he had been taught by his parents, but it's the only one I had. I tried to change the subject to get his mind off the pain. "You want to help me?"

He shrugged his shoulders indifferently.

"I'll take that as a yes. Here, take this wrench."

He fumbled with the wrench and began torquing it the wrong way.

"Wait," I said, taking it from him and manipulating it from left to right with the soft, regular rhythm of the clock. "You have to turn it this way." Ali took over and together we changed out the oil and replaced the air filter.

Raheem came in and saw the two of us diligently at work. He put down a box of spare parts and with the wink of an eye, he stepped outside, leaving the two of us to bond (two fatherless children, learning from one another, torn yet together).

When we were finished, I put the key into the ignition and looked down at Ali. "You ready?"

He gently nodded.

I turned the key, and that old rusty bus, which had been sitting in the hot Iraqi sun for the better part of Ali's life, finally started. It lumbered to life like an old man getting up to pee. And just like an old man getting up to pee, it leaked a little along the way.

As I smiled, I saw the creases around Ali's brow soften. A look of satisfaction took over his face. It was clinching proof that he could mend or create whatever he wanted. For a boy who would never see home again, he looked like he could build one with his own two hands.

I took out Rev's camera and took a picture of the two of us: a stoic little boy, and a wide-eyed, ignorant Marine. I showed Ali and he touched the screen and smiled.

"I got something else for you," I said.

"What?" he asked with a hint of excitement.

In a place where the drop of a ball can begin an impromptu game of soccer, what else would I give a young boy, but a soccer ball. The second he saw it, his face swelled into a smile, and his eyes harvested all the light in the room. It's amazing how children have the ability to resurrect themselves from nothing. In that moment you'd swear he was just another boy from back home.

"You want to play?"

He gave me a nod, putting his problems on the shelf for the time being and picked up the ball.

Together, we stepped through the rear gate, into the alley behind the orphanage, where children were playing, barefoot through minefields. They stood atop mounds of debris, which lightly blown sand and dust revealed to be a school sign. They constructed make-believe forts and picked through the black gutter water for any treasure they could find to sell. It was a playground out of perdition.

The children saw me in my uniform and tensed up. Putting my arm around Ali, I gave them a smile. Seeing this gesture of affection seemed to put them at their ease.

Ali took note of a little boy across the street, sitting in the lap of his father, playing cards. The man pulled his son close, holding him for what seemed like it may just be forever. Ali continued to stare, his interest cut with jealousy. You didn't have to be a mind reader to know what he was thinking: Why me? Why not that boy? Why not that family? Who decides these things?

I'm afraid I still haven't figured it out.

Helping him take his mind off of all the questions, I kicked the ball toward him and we played soccer in the ruins of his city.

He took everything his father had taught him and kicked it back with a strained blast of dust.

"Good kick," I said, slashing the ball up the alley.

Ali sprinted after it, past the twisted, mangled rebar, to the top of the mountain of debris, which was most likely someone's home. He reached for the ball, paused, bent over and picked up something else. As he continued to stare at it—his silhouette pressed against the afternoon sky—I made my way toward him. The sun refracted off of the object, shining a sliver of light onto his face.

I spied a lone bullet in his hand. I could see beads of sweat gathering on Ali's brow, and his little eyes tightening at the memory of the tragic event that claimed his family. The event I was responsible for.

A storm was starting to come up. The wind rode through Ali's clothes. His face turned skyward, his eyes shut tight, and he said a prayer on top the mound, as if being higher up would expedite his words to heaven.

To this day, I have no idea what he said, but I'm sure it had something to do with peace or hope. Something to help him cope and understand why things are the way they are. Something he couldn't get from this place, or from the other boys, or from Raheem or me or Nadeel. Perhaps he was praying for a miracle, a resurrection, praying to make the impossible, possible. It's a good thing as any to pray for, I suppose. After all, religion and science met with the Big Bang. They started on the same day. So why couldn't it be possible?

Then suddenly, I was reminded why.

Off in the distance ignorant fingers convulsed over the trigger of a heartless machinegun. That's why. Because what God can do, man can undo, in a matter of seconds. Man is equal parts destruction and creation, and once he destroys, he cannot recreate. He is a hollow creator, one not to be worshipped.

The street echoed from the stutter of the machinegun. The sounds startled Ali and he dropped the bullet, which clinked down the mountain of debris, landing by my feet.

I felt a heavy burden all of a sudden. The secret that I had been keeping from Ali—the secret I could no longer keep, not with a clear conscience—was forcing its way up my throat. I was sick and tired of all the over-baked lies and undercooked truths that I had served up to this kid on a dirty, porcelain platter. As I looked at him, thinking about all the billions of alternate realities, branching off into the millions of possible destinies, he got stuck with this one—this faded glimmer of a life, all because of me.

"Come down," I said. "It's not safe up there."

He slowly climbed down off the mound and dropped the soccer ball by my feet. The moment had clearly reaped him of all desire to play.

Honesty accounts for something in life; hell, it's the only thing that really matters. As much as I wanted to hold my tongue, or scream inside *don't tell him, he's not ready for it, he doesn't really want to hear it, he can't handle it,* it's the only right thing I've ever done in my life. So I told him the truth. I told him how it was me; it was my shot and if I hadn't taken it, it would've cost me my life. I told him about the aim, the wind factor and the trajectory to help my case. A desperate attempt, I know, but all I really wanted in that moment was his forgiveness.

As I laid out the truth, the little remaining color in Ali's face drained away and he became as pale as a ghost. He took a few steps back, serious, scared, his eyes lowered. It was one of those fragile moments where things could've gone either way. He could've either accepted my apology and accepted the truth, accepted his fate, accepted the improbable weight of the tragedy, or he could've given into the anger, coiled his fists, spat in my face and declared me dead.

Sadly, he chose the latter. His eyes rose with angry disbelief.

I reached out to him, drawing him into my arms, pressing him close to me.

He pushed against my chest, his little hands strong and solid, as if they were guarding an inner chaos that could've rushed out at any time and destroyed me right on the spot. "No!" he shouted. His words were fragile, slowly breaking every time he opened his mouth. "I-I-c-ca-can't."

My eyes cried silent apologies, giving him glimpses of my crippled soul, but Ali wasn't having it. He put up his hands to protect himself. Unfortunately, they offered no protection against the emotional hail hammering him head on.

If only I could've given him some of my strength and he could've given me some of his innocence. Then perhaps we could've both made it through that moment. But no such exchange took place. It was now official. His heart was shut tight, letting no more love in. He had made the mistake once. This time, he stood there shaking his head, like *never again*.

I made one last attempt to reach out to him, to bring him back off the road of hate. "It didn't just happen to you," I said. "It happened to me as well. It's my memory too. I was there. I have to live with the knowledge that it was me, that it was my fault, it was my shot. Nothing happens in this world, without it taking something or giving something to you, and it took something from me as well. I swear to you, I'd change it all in a second if I could."

His lips said nothing, but his eyes denounced me dead.

"Ali...."

He shook his head again, begging me to stop talking.

As I took a step toward him, he bolted down the alley, back toward the orphanage.

I didn't give chase. I'm sure the last thing he wanted was to be pursued.

By the time I made it up to his room, Ali was lying in bed, face down in his pillow. Nadeel was seated on the bed, holding his hand and pleading, "What is it, Ali? You can tell me." She held his hand as he cried the heartbroken tears of someone who had lost his one last hope. Nadeel saw me standing in the doorway. As she turned toward me, tentative, eyes searching for an answer, something unspoken passed between us. She got up off the bed and pulled me into the hallway. "What happened?"

I tried to find the words to tell her, but all that came out was, "His family…it was my fault." I didn't have to finish; my discomfort was enough. It did a better job than my words ever could.

Nadeel didn't know whether to slap me or cry. She did neither, burying her emotions behind a professional mask instead. "This is the way of things here. This is the plague you have brought with you. What did you think would happen?"

I opened my mouth, yet nothing came out.

Nadeel shook her head, and as soon as her eyes flatlined, I knew any chance for sympathy was dead. The vulnerability was gone, and Nadeel with it. She swept up her littered affections for me and walked away, disappointed.

I breathed a deep sigh. I had just lost everything. That's when I realized: When it comes to the final nail in your coffin it doesn't matter if it's dull or sharp, it'll still hold, because a lifetime of prior nails have helped seal that coffin shut.

I took one last look at Ali. He lifted his head off the pillow and stared back at me. His eyes were deserted like so many homes in his city.

I had burnt him with my actions and he had burnt me with his words. *Perhaps we're even.* But no. Not even close.

Crouched low in the doorway, the other boys stared back at me, horrified by the news. Here, tears spread faster than gossip. By the time I made it down the steps, the entire orphanage knew. It was on my face, it was in my eyes. The scene had exhausted me. I wanted to stretch myself on the ground like I used to do by my mother's feet when I was a child. I remember how it felt like being under the tree of life, being shaded from pain and regret. Her hands were an expansive canopy of leaves, and her feet strong roots, offering a kind of stability that couldn't be found anywhere else. But that tree was gone now, just like Ali.

I slunk back to the Humvee, where Alvarez was pressed up against the front bumper finishing his third smoke. Embezzling Nadeel's words, he said, "What did you think was gonna happen?"

He was the last person in the world I wanted to hear from, but he kept at it.

"Did you think you and the kid were gonna drive off into the sunset together?" He smirked and stared at me.

I stared back at him in an unflinching way, ready for anything.

"Get in the truck the two of you," Rev said, "we have to get back."

Alvarez peeled himself off the bumper and got into the driver seat, while I got into the back of the Humvee.

Once inside, Rev gave me a glance like one throws a question in the air.

I was slow to respond. "I wanted to leave this place the second I got here, but now I can't seem to leave the idea of these people, these children."

Rev reached over and put a hand on my shoulder. "It's not going to be easy."

"You think it was wrong for me to tell him the truth?"

Rev smirked.

"What's so funny?"

"*You* asking *me* that question."

"What about it?"

"Do you know what Ernie stands for?" he said, bringing up his first name, which I rarely heard being spoken.

I shrugged my shoulders. "I always assumed it was Arnold."

He shook his head. "No. It's Earnest. Not like Hemingway, but with an 'A', like the word. My mother said I was born with an earnest face. But I wonder what she would say about me now. I don't see an earnest man when I look in the mirror." He shook his head. "You know what Benjamin Disraeli said about being earnest?"

"No. What?"

"He said, 'what is earnest is not always true; on the contrary, error is often more earnest than truth'. So maybe I am earnest, after all. And maybe you are too."

I thought about his words. I let them simmer on low, hoping to make them more appetizing. "I don't know anything about earnestness," I said. "There's too much moral abortion here. I know the right thing to do, but I can't bring it to fruition. It dies after conception, somewhere in the birth place of my mind."

"You have to trust in God, my friend."

"There's no God here that much is for certain."

He looked at me questioningly.

"Sorry, Rev. I didn't mean…."

"It's alright," he said with a smile. "God is both the eagle that you ascend on and the pigeon that craps on your window."

"Is that right?"

"That's right. He'll take your gratitude *and* your blame."

"What if I got no gratitude left in me?"

"Then He'll take double the blame, I suppose."

I smirked. "I've never known a sympathetic God. As far as I know, sympathy and God don't live on the same block."

Rev shook me by the shoulder like a big brother would. "Unfortunately, before the garden of peace stands the iron gates of absolution locked and bolted shut."

That one went clear over my head. "What are you talking about, Rev?"

"Forgiveness. That's what you want, isn't it, from the boy?"

"I'm not sure that's going to help me now."

"Sure it will. Forgiveness goes a long way. That's why confessionals exist in the first place, right? Everyone wants forgiveness. They're begging for it."

"Yeah, but who really steps out completely free of sins? Does anyone really get that courtesy? No one I've ever met. I've seen people trying, some their whole lives, but none successfully. You hold out, waiting for those moments of peace, but before you know it, half your life's gone by and those moments were far and few or came and went too quick to remember and too short to matter. Either way, it wasn't what you thought it would be. Hell, it wasn't even close."

Rev remained undeterred by my blasphemous thoughts. "More of a reason to believe in something," he said, "something bigger than yourself."

I gave him that look that said *I just don't know anymore.*

CHAPTER 12

Restless from wrestling with my thoughts, I tightly forced them to the back of my mind, and spent the next week concentrating on my duties. As the support element, we were pulling security for trucks carrying food, water, parts and mail. All around us were starving people, without clean water, displaced from their families and their homes, and yet we were receiving letters from our families, wishing us well, sipping clean water and eating hardy. If all that wasn't enough, I finally got the news I *thought* I wanted to hear.

"Only a week left in this hellhole," Rev said.

"Yeah. One more week."

"Hell yeah," Alvarez chirped in. "Can't wait for the girls back home, and to sleep in my own bed."

I gave him an unenthusiastic, "Yeah…home sweet home." But home didn't have the same meaning for me anymore. I had been racking my brain for the last month trying to figure out what I was going to do back home. I had no diploma, no résumé and no prospects. The idea of home frightened me, just as much as the idea of Iraq did when I first arrived.

But I was getting ahead of myself. I still had a week left, and a week in Iraq is like a lifetime anywhere else. I could get shot tomorrow or blown to bits just before the convoy leaves for the airport. Instead of fearing the uncertainty of tomorrow, I had to focus on the uncertainty of today.

The thought quickly got pushed out of my mind when the Humvee in front of us came to a stop.

"I think we got a possible IED on the road," Alvarez said.

Maybe today's the day I die after all.

"Damn window-lickers," he continued, "they think everything looks like a bomb." He was referring to the IED hunters in the lead Humvee, whose job it was to stare out the window, looking for bombs.

I noticed the time on the digital watch stuck to the dash. It was 11:34. That same goddam number that was always following me. I'd always pause for a second to stare at it. Definitely not a comforting number or a comforting thought.

A few Marines got out of the lead Humvees to investigate. Alvarez and I joined them. We kept a trained eye on our surroundings, making our way toward the possible IED. I looked down, carefully watching my footfalls. Through the windows of the two-story high mud-brick buildings, I could see eyes watching us. There were more than half-a-dozen: some visible, then a few more from secret cracks and peepholes in rotted out buildings. The weight of all the eyes was heavy. I remember how everything felt like it was moving in slow motion.

Suddenly, I noticed a wire protruding out of the dirt. "Watch your 5 and 25," I said to Alvarez.

He gave me a quick nod.

My eyes followed the wire, as it snaked through the ground, tracing out a lazy line. My mouth went from 0 to 100mph. "Don't move! We might have a possible secondary. Repeat we might have a second IED."

Through the radio, I heard Rev shouting, "Copy that. Where is it?"

I followed the wire, which at times disappeared into the ground. To my surprise, the long line snaked right under the lead Humvee. It was attached to a large artillery shell that was sticking its head out of the dirt. "Oh fuck!"

"Where is it?" Rev shouted.

Alvarez beat me to it. "We're parked right on top of it!"

It was the kind of explosive that was armed with a blasting cap and could be set off by a radio frequency from a garage door opener or a cellphone. I immediately began looking around for a trigger man. It was a bad day to be holding an electronic device in your hand.

No one dared to open their doors and exit the vehicles. "Everybody, slowly get out through the turret," Rev said to the lead Humvee, "one by one."

What I remember most about that day is the heat of the sun on my neck with just the slightest breeze moving around me. It could've been any summer day back home. I remember eyes drifting about and mouths moving slowly. And then, BOOM, gravity, suddenly gone. The inside of the first vehicle became a pinball machine: heads banged into each other, hands became safety-pins holding bodies in place, bones snapped like kindling and human molecules separated at the seams. Everything was now dangerous debris, shooting off in every direction. The occupants hit the roof of the Humvee, and the roof hit the ground, crushing the body in the turret.

Time stopped. My senses became acute. If someone had checked my temperature, it would've been 120 degrees. My ears were still ringing, hurting. My eyesight was blurry. My face was sore, as if I'd just been punched in the nose by the undisputed heavyweight champion of the world.

All around me, dazed Marines slowly stumbled back to their feet: Alvarez, a Sergeant, three Privates and a Corporal. They were all I could see. Everyone else became a prairie dog, scurrying back down whatever alley they came from.

Amidst the chaos, I turned toward our Humvee and the sole occupant, Rev, who was still in one piece. The lead Humvee had taken the full brunt of the explosion, along with a couple of storefronts.

Still in the kill zone, Rev patted the tattoo on his arm: his saving grace. As he did, grace was suddenly under fire. A second explosion ripped him in half, along with our vehicle. The blast left a crater ten meters wide and ejected debris at least sixty feet into the air. The blackened sand looked like a Jackson Pollock painting—and not one of his good ones.

The steel carcass of the Humvee sat in the undulating heat waves, searing like a freshly lit barbecue. The putrid smell of blood and burning flesh quickly filled the air. Smoke and dust were everywhere. It was hard to see if Rev was still alive, even though I knew nothing could have survived a blast like that.

Alvarez's eyes were wide open, dilated, disoriented. He had taken a fraction of the explosion. He clutched his torso as if it were about to fall to pieces. He was stunned, but he knew well enough to press against the wound on the side of his face. "I can't stop the bleeding!" he shouted. The blood began seeping out through the cracks of his fingers.

The Corporal, a man by the name of Blackwood, rushed to his aid, dragging him across the ground. "Look at me," he said, "you're going to be alright!"

Once the shock wore off, there became a calmness in our movements. The adrenaline had leveled off, or rather been exhausted completely.

Before the smoke of battle had lifted, I saw Rev with blood running down his face. "Jesus Christ!" He was still alive. Barely. Not the kind of *alive* you want to be. The kind of alive where you beg someone to put you out of your misery. He was down; his heart was hemorrhaging in his chest. His lungs nearly jumped out of his throat, begging for a small breath of air. Blood bubbled in his mouth and his eyes slowly closed for the last time. Rev was dead, yet there was no moment of silence, everything just continued to get louder.

Through the scope of my rifle, I searched for a triggerman, and noticed a suspicious old Datsun truck parked in the middle of the road. Fifteen feet away from it, was a lone staggering figure.

"I got something at my three o'clock! Possible triggerman."

The man saw me looking at him; he quickly jumped into his truck and peeled away at a hundred miles per hour. As I took aim at the truck, a late-model Range Rover with blacked-out windows, queued up from an adjacent alley. All the windows rolled down simultaneously, and shots sprayed out, turning bodies into human pincushions. One more Marine was dead and two more wounded, among them: twenty-four-year-old Daniels from Kentucky, and Creed, a twenty-year-old boot who was greener than the grass on a freshly mowed golf course. He had taken a shot in the face, but he was still alive.

Alvarez pushed Blackwood out of the way and swung his M16, while trying to get back up to his feet. He let out ten shots in succession and not a single one hit the target. That's Alvarez for you.

I took cover, returning fire. But it was too late. They were gone.

"We're too exposed out here," said Blackwood. "We gotta get moving, quickly."

"Request an immediate evac," I told him. "Let's get the hell out of here."

Alvarez finally managed to get back onto his feet. In the rubble, he found the naked belly of a very pregnant woman. A civilian casualty. Alvarez was in an uncharacteristic state of shock. "Is that you?" he said, vacantly.

"What?" I replied, looking over my shoulder at him.

"Is that you?" he said again, his face cracking at the seams.

In a single terrible moment, I realized that he wasn't talking to me. He was talking to the dead body.

"Jill! Is that you?" He moved uneasily toward the pregnant woman. His balance was messed up from a blown inner-ear and his massive frame was shaking. Having run himself into the ground, he collapsed against a brick wall, holding onto it. He buried his head into his shoulder, pitifully.

"What the hell are you doing?" I asked.

"That's my sister. They killed my sister. They killed her."

"What the hell's he talking about?" Blackwood shouted. "That's not your sister. That's an Iraqi woman."

"That's my sister, Jill."

He was losing it. Alvarez, a man who had gone over the edge more times than a bungee jumper, couldn't bounce back from this. Then again, war has no pause button, no half-time, no intermission; it's a total and utter cluster-fuck. It couldn't have been made more apparent in that moment.

Alvarez's stone-like demeanor cracked, and he began sobbing like a twelve-year-old girl. He took out the cartridge from his rifle and began beating it against the corner of the building, shards flying off in every direction. To him, this was the real weapon of mass destruction, this *thing* capable of destroying lives. Each time he battered it, he insanely recited, "Oooh-rah! Oooh-rah! Oooh-rah!"

The Sergeant approached him and shook him by the shoulder. "What's the matter with you? Get your shit together, Marine!"

He clattered to the ground in tears, a big country boy. His mouth, like the rings of Saturn, spun words around him as particles of ice and dust. "Fuck this place!" he said. "Fuck it to hell! We kill people for a living. That's what we do."

The band of brothers that we were supposed to be, the Marine Code, and yet, not one man moved to console him. The Sergeant slapped him up side the back of the head and said, "Get your shit together!"

He was having an eye-opening, awe-inspiring realization, but that didn't matter. To the Sergeant, it was nothing a hundred milligrams of Thorazine couldn't cure. It was get your shit together Marine. It wasn't exactly the hug or the pat on the back he needed or wanted, but it was the only response he would get. We were, after all, at the bottom of the food chain, the expendables.

Alvarez's madness was catching; I could feel it. You can only see so much death before enough is enough. I threw in my two cents, which is all that my words were worth. "Give him a second," I said. "Come on, Alvarez, get up."

Too many men go off to war without discovering first who they are. It makes for a perfect drone. Shallow drones like Alvarez had no tools to help them in the face of disaster. All he had were his orders, and when orders cease to make sense the brain shuts down, emotions go haywire.

For the first time, I found myself feeling sorry for him. Then I quickly realized it wasn't him I was feeling sorry for. It was me. It was us. Because empathy isn't putting yourself in another man's shoes, it's buying a pair in your own size.

As Alvarez wiped away the first real emotion I had witnessed off his face, in came the cavalry to the rescue. Our orders came over the radio. "Move to your extraction point for pick up."

"Roger that!" I replied.

We moved to a safer place and deployed green smoke to mark the landing area. I could hear the Medevac chopper coming toward us. It quickly turned the dirt roads of Iraq into small dust funnels.

Medics assisted the wounded. They put five men and one woman in a body bag and Alvarez on a stretcher to be loaded into the bird. As they hauled what was left of Rev into the chopper, I checked myself for the first time, to see if I had any injuries. There wasn't a scratch on me.

It didn't take long to fill up the aircraft, maybe two or three minutes. There is something to be said about military precision. They laid Creed in a corner of the craft, and sprawled Alvarez in the back. He was crying and groaning in pain, but nobody spoke real words. After a little while, I looked to Creed again and he was dead. His head was limp, and his mouth filled with blood.

I turned my attentions out the side of the chopper as it flew low along the Tigris, where slender handmade boats peacefully sailed down the river, filled to the rim with reeds. It was a timeless image. It could've been a century or millennia ago and nobody here would've noticed the difference—a time long before bombs or automatic weapons. I found myself wishing for such a peaceful time, for such an undisturbed life, isolated from all outside influence. Then again, peace isn't why they recruited me, and Alvarez confirmed it with his screams of war. "I'll kill these assholes! I swear."

As badly as he was injured, I wasn't sure if he'd ever get the chance. We brought him back to the Combat Support Hospital, where throngs of military personnel and wounded survivors were being tended to. He was carried in by stretcher and moved to one of the beds that was partitioned off by curtains, where a crowd of surgical gloves tended to him and the other survivors.

Feeling overwhelmed, I stepped outside, running the ordeal over and over in my mind. I asked myself questions and desperately tried to find the answers. I searched deep within and found the only thing that remained of Rev: memories. I thought about the first time I met him. I was under the assumption he was going to be more like my Drill Sergeant, a complete hard-ass, but the two were nothing alike. The first month I arrived, Rev could tell I was scared and unsure of myself. He went out of his way to make sure I felt comfortable. He let me know that we were more than just a team, we were now brothers.

We would chase the evening hours, playing chess and talking about our lives. I would get entangled in his stories about the town he grew up in, back when he was 'to curious for his own good', as Rev would say. It was a small town very much like my own. He grew up on a trampled-down farm by the side of a country road, where large, round ton bales dotted the countryside, shining golden bright in the afternoon sun. A place where rivers changed with the seasons and the water was as fresh and clean as the air.

He also told me about his wife, and how nervous he was when he proposed to her. It wasn't because he was afraid that she would say no, it was because he was afraid that he wouldn't be able to give her everything he wanted to. He was afraid of falling short. It was just like Rev to worry more about other's needs than his own. I remember how one night Rev showed up in the barracks with a bottle of Jack that he had found in an abandoned warehouse, while we were on patrol. We spent the night telling old stories and taking swigs until four in the morning.

I remember how it pissed Alvarez off something awful. But Rev was the only person Alvarez respected. I could tell he was holding back *some* of his ignorance when he was around him. One could say it was because of Rev's rank, but no. That's just the kind of man Rev was. You wanted to impress him, you wanted him to like you. He was our moral compass, after all, with the courage to say the things that the rest of us only think.

I must have been out there for at least two hours, reminiscing and going in and out of tears, when suddenly the office door opened and Ryan Benson appeared, looking a little distant.

"Sir, how's Alvarez doing?"

He shook his head and said, "He's done. He's going to be Medevac to Germany, immediately. Doctor said he has traumatic brain injury."

I knew most Marines on the base were going to think *good riddance*, but I couldn't help but feel sympathy for Alvarez. The big bad wrestler had finally been pinned for the final three count.

"And Rev, sir?" I asked, hoping to share some of my sadness.

Benson looked remorseful. "Mortuary Affairs will be taking him home. He was one of the best we had. He'll be sorely missed." Benson didn't waste any time in undo sentimentality. He moved on, while I stood there, vacant and alone, sickened with anger while stricken with grief at the same time. I had lost more than just a friend. I had lost a brother.

CHAPTER 13

Two days and a wake up and my tour in Iraq was going to be over. Nothing about it felt right at all. Rev was dead, Nadeel wanted nothing to do with me and Ali hated me. Unfortunately, there was no planned mission to the orphanage between now and the time I was to leave.

As I lay in bed, thinking about my last conversation with Ali, I knew I had to mend that broken bridge before it came crumbling down. I pushed the heavy sheets off of me and stepped outside for some air. Manning, the young boot I had saved from Alvarez's tirade, was heading toward the gate.

"Hey Manning, you got perimeter watch tonight?"

He stopped and turned around. "Yup, another exciting night."

"I need your help," I told him.

"What is it?"

"I need to get on the other side of the wire."

"You wanna go AWOL? Are you crazy! If someone catches you, we're both screwed. I can't take that risk."

"Hey, if it wasn't for me, you'd still be under Alvarez's boot, so you owe me one."

He knew I had him. I was the only one who had his back.

"No one will find out. I'll be back as soon as I can. I swear."

Manning looked unsure.

"Come on, I'm out of here in two days anyway. I need this."

He took a look around to make sure no one was eavesdropping. "If you're not back by zero-two-hundred you're on your own."

I checked my watch. It was already midnight. "That doesn't give me much time."

"That's all I can give you. Take it or leave it."

Of course I took it. Even if it only gave me two hours outside the wire, in one of the most dangerous places in the world.

Getting past the perimeter wasn't hard. It was getting back in that was going to be downright impossible, especially if I showed up late. Then I might as well show up in cuffs.

Manning did his part and got me across the wire undetected. I had no vehicle or gear, and just a 9mm to protect myself. It wasn't exactly the ideal situation, but it was the only opportunity that I would get.

It was surprisingly quiet on the streets, but quiet can turn to chaos in the blink of an eye. I had to watch my back constantly. There was a lot of money being offered for captured military personnel. Enough that even our *allies*—a word I use very loosely—would be sorely tempted to grab one of us if found alone in the middle of the street. Not only did I have to watch out for the enemy, I also had to watch out for my own troops as well.

I wasn't gone but a couple of hundred meters when a column of Humvees drove by, with a sense of barely contained chaos. I hid in the shadows the best I could, but out here, even a shadow can't save you. Many friendlies had been shot in broad daylight, while still in uniform. A man in civilian clothes in the middle of the night could easily become a PR disaster in a matter of seconds.

I remember the long, suspenseful walk from the base to the orphanage, which was a good five miles away. I remember moving rapidly through small allies and locked-down storefronts. The only sound I could here was the echo of my footsteps on the deserted cobblestone street. Then suddenly, I became aware of someone walking up behind me. My hand instinctually went to my holster. I stopped abruptly, turned around and withdrew my 9mm. Twenty-feet in front of me stood a teenage boy. He was unarmed. Terrified.

Across the street, an old woman peered nervously out her window. The second I made eye contact with her, she stepped back, drawing in her curtains.

I turned back to the boy; he was afraid. I lowered my gun, and in broken Arabic I told him to get off the streets and go home. He did so, as quickly as he could. Something I wish *I* could've done. I pressed on for another mile, however, before arriving at the orphanage. I stopped outside the seven-foot wall, regarding the gate with dread.

With one foot on the wall, I got ready to scale it, when I heard a shotgun cocking behind me and a voice on the other end of it, yelling in Arabic, "Ailtaff hawlah!" (Turn around!)

Shit was my first thought, *fuck* was my second. I took a breath and slowly looked over my shoulder, while reaching for the 9mm at my hip.

"Don't move!" the voice said in English.

I thought twice about it. Turning completely around, I saw that it was Raheem. He was holding back his panic. He couldn't yet make out my face through the darkness. He saw my hand drifting dangerously close to my gun and he squared his shoulders, yelling again, "Don't move!"

"It's me, Raheem," I said, in the clearest tone I could muster. "It's Santoli."

He lowered his gun and let out a breath. "I thought you were one of the *them*," he said.

"One of who?"

He looked around to make sure we were alone. "These orphanages have become targets for terrorist, who seek to recruit the boys as 'Children of Heaven'. The last suicide attack was committed by an eleven-year-old, did you know that?"

I slowly and sadly nodded.

"That is a frightening thing, when a fact like that doesn't surprise anyone at all." Raheem took one look at me and instantly knew why I was there. He also knew the risk I was taking. "Come on in before someone sees you." Opening the small door within the gate, he pulled me into the courtyard.

We walked through the foyer of the orphanage and he quietly pointed up the stairs, both to let me know where Ali was, and to say—in his own way—good luck. Clearly a man who believed in second chances. But definitely not third, and he let me know by grabbing me firmly by the sleeve. "Be honest with him. He's heard enough lies."

I nodded respectfully and made my way up the stairs. The orphanage was eerily silent. I entered the room and found myself standing between two long rows of beds, each with a little boy, and each boy alone with his thoughts. Ali lay motionless in the next bed. I put a hand on his forehead, which was just as hot as his temper. He pulled away from me and watched me with a cold eye like I had intentionally cheated him out of a better life. He remained hopeless yet hoping the worst for me.

Suddenly, I noticed a figure looming in the doorway. It was Nadeel. She had that look in her eyes that let me know there was still much left to say. She knew that a part of me was in terrible pain. With a gesture of the hand, she pulled me out of the room and into the hall.

"How is it that you are here?" She asked.

"There were things I had to get off my chest."

She moved down the stairs. "You shouldn't be here."

"Wait."

She stopped for a second.

"I'm going home in two days."

She turned toward me with her indecipherable face. "You should be happy."

It wasn't the response I was hoping for. "I should be, but I'm not."

She looked at me like she couldn't imagine why.

"All I can think about is Ali, this place…." I looked deep into her eyes, "and you."

It was the moment of truth. It was now or never, and I listened quietly to see what she would say.

She pulled back, barely acknowledging my words. "The streets are dangerous; you should go now before you're found out."

"The streets? That's it?"

She turned around and continued down the stairs.

Come on! Are you serious?

Why do women do that? I'd rather she yell at me, tell me to go to hell or drop dead, but don't give me the silent treatment. Silence is a death sentence. But then again, maybe that's why she did it.

I ran after her and grabbed her by the wrist.

She turned to face me, but no words fell out of my mouth.

"Whatever you were going to say, don't say it." It was as if she read my mind and rejected the very idea of it.

"Why not?"

Nadeel shook her head and pulled her wrist out of my grip, looking almost circumspect. "Because it doesn't matter."

I let my jealousy get the better of me. "Because you're getting married to a man you barely know?"

She was unable to look me in the eyes. "He's a good man," she said, coming to his defense.

I shook her arm and repeated. "To a man you barely know."

She yanked her arm away from me and in a stern, indignant voice, she replied, "Then I suppose the two of you have something in common."

I was taken aback. "You know me."

"How could I know you when you have your heart completely covered up behind bricks and mortar, holding onto pieces of the past like a child holding tight his blanket?"

I dropped my head. "My past is filled with resentment."

"You have brought hate into an environment already filled with it. How can you expect these boys to let go of theirs, if you can't even let go of yours?"

"You want to analyze me, feel free; it's nothing I haven't heard before. But what about the man you're going to marry, do you know everything about him?"

She slapped me and said, "You're better than that, and if you're not, then *be* better than that. This place isn't like your America. I can marry someone without knowing them, but I could never love someone without knowing what was in their heart."

I watched her undo all the work I had put into showing her the real me. It turned out that this whole time, Ali was the linchpin, holding the three of us together. The second he was pulled out, this entire life fell apart.

I threw up a Hail Mary pass and said, "Is that it? Is that all you have to say to me?"

She sighed as if this were all a game and she was too tired to play it. "I'm glad that you're leaving. Better you head home, before this war claims you as well."

As I heard those words, a quick flash of the nearest galaxy popped up in my head: 25,000 light years away. That's how far Nadeel seemed from me. She was physically the closest thing to me, yet mentally further away than I could ever imagine, further away than I could ever hope to reach in my lifetime.

Her lips came together purposefully. "Go home to your America," she said, receding backward, her unspoken words carelessly thrown away, never to be heard. "There's nothing for you here."

The tone of her voice reminded me of the first time we met. It was as if we had rehearsed it all before, and again, I found myself on the losing end of the argument. She was right. It was time to go home.

Raheem appeared at the bottom of the stairs. I don't know if he had been eavesdropping or just had perfect timing, but I was glad to see him.

"Come, Mr. Santoli," he said. "I will drive you back."

Feeling defeated, I quietly followed him out and got into his truck. Taking one last look through the back window, I saw Nadeel's face just before the door closed.

"I suppose you wish we never came here as well?" I asked Raheem.

He seemed at peace with the world, in the driver's seat, literally on the edge of a warzone. "You did not bring war here. Most people forget that this is the ancient land of prophets where the Bible states that Cain killed Abel: two brothers at each other's throats. My father would remind me of that story every day. He would remind me that peace is a rare thing, and war is abundant. I saw this first hand. When I was a young man, one night, there was a knock at the door, and my father was taken away by Saddam's people and quietly executed. We never saw him again. His body is probably buried in Abu Ghraib, still in his pajamas.

I have seen Iraq during times of war and times of peace, and the only difference now is that the death is in the streets, instead of hidden behind closed doors. Those of us who lived under the boot of Saddam Hussein truly understand what tyranny is. The difficulties of today, although they are very profound, pale in comparison to what we had to endure. We are far from free. Our oppression is far from over. We've kneeled before Saddam, and we may still be kneeling, but now we have a cushion to kneel against." He turned to me and in a brotherly tone, he said. "I don't know why you are here, and you might've been brought here by false hope, but it's *hope* nonetheless. That in itself is a good thing."

I sat in silence letting the power of Raheem's words seep in. There were two zeitgeists emerging simultaneously, both hope and hopelessness splitting apart a country, and at the center of it, men like Raheem and I, fighting for one, while secretly fearing the other. The love of Nadeel or Ali could have kept me together, fighting the good fight. But sitting there in that truck, feeling alone and vacant, I gave into the hopelessness and for the first time in months, I was glad I was going home.

Two streets away from the base, Raheem pulled over.

"Thanks for the ride, my friend," I said. "Take care of yourself."

Before I could get out, he leaned in and said, "She cares for you, but she is stubborn."

"I've noticed," I replied.

The look on Raheem's face was thoughtful. "I thought you should know, before you leave."

I stepped out of the truck. "I appreciate it."

Raheem gave me a small smile. "Be well." and with those two simple words, he was gone.

I glanced down at my wrist; it was zero-three-hundred. As I slowly approached the gate, I could see that Manning wasn't at his post. His shift had ended and someone else had taken his place. I was officially screwed. The only way *in* was to tell the truth and suffer punishment.

I was almost to the gate when I heard a voice from behind me. "Out pretty late, aren't you?" It was Ryan Benson. He was a having a smoke against the wall just outside the gate—a place I had never seen him before. He was a desk jockey, a pencil pusher, the kind of man who wouldn't step across the wire, unless the base was burning down.

"Let me guess, just taking a brisk walk?" he said sarcastically.

I thought about lying to him, but I got the feeling he already knew the truth and just wanted to hear me say it. So I did. "I'm sorry. I had to say goodbye."

Benson breathed out softly. "Santoli, you must have lost your mind. Your actions nearly threw Manning under the bus with you."

"My actions are inexcusable sir, and whatever punishment you hand out will have been worth it."

He approached me slowly, exhaling a cloud of smoke. "I know what people say. I know what they call me: a paper-pushing asshole, a douche bag, a piece of shit. But I wasn't always stuck in that head shed, watching drone-fed images on a little monitor, deciding whether or not those little blips live or die. I've seen my time at war."

I remained tense yet watchful, waiting to see where this was all going.

Benson's demeanor shifted from hard to soft immediately. "You know I've been on six tours now and I've never asked a single Marine what their time in war was like. I never gave a shit, because I was sure it was no different than mine. Same shit. Same stories of bloodshed and gore, and bodies and death. I've asked them what their life was like before, and what it was like after, but you're the first man who's got a story that I want to hear—a story that's bigger than just you. This war is ours to lose and we've done a pretty good job of it, but *you* had a real victory here. You made a difference. That's why the rest of us came over here, for that same chance, to change something."

I had to stop him. "I'm not sure I changed anything for the better, sir."

He smirked. "Just from my drive in from the airport I saw at least ten graffiti-covered apartment buildings. There are American gangs in the military, dressed in our uniforms, tagging up Iraqi streets. This is what the world has come to. Only time will tell if you've truly made a difference, but I know that you're not here pretending to be something you're not. You've always embodied what a Marine should be, and I respect that."

Before I could open my mouth and say something stupid, he interjected. "Now come on, before anyone sees you."

"Sir?"

His lips gave me a stern warning, but his eyes gave me a standing ovation. "Semper fi," he said. "Always faithful." He looked to the guard at the gate, who without question, opened up and let us in. Benson knew I was going to pull something and still he let me do it. I never quite looked at him the same way after that. It turned out he was more than just a pencil pusher. He had seen a lot more pain than I had ever given him credit for. He deserved some peace of mind behind a desk.

Benson never told anyone about my AWOL incident, and before I knew it, I was headed back to Kuwait, where I spent a week *decompressing.* That's what they called it, but it felt more like being a convict out on parole. The food was a lot better, and there was even therapy (mandatory, I'm afraid). Also a briefing on post-traumatic stress, along with a video on how to integrate yourself back into society.

Although there was no more waking up at the crack of dawn, it was a hard habit to break. I would sit in the window and watch the large Middle Eastern sun devour the landscape, all the while wondering about Ali and his bleak future. I wished for one more conversation with him, not to explain my actions (I had already drowned myself in an ocean of excuses), but to tell him I'm sorry that I couldn't stay and wait out his anger and watch him grow up to be a good man. I wanted to tell him to let go of the vindictive feelings before they get the better of him. Perhaps it was for the best that I was leaving; it would've taken a lifetime to tell him everything I wanted to. And from the way he looked at me the last time I saw him, I knew that a lifetime was asking for too much.

So, I collected myself and hesitantly boarded the waiting courier plane heading back home. As I prepared for departure, down on the tarmac, caskets—too many to count—were being loaded into the cargo hold. I thought of Rev, who was probably six-feet under American soil by now, where his medals would soon turn to rust. Not the homecoming his family had envisioned, but it was the one they got. Maybe my heart will heal itself someday, but I will never forget what I have seen, and more importantly, who I have hurt in the process.

CHAPTER 14

Over six thousand miles later, I found I was still in Iraq. It looked like America, and at times it even felt like America, but something was missing: Me. What they forget to tell you is that you don't really make it back home. Something comes back: the representation of a body, the remnants of a mind, the illusion of a soul. But it's not at all who you were, or who you promised would return. I thought coming home would be easy, but it was the furthest thing from it.

As I arrived at the airport, I was greeted by faces I hadn't seen in a long time. Truth be told, they were faces I could've gone my whole life without seeing. Faces like my cousin, Kelly, whose mouth always reeked of cigarettes. Kelly didn't have taste buds he had taste-butts, and his lips were just as ashy as the rim of an ashtray. He was tall and skinny—the kind of skinny that made him look like a crack head. In the most obese country in the world, he might as well have been labeled malnourished.

He had brought our old buddy, Roger, with him. I hadn't seen Rog since I left the lumber mill to join the Marine Corps. He was one of those people who fancied himself an intellectual of the world, a man of many talents, though he had never been more than an hour out of town. He was an agoraphobic, just on a bigger scale. He once told me that the size of the world scared him. After being away in Iraq, I now know what he meant.

Roger spat out tobacco juice between his wide spaced front teeth and gave me a firm handshake. "Good to see ya, buddy!"

Kelly smiled at me. "You look good for a man who just returned from a warzone." He then said, "Welcome back to reality," as if my time in Iraq were spent in an illusion.

I shook their hands, but I remember thinking what's the point of renewing old acquaintances? They fell apart once, who's to say they won't again.

As I looked around, I saw other Marines embraced with signs that had sentimental messages written on them: *we're proud of you, hugs and kisses, and happy that you're home.* It was ironic given the fact that just beyond a pair of revolving doors, protesters were flashing their own signs and chanting, "US out of Iraq now!"

I was over there fighting for this country, yet the average person didn't care. They thought I was stupid, as if my duties to serve for my country had anything to do with my own political views on the war itself. I fight *for* my country, not necessarily *with* my country. I'm not the hand, I'm just the hammer. I never thought I would learn heartache and pain with such understatement. But they didn't care about any of that. It was black and white to them, and like I said before, war is anything but.

I walked through the crowd, wishing for my rifle, my Kevlar vest, my helmet, anything to protect me from the mob. Even though I had forfeited my uniform for civilian clothes, they looked at me as if I had past sins left to pay.

"Come on, let's get out of here," Kelly said, his protective side acting up—the same side that had gotten him into trouble most of his life. "Ignore these assholes; you're a hero! Don't you forget that."

As I reached for the handle of Kelly's car, I felt a sharp pain shoot through my forearm: Carpal-tunnel, from all the trigger pulling. *Some hero*, I remember thinking; I couldn't even get into a car without twitching.

I sat in the passenger seat of Kelly's rusted out El Camino, my hands still holding an imaginary rifle. My fingers felt more comfortable in the pose. It off-set the pain greatly.

"Grandma's gonna be really happy to see you," Kelly said.

I could tell from the inflection in his voice that he was up to his old shit. Kelly was always in and out of jail for misdemeanors, minor disturbances and drunken, lewd conduct. He was glad that I was back to take all the attention off of him. After my mother passed away, we grew up together with my grandmother. He always looked up to me like an older brother—a responsibility I never wanted. I'm not exactly a role model. And the one person who desperately needed a role model was Kelly. He took a swig of whisky and smiled at me, his front two teeth knocked clean out by a right hook from a bar brawl. "I saw your old girlfriend, Sophia, around town last week."

As soon as I heard her name my ears pricked up. Sophia, the only woman who I still thought about from time to time. I'd like to say the one who got away, but that statement wouldn't be true. More like the one I drove away.

"What is she up to?" I asked, trying to sound as least interested as possible.

"She says she misses you and would love to see you again."

As I reflected on his words, Kelly raised an eyebrow, suggesting he was either concerned or plain messing with me.

I grabbed an empty coffee cup from all the junk that littered Kelly's dash and I threw it at his head. "You're an idiot."

He burst out laughing. "I had you going for a second, admit it."

"Only thing I'll admit, is that you're an asshole."

But Kelly was right. He had me for a second. Then again, there's not a person in the world who doesn't want to hear that their ex still thinks about them. I knew she had moved on, however. So had I. From one unobtainable woman to another. I guess that's my type. I instantly began comparing Sophia to Nadeel, even though there was no comparison at all. But what difference did it make; I had neither. I would probably never see Nadeel again. Iraq isn't exactly a place you voluntarily return to, or at least that's what I had told myself.

My life was here, in Galena, Illinois. It was the kind of small-town you expect to find in the Midwest: that sad little grocery store that everyone went to on the weekend, the swap-meet where one could find a decent pair of knockoff Gucci shades, the strip mall, where materialism reigned: hardworking people, spending money that they didn't have on things that they didn't need.

But then again, the media is used to redirect our attention toward materialism rather than world issues and human suffering. I mean who cares about the 800,000 orphans in Iraq, or the 100,000 people who died during the Syrian crisis, or the 480,000 people killed in the Darfur genocide, when you can buy yourself the latest appliance which drains away fat and helps you trim your waistline for only three easy payments of $29.99. That's the kind of life I had to look forward to.

In the past I remember how things were so simple. I could've imagined buying some run-down place over on Franklin street and fixing it up like new, getting a job, settling down with a woman who complimented me, having a few kids and calling it a life. But as we drove against the dissolving landscape, I knew it wasn't going to be so simple anymore. I felt like a stranger in a no name town. Not Kelly though; he could've spent his whole life going through routines. He had gotten comfortable with his life, which meant he had stopped trying to reach for anything better. As far as he was concerned, he had it all.

Kelly wheeled into the small driveway of our grandmother's old rancher home, where we used to play hockey. That was back when Kelly had dreams of being an NHL defenseman. He was pretty good back then, I remember. We would pretend that we were stepping onto the ice as professional players, with our make-shift pads, made from pillows and duct tape and old bicycle helmets to protect our heads. In the winter, when the pond froze over, we would spend our nights skating under the stars, on our own personal rink, with the city lights sparkling around us. I still remember those small, wonderful experiences that helped shape my childhood.

As I stood there reminiscing, one of the teens, who was playing hockey in the streets, ran over and shouted at Kelly. "Is this him? Is this your cousin?"

Kelly smirked. "Yeah, this is him."

Apparently Kelly had been telling stories about his brave cousin who went off to war. But that's all they were: just stories.

"Have you ever killed anyone," the boy asked, with a smug look on his face. He was a young punk, with a self-imposed crew cut and a t-shirt with an American flag on the chest. I found his tone disturbing. He asked with excitement pulsing through his eyes and the slightest grin, as if shooting someone was a good thing. But he wasn't asking if I had killed 'someone', he wanted to hear how I had killed 'the enemy', so he could take some gratitude home with him.

I answered him, honestly. "I killed a kid, thirteen-years-old, shot him dead, right through the chest." I said it with pride to see how he would react.

I watched his face alter in a surreal fashion. It was as if we had traded places for a second. My answer allowed him to feel the same emotions I felt when he asked me the question: grief and sorrow.

However, the emotions didn't stick. He resurrected his cold

demeanor and said, "You're teaching those terrorists that you can't mess with Merica."

Suddenly, I lost it on him. "There's an 'A' in it jerk off! If you want to stand up for a country, get the name right. I was over there fighting for America!"

Kelly took a step back.

The kid stood there with a stupid look on his face, unaware of what to say.

"Run along now," I said, desperately trying to be free of him.

Kelly smirked, smacked the kid on the back of the head and said, "You heard the man, now get the hell out of here jerk off." He then turned back to me and shrugged his shoulders. "That was a little harsh, don't you think?"

"Since when do you care?"

Kelly smirked. "I'm just sayin'."

"There's no harshness in the truth."

Kelly patted me on the back. "I think you need a drink. It'll take the edge off."

"No…I'm good."

"Suit yourself." He proceeded to take a few shots of whisky from his flask.

"Still the same Kelly, huh?"

The way he looked at me, I could tell the comment stung a little. He then smirked and went right back to drinking. "Well you know me, same old fuck up. Come on, let's get this over with so we can head down to the bar. I know some of the old boys would love to see you."

More acquaintances that weren't worth rehashing. "Sure," I said, putting my best foot forward.

As soon as we walked through the door, I could smell my grandmother's seafood gumbo, boiling on the burner. During my deployment, I was missing it so much. When I finally had it, the sensation passed, and I thought to myself *all that time spent thinking about a flavor.* It's funny how we hold onto these sparse, unimportant things in our brain that serve no purpose but to tease us.

Like all Italian women, my grandmother just wanted to feed and swoon over her grandson—a hero in her eyes. She loaded up plate after plate, making sure I had more of everything. "Eat! Eat!" She said. "You look so skinny."

I couldn't argue with her statement. The last time she saw me, I was at least twenty pounds heavier.

"Come on, let's go get that drink," Kelly said before my plate was even empty.

My grandmother shook her head, as if Kelly would never change his ways.

"Give me a second," I said to him, heading to my room to drop off my duffle bag. On my night table was a pile of unopened mail. Gone this whole time and not a single important message, just Publisher's Sweepstakes, old bills, flyers and junk mail. That's all I had missed while I was gone.

Kelly ducked into my room and said, "Come on, cuz, let's get out of here." He couldn't wait to get out of the house and away from my grandmother's judgmental eyes.

The last thing I wanted to do was sit around opening up old mail, so I grabbed my coat and we headed out.

On the drive into town, Kelly told me how happy he was that I was back home, most likely to bail him out of trouble. Everyone kept using that word: happy. The locals were happy to see me, my so-called friends were happy to hear some war stories, and even my barber was happy to see my poorly shaved head again. He would always slap me on the back and say, "Hello, my friend." One of those impersonal greetings that middle-eastern barbers throw at you. It seemed like I was the only one who wasn't all that happy.

As Kelly and I made our way through town, I was on edge, constantly looking down alleyways and scanning rooftops for insurgents, IEDs, or any suspicious activity. I noticed things I otherwise wouldn't have before. Even though I had walked down that street thousands of times in my life, this time was different. I didn't feel safe without my rifle. My alertness was at red. I couldn't bring it down. I couldn't cool it off. I felt dangerous. My emotions came rising up like the fat that settles on top of gravy. I closed my eyes and took in three long breaths to settle my thoughts. I told myself neither fight or flight is required right now. I then repeated the mantra that I came up with during decompression. "You're safe now, there's no one trying to kill you. It's all in your head." By the time I opened my eyes, the fat had been mixed back into the gravy. Not all the way, but enough to make it edible again.

Kelly had no idea of the private war that I was waging in my mind. "You're gonna love the girls in this place," he said, heading toward a local bar. "They're a little young, but they know how to party."

The bar was filled with rowdy and excited people, which only added to my anxiety. Everyone was cheering over the football game, but war had muted that kind of excitement for me. It's hard to get excited about watching a man running from a group of men in tights, while carrying a football, once you've seen men in uniforms running from men with guns, who were shooting at them, while carrying civilians out of harm's way. The only sport I could even stand to watch anymore was hand to hand combat. Anything where blood and brutality were involved and sacrifices were made.

Kelly, however, was right at home here. We had barely sat down before he made eye-contact with a young girl. Approaching her, he put his hands on her hips and kissed her neck, then bought her a drink at the bar. I had forgotten how easy it was to interact with women here. Even in the heat of the moment, Nadeel was never able to completely let go of her responsibilities. I could never just move in and kiss her, not that I would, even I'm not that stupid. But here, a move like that, could lead to more.

Kelly looked up from the random girl's neck and gave me a wink. He then brought her over to our table and introduced her as Sam. She smiled and her eyes glazed over like she had one too many drinks already but was dying for another. Free, of course. Women like her don't want to pay for drinks. She was willing to spark up a conversation with any loser who would buy her one. In this case, it was Kelly. He sat her down next to me and then excused himself to hit the John.

Before Sam could open her mouth, a car backfired outside and my head swirled around faster than a top. There are some sounds you just never forget. The sound of your mother's voice, the sound of a 64 Plymouth roadster, the sounds of that first orgasm, and of course, the sounds of war: the screeching, the banging, the clapping, the barking, the crying, the wailing, the breaking, the toppling, the exploding and the booming. They become so inherent that the second you hear anything that remotely sounds like it, you're instantly on edge. Your hands immediately revert to that of a Marine's, your shoulders pull back, your jaw clenches up and your legs brace themselves. It's a visceral response. You react without thinking.

"You alright," Sam asked me, slurring her words.

"Yeah. I'm fine."

She threw me a fake smile and said, "OK."

There's nothing worse than fake smiles and verdicts. Both are judgments beyond your control. The last thing I needed or wanted was to be judged in that moment. Needless to say, I was glad when Kelly came back. I quickly excused myself and stepped out into the back alley, in desperate need of some fresh air. I cinched in my coat and noticed a quiet observer off in corner of the alley. It was a coyote. It watched me, never blinking once. From the strays in Iraq to the coyotes in the streets, only dogs understood me now. They saw something no one else did. When they looked at me, they recognized one of their own. That was the secret that the dogs knew that I didn't at the time. We were both lone predators, lost in a world that didn't understand us. The coyote was a metaphor for my life: everything from their ghostly choir of thin cries, to their scavenging ways. We were both just trying to survive in an ever-changing world.

The coyote suddenly disappeared, and I instantly felt tired. All the sleepless nights hit me like a sledgehammer to the back of the head. I could've passed out right there in that alley. War takes away all of life's problems and replaces them with just one: stay alive. When it comes to war, a finger is all you need. One push of a trigger can change your entire life. All other problems seem unimportant. Here, however, all the little unimportant problems hit you all at once, one stiff uppercut, pushing your jaw up into your brain.

When I went back to the table, another girl had joined Kelly and Sam. Kelly winked an eye and said, "This is Sam's friend Gabby."

As I shook her hand, she licked her lips and smiled. I looked back at Kelly and he had that look in his eyes that let me know it was going to be a long night. That was the other thing about Kelly, he was willing to go to the ends of the earth for a girl. And I don't mean in a romantic way, I mean he would literally spend whatever he had to and go wherever he had to in order to make sure the night ended with sex. He once drove four hours both ways for a late-night booty call. So when he winked at me, I just knew where the night was going.

Kelly waved at a man standing by the bar, and he began walking over.

"Who's that?" I asked.

"That's the candy man," Kelly said with a smile. "You ladies like candy, right?"

The women chuckled.

I gave Kelly a sigh to say *I'm not sure if I got it in me to party*. "I don't do that anymore."

"Come on, it's your first day back. We have to let loose, just a little."

Gabby took a hold of my hand and said, "I heard you were a good time."

Behind her, just out of Sam's view, Kelly threw me an obscene gesture, miming fellacio.

I rolled my eyes. Then turning to Gabby, I said, "I used to be."

She let go of my hand. "It's a shame. I thought we were going to have fun tonight."

Kelly quickly took over the conversation. "We are...we are. We're definitely partying tonight. Isn't that right, Cuz!"

Kelly mouthed the word *please*. I officially had no choice. Wingman rules prevented me from saying no.

As more and more shots got fed into me, and the night progressed, I slowly regressed back into the man I used to be—the man I thought I had left behind. I excused myself from Gabby and went to the can. As I opened the single-person bathroom, Kelly and Sam were doing bumps of coke off the sink counter.

"Shit! You scared me," Kelly said, wiping the powder from his nose.

Sam burst out laughing, high as a kite.

"Could you please do that shit somewhere else? I have to piss."

"Come on in and join us."

I smirked. "No thanks. "When are we leaving?"

"Leaving?" Kelly shook his head. "The night's just getting started."

"Come on man, I just got back today, I'm tired."

"I was hoping we could party like we used to."

As I stood there, staring at Kelly, I realized that come tomorrow morning, I'd have to officially start planning out my life. Not looking forward to the process, I gave in and threw him a nod. "Sure, why not."

Like Kelly said, the night was just getting started. I believe I blacked out right around last call. The rest of the night was a blur. I remember flashes of random moments: stumbling out of the bar, Kelly picking a fight with the bouncer, and making out with Gabby in the back of a car.

The next morning, I came to, a little disoriented, staring up at a bright, red ceiling fan, and a room filled with posters of shirtless men. I was in a strange bedroom, my clothes strewn about the floor. Quickly getting dressed, I staggered into the kitchen, where Kelly was making breakfast, in nothing but his underwear and a woman's robe.

He winked an eye. "Hey stud, you have a good time last night?"

"I'll tell you the second the room stops spinning."

Gabby and Sam sat at the table pouring bowls of cereal. Gabby smiled. "So what are we doing today?"

"Uh...actually ladies, you'll have to excuse us, but we have to get going." I threw Kelly that look that said *I've had enough, now it's time to go.*

He got the point. "Sorry ladies, we had a great time last night, but my cousin's got somewhere else to be." Kelly quickly put on his pants, and we emerged from Sam's building, squinting at the blinding sunlight, trying to find the keys to the El Camino. Once inside the car, Kelly slapped my thigh and burst out laughing. "Just like old time."

"Congratulations, Kelly, you just set me back three years in my evolution, all in one night."

"You're welcome," he said, lighting a cigarette.

CHAPTER 15

I spent the first few months back saying *no* to reality and *yes* to bartenders, saying no to therapists and yes to painkillers. *Last call* became just another phrase, and each night that went by, the stars seemed more and more dim. I remember how bright they were out in the villages, big giant pinpricks of light. But here, there was too much false light, blotting out the real. I've always hated false light. I would avoid it as much as I could. Even in my room, I would keep it real dim.

I would wander around the house like a zombie, looking through every window, checking every lock, listening to the neighborhood. It was all too quiet. One would think that's a good thing, right? Maybe for the average person, but for me, the silence was too much to take. I couldn't even sleep unless there was artillery fire somewhere off in the distance. The lack of all that sound had made me a light sleeper. I would stay up late and have conversations with shadows. I would see things that weren't really there, things that would manifest themselves out of nothing: a coat on a hook somehow looked like an insurgent creeping in around the corner, the ceiling fan above my bed looked like a trained assassin waiting to get the drop on me, and the long, hanging plant in the kitchen looked like the dead body of Zaid, hanging from a noose.

There were nights I would wake up and couldn't recognize my room immediately. I'd get up and sit in my armchair, staring at the small veins of light projected on the walls by the lamppost outside, desperately waiting for dawn to arrive.

My grandmother would get up real early like old folks do, and she would see me sitting by the windowsill, murmuring to myself. She would sit with me for a while and ask me if I wanted to talk about it.

"There's nothing to say," I would tell her.

She would pat me on the back and tell me to go visit my parents. "It might make you feel better," she would say.

Maybe. It had been a while since I went down to the cemetery.

She would then send me back off to bed. But it was only when the sun was coming up that I actually felt tired enough to doze off for a couple of hours.

I remember how I didn't have a single dream while I was in Iraq, yet back home, I would have the same reoccurring dream every time I fell asleep. I would always find myself under a bright, beautiful sky, standing on the rooftop of an old Iraqi home. A very familiar home. Ali stood before me, a yellow homemade kite by his side, with a white dove painted on it. I held it, while Ali ran with string in hand, and together we let the wind carry it away. His heart flew with the kite, higher and higher, until it touched the cerulean sky. Ali let out a joyful cry and I cheered along with him.

This little fragile kite made of tissue paper, bamboo strips, and a thin cotton string, was strong enough to carry both of our spirits on it. We let go of all our fears and embraced the peace around us. It crisscrossed through the sky and embedded itself against the sun, which shined through the thin paper, casting a yellow light on the ground, bathing Ali in its sweet, luminous glow.

I sat a spell and watched Ali rejoice in this sweet little world where people kept their promises till the end. A place filled with painted doves on kites and Xeroxed smiles on origami planes, spreading happiness simply through the wind. The kite reflected Ali's hopes: to be completely free, unbridled by war. Ali looked as if he could've lived there forever.

Echoes of our laughter, pulled children out of their homes and onto their roofs. All of a sudden, the sky was full of paper kites, with long trailing ribbons. The carefree kites soared with childhood dreams, and danced in the wind.

Ali looked over at me and smiled, and as he did, the wind suddenly became stronger and our fragile little kite began wavering.

"Hold onto it tight," I said to Ali.

He tugged at the string, trying to pull it out the turbulent current. Just then, the kamikaze clouds moved in, blotting out the sun, and our little kite took a nose-dive like an epileptic bird.

"Pull the string," I said to Ali, in an effort to save it.

Ali tugged the string and the kite caught a gust of wind for one last rise. The wind was so strong that the kite, broke free from Ali's hands, and drifted skyward, taking Ali's dreams with it.

Just as Ali turned toward me, an otherworldly light seeped in from someplace far off, sharply silhouetting the landscape. A boisterous boom like a hundred snare drums went off, and a mushroom cloud rose from the distance. A sound began to build like a living wind. The sky erupted and a blast wave devoured the children, who all ignited like sulfur. I pushed toward Ali, but I was moving in slow motion. Why is it that you can never really run in a dream when you need to? It says something about our insecurities of never being fast enough to stop pain.

As the wave reached me, it passed through me like I wasn't really there, like the consequences of that place had nothing to do with my life whatsoever.

Ali screamed without a voice. The force of the blast was too loud, the wind too violent. His little voice was eaten up the second it left his tongue.

The wave passed just as quickly as it came. In the post-nuclear desolation, charred remains of children stood like horrific sculptures. I couldn't tell if it was Iraq or Pompeii. Everything was silent and overexposed like white, Christmas morning.

I stepped toward Ali and I remember thinking how nothing could dim those bright eyes of his. Well it took a nuclear blast to do it. He looked like he was made of carbon paper, and the second I touched him, his ashes scattered into the wind.

That's when my eyes blinked awake and I woke up in bed covered in a cold sweat, breathing heavily. All was quiet and normal. There were children playing outside; I could hear them through an open window. They played fearlessly, unafraid of a nuclear explosion or war in the streets. Maybe Kelly was right, maybe this was reality. *If this is* real *then where the hell was I this whole time?* I wasn't sure whether or not I had dreamt up these mental pictures imported from hopeless places, or if they actually happened. In a civilized world, how could that be real? How could any of it?

My eyes suddenly noticed the clock sitting on the nightstand. It was 11:34 AM. For the first time in my life, I noticed that it spelled the word 'hell' upside down. Not exactly a comforting thought.

When the dreams became too much, I turned to doctors, who recommended I complete a treatment program for post-traumatic stress disorder, at a place where wounded warriors went to put their lives back together, or at least tried to. I'm not sure that you can put a broken vase back together. You can glue it or tape it up, but I'm not sure it'll ever hold water again. I was told therapy would help, but I knew that it was going to be a long way back to normal.

One cold, grey morning, I got into Kelly's car and took a three-hour drive down to Lemont, where they had a great post-traumatic stress treatment center in town. I sat in a room with men—strangers to one another and to me—who tried, sometimes through tears, to communicate what the intensity of an ambiguous war had done to them.

There was Edward, a twenty-year-old kid, who wasn't even old enough to have a drink, yet old enough to pick up a rifle and fight for his country. The slow way in which he moved, he looked like he was fifty. "I don't understand why I panic or break out into sweats," he said with a shaky voice. "The war is over for me, or so I thought. No one can relieve my mind of all the horrible memories. I went over to Iraq to find monsters, and I definitely found some, but none of them were as frightening as the one I became. I'm afraid of me now. I've seen too much and felt too little. I've talked too much and listened not enough. I've wished too big and hoped to small. I'm tired of it all, of all the lies I tell myself and even more so of the truth."

Then there was John, an amputee, who was having a tough time with his survivor's guilt. "Why did I make it back and they didn't?" he said, as if he should've been lying in a plot six feet deep. "There's nothing for me here. I don't feel deserving of life. I know the day will come when I have to answer for all I've done. And when that day comes, I'll be ready."

Next to him was Paul, a twenty-eight-year-old who was wheelchair bound. In his lap was a diary, from which he read aloud. "This once strong soldier is now frail and weak, left to page his rage with ink and paper. When the pain gets really bad, out come the needles and I'm left sitting in a wheelchair, wearing a permanent psychotic smile, off in la la land. If you're wondering how much Xanax it takes to wipe away one bad memory, the answer is 0.5 milligrams given three times daily."

And finally, there was Adrian, the thirty-year-old who had two blown out ears and TBI (traumatic brain injury). "I went off to war thinking I would come back with some stories to tell. Now I can't stop talking about it. But no one wants to hear my stories; they change the subject or walk away from me. They find them too violent. I'm a broken record. Even I'm sick and tired of reliving those memories, but unfortunately, I can't walk away from myself. I've concluded that life is a one-piece wallpaper that covers the world, its pattern is tacky and played-out: pastel florals on earth tones. It's enough to make you sick. Sometimes I want to put a gun in my mouth and paint the walls with my brain matter, if only to add some color to it."

The battle was still waging in their minds. I guess time doesn't heal all wounds; for some, it just preserves them like dinosaur fossils, to be witnessed later.

They then turned the mic to me. "Tell us about your experience," they said.

Yeah, let me spill my guts about how many guts I've spilt. No thanks. Memory lane runs parallel to regret road, and I didn't have the fuel to travel down it in that moment. So, I sat there with my hands in my lap and said, "Pass," like it was a gameshow quiz.

"Come on," said the man in the wheelchair. "Lay it all out; you'd be surprised by how much better you feel. If you can't talk to us, then who can you talk to?"

I still felt reluctant to speak, but as I heard the sincere tone in their voices, as they said, "It's alright, you're amongst friends." I slowly began to tell them my story. They each offered up their sympathetic ears and listened carefully.

I started with Sophia and ended with Nadeel. I paused on my mother and ran right past my father. I told them about Alvarez and they smirked, because they had all met his type before, and then I shared my feelings about Rev and they smiled because they had all met his type as well. I mentioned the orphanage and Ali and instantly saw some of the men tear-up. However, throughout the whole process, I didn't cry. I think you cry when it's all over, something felt unfinished to me. I'll definitely cry when the time comes, but it'll be on my own terms.

After the meeting concluded, I met with the doctor privately, who said I wasn't diagnosably impaired.

And when I said, "I guess my nightmares and suicidal tendencies don't account for anything? I guess I'm just a poor schmuck self-diagnosing himself, right?" She blamed it on sleep deprivation and substance abuse. But she had it backward. Those were caused by my impairment and not the other way around.

My father would always talk about the inadequacy of what the military calls reintegration counseling. It was always a struggle for him to rejoin a society that seemed unwilling to comprehend the price of his service. I didn't understand what he meant until that moment. Then again, I'm not sure how you can integrate strychnine into cake batter.

The only thing that I was thankful for, were the pills the doctor prescribed in the end: painkillers and antidepressants. Exactly what I needed.

As I left the hospital, just glad to be out of there, out in the parking lot, I saw a man looking back at me. Just another wounded warrior, I thought. I didn't recognize him at all. Then I studied his face a beat, just seeing the cracks and tears that weren't there last time I saw him. There was no mistaking him. It was Aries Alvarez, the self-proclaimed God of War. I was surprised to see him so far away from home. He was clearly searching for answers.

It was plain to see, that the tough Marine who wanted war, apparently got too much of it. That's the thing about war; you can't pour yourself a cup of it and think that'll be that. As soon as you tip the kettle over, it pours out, hot, steaming, burning, black, toxic, bitter, overflowing your cup, searing your hands, emptying itself all over you. More than you wanted, more than you could handle, more than you could ever have imagined in your wildest nightmares.

Alvarez was now beyond full, just a shell of a man, without ego or bravado. His face was now calm and benign, and his twenty-inch pythons were now mere garden snakes. He looked so frail that a stiff breeze could've knocked him down. War had silenced his raging voice, cooled his boiling temper, relaxed his fierce eyes and humbled his bigger than life ego.

He saw me and smiled like we were two children on a playground, with no toys to speak of. I smiled back, but neither one of us spoke. We didn't have to. We had said it all, seen it all, done it all. We were two ships passing in the night, flashing our warning lights, making sure we didn't collide and destroy each other.

With a sad wave of the hand, he turned around and staggered across the deserted parking lot toward the bus stop. That was the last time I ever saw Aries Alvarez. Years later, I heard he got married, and while asleep one night, both he and his wife were shot in bed by a couple of home intruders in a drugged-out rage. It would seem that war found him even in his dreams.

CHAPTER 16

When my grandmother mentioned again how I hadn't visited my parents grave in a while, I finally decided I would go—for her sake. I say for her sake, because the thought never came up on its own, it was always forced by her lips. Grandmothers, regardless of how soft their voices may be, have that heaviness to their words. I would assume at that age, they know what regret is all about and what it can do to you. She knew that I had a lot of pent-up emotions inside me in regard to my parents: words I never got to say to them and things I never got to do.

All the memories of my father are a complete blur. He didn't give me much, just a split-second childhood, followed by fifteen minutes of adolescence and a quick, *hypocritical* lesson in manhood: men don't hit women, men keep their word, and until you get to know a man's intentions, always keep your eyes on his shoulders. They'll tell you everything you need to know about a man: how strong he is, how confident he is, and whether or not he's going to throw a punch your way. That's all I remember about my father—that and war.

I realized early on that no matter how hard men try, they cannot escape the clench of war, be it external or internal. It's seeded too deep in our blood. For me, it's been stirring since the beginning. Florida, September 3, 1979. I was born in the eye of Hurricane David: a category five hurricane, which killed 2,068 people. My mother used to say, if all the forces of nature couldn't stop me then nothing ever could.

I remember her auburn hair, her crooked smile and the ease in which she would put ketchup-soaked meatloaf down on paper plates, day in and day out. I don't remember a single porcelain plate in my house. Peeled oranges were her favorite dessert, or perhaps the only one she could afford to serve. I remember tasting in them rays of sunshine and spring time dew. I can't even smell an orange without feeling her gentle touch. That was my mother: a generous person through and through.

My father, on the other hand, was a different story. He thought generosity was a disease you catch from being around missionaries or Jehovah's witnesses. The last time I saw him—alive that is—was when my mother threatened to leave him, and he backhanded her exactly the way I had seen him do many times before, knocking her to the floor. I guess his advice on not hitting women was more of a guideline—do as I say and not as I do. My mother packed her bags and told him it was the last time he'd ever put his hands on her again. She was right.

I'm sure Freud would have a thing or two to say about the state of my mind, in regard to my upbringing. Even though my parents were gone, I still found it hard to stand before them. Before going to the graveyard, my grandmother insisted I put on a shirt and tie, as if anyone would notice or care. But there are worse things than to oblige an old woman's request. So, I put on a clean, white shirt and the only tie I could find, a blue paisley silk one that Kelly had worn to his arraignment last year, after punching out an off-duty officer at the bar.

I borrowed Kelly's car and travelled down the dusty nameless road that I had been down only four times in my life. The first time was when my old man passed away. I remember we got the call at 4 AM. Everyone was sleeping. I was jolted awake and was struck instantly by that terrifying feeling you get when someone calls you that early in the morning. No good news is ever delivered at four in the morning. And this time was no different. It was the hospital. Someone had found my father lying unconscious at a nearby motel and called an ambulance.

They say he had been lying there for several hours from an overdose. Even though my mom predicted it, and on several occasions, even said to his face, "They're going to find you dead someday if you don't clean up your shit and get your life together," hearing her prediction come true didn't numb the pain any. I had made the mistake of picking up the phone at the same time and overheard the news, followed by my mother's hyperventilated sobbing. I remember how heavy I felt. I could feel myself sinking into the mattress. My body instantly became soaked with sweat and I pinched my arm, hoping to wake up from a dream. Not such an impossible wish. I had dreamt he had died on many occasions, and then woke up crying and feeling relieved that it was only a dream. But no such luck that night.

The second time I found myself on that miserable road was when my mother died. It was February. I remember how cold it was. Winter months make any news that much harder to bear. She died of a myocardial infarction: a fancy word for heart attack. She was working the late shift as a custodian at the nearby elementary school. After complaining about chest pains, the other woman who was working with her, made the mistake of driving her to the hospital, instead of calling an ambulance. By the time she made it to the hospital, there was nothing the doctors could do for her. When my grandmother told me the news, my first instinct was to call her on her cellphone and ask if she was still alive. My grandmother grabbed me and held me close, and I cried the whole night, just like Ali when he heard the news about his family.

The third time I was on that road was when my grandmother insisted I go visit my parents. And the fourth time, was on that day, again, to my grandmother's request.

I hated that road. It was no wonder it had no name. Everyone in town just called it the old deserted road. It was just as lonely and desolate as all the poor souls that travelled down it, and the ones that were buried at the end of it. It shouted *turn back! Go home! There's nothing for anyone down here.* What else do you do with a road like that but put a cemetery at the end of it? No wonder I never wanted to go down it.

Regardless of whether I wanted to or not, I did. And it brought back every memory I had with my parents, all the ones when they were still together—which weren't many, but they were sweet. I remember a couple of Christmases, one random Halloween and a nice birthday BBQ in the sun, made complete with the smell of burnt meat, toasted burger buns, mustard and ketchup. That was my life, simple and expected.

As I pulled into the vacant parking lot of the cemetery, I sat in the car staring at a random funeral procession. My eyes moved past a row of black suits and dresses, to a child holding his mother's hand—three-quarters of a family. I could tell his father was in the casket. Our eyes met for only a second, but I recognized the look on his face. I'd had that look before, and it lasted a lot longer than people told me it would.

Even when it departed, it left a chip on my shoulder the size of a cantaloup.

My eyes ran away from his and to the rear-view mirror in front of me. "Let's get this over with," I said to myself.

I walked through the cemetery like a ghost, half-expecting to see my own gravestone popping up from the shrubs. I approached my parent's side-by-side graves and stood in between them, unaware of what to say or do. Even though the old man skipped out on us, he kept the same burial plot. It was irony, I suppose, that the man my mother wanted to escape her whole life was now buried next to her for all of eternity.

Suddenly, I was young again, standing with my father by the pier, watching the boats come in. His grip around the bottle was tighter than the one he had around me. He looked down at me and I could see the dread in his eyes. I was too young to understand it then, but I knew it all too well now. I would see it from time to time in the mirror: that war-time dread that lives in the corners of your eyes that you can't wash out, even with cold water. I inherited more than just my father's eyes; I inherited his dread, his war, his pain. Maybe it was my way, subconsciously, of relating with him and finding some common ground that we could both stand on.

We want our parents to be proud of us. Regardless of how their life turned out or how much of a fuck up they were, we still want their pride. I never got the old man's pride. I got his disappointment, his grief, his pity, his anger, but never his pride. I'm not sure if it would have changed my life or made a difference in any way. I guess I'll never know.

Having met my obligations to my grandmother, I said goodbye to my parents and headed back home. On the way, I stopped to pick up my prescription. While parked in the supermarket parking lot, I saw a pair of recruiters, trying to talk a couple of high school kids into joining the military. As I stepped out of my car, I overheard one of the boys say, "What can I expect by joining?"

Without a beat, the Recruiter replied, "Most of the time it's serious work: fighting terrorists, rebuilding a country, saving lives, but there's also a point. You're changing the world, and that's not a feeling you're going to get serving hot dogs at the ball game."

"I don't know," the boy fired back, "what about school? I really wanna become an engineer."

The Recruiter had an answer to anything the boy could possibly ask. They were trained with every rebuttal known to man. They were better than any salesmen, because they weren't selling a timeshare, they were selling pride, courage and glory. Pretty much everything but the truth. I wanted to slug the recruiters in their nose and tell them to leave the kids alone. That too many men had gone to war under false pretenses. But before I could, one of the boys' moms came out of the store and pulled them away from the silver-tongued devils and made a b-line for her station wagon. It was for the best, I thought. One Marine versus two is not exactly the best odds. I definitely didn't feel like taking an ass whupping.

As I continued past them, my hands slowly tightened. They looked me right in the eyes and gave me a simple nod as if they knew that I had already been recruited, already went off to war and came back and didn't want to hear even a single word from them. Marines can recognize another Marine by the look in their eyes. I think most men my age have a benign look, whereas Marines have that look that says don't fuck with me, I'm ready to die, right here, right now. And it isn't a simple threat; it's a promise. Having passed them, I didn't look over my shoulder and they didn't look over theirs. By the time I entered the store, my hands had loosened up, and I began feeling a tingling sensation in the fingertips as the blood slowly emptied out.

After picking up my prescription from the pharmacy, I was on my way out, when someone I hadn't seen in a very long time emerged in the aisle. *Oh shit!* It was my ex-girlfriend, Sophia, with a little boy in a shopping cart. My stomach was in knots. It was that feeling you get when you see an ex and you don't quite know where to put your hands or place your eyes. I took a closer look at the boy, while secretly doing the math in my head. *He isn't mine, is he? No. Too young.*

Sophia looked happy, as did her son, who was sitting in the cart, tucked between boxes of cereal. She brushed his cheek and the boy laughed and reached out to her. I watched them, unseen.

I remember in the past thinking she wasn't fit to be a mother, but she looked different now. Maybe she finally grew up and got her head straight.

The closer she got, the more nervous I became. She hadn't yet seen me. Then finally, the moment of truth: we were barely five feet away from each other when we made eye contact.

She walked right by me without any acknowledgement whatsoever.

Seriously? Did she not recognize me? It's a strange feeling when somebody you used to know, love, care about or sleep with, walks right past you like you never existed, like you had absolutely zero influence in their life. Then again, maybe I never did, not to her anyway. I'm sure when she thinks about me (that is if she thinks of me at all), it's very much like someone remembering the mumps. They remember having them, but they don't remember what they looked like, how bad the pain was, or any of the sensations or feelings associated with them. 'I already had them,' is what people say, which makes them safe going forward. Maybe I was the mumps for Sophia. She already had me. The worst of it was over. She was free to be herself now, free to love unconditionally.

I took a second look at the boy and I saw a lot of Sophia in him. She had a lot of dominant features. *Is that what our kid would've looked like?*

I felt so removed in that moment, and the cold draft from the freezer aisle didn't help things any. It was like I was caught in a vacuum of space: completely alone, void of matter or substance. It took the voice of a fifteen-year-old stock boy to bring me back to reality. "Sir?"

"Huh?"

He looked at me concerned. "Are you alright?"

I nodded. "I'll be fine, thanks."

After such a long day, I finally made it home. Kelly was sitting on the stoop, wiping sleep from his eyes. It was four in the afternoon. "You have got to be the laziest guy I have ever met," I said, smirking at him.

Kelly took out a roach from his hiding spot—in-between two loose bricks—and lit it, trying to get high off of a few crumbs of weed. He looked up at me with his bloodshot eyes and said, "We all got our roles to play. You're the hero, fighting for the American dream, and I'm the villain, reaping all the benefits."

There it was again, that false title. "Hero?"

"Yeah. Hero."

I wanted to laugh. You could've measured my courage in teaspoons. "What kind of heroics do you think I was up to over there, saving children from a burning building? No. I was the one burning it down."

"What are you talking about?"

"Never mind. I'm sure it's the last thing you want to hear."

"Come on, give me a little more credit than that."

I gave him the benefit of the doubt and took a seat next to him. "You really want the truth?"

He said, "Yeah."

So I let him have it. "During a raid in Iraq, a misfire caused a grenade to crash through a civilian home, killing an entire family, all except a young boy named Ali. He lost his mother, his father, and his sister, all on the same day."

Kelly scratched his head; he didn't really know what to make of the story. I think that's all it was to him, just a story. "That's war for ya," he said taking a drag.

"They were civilians," I protested.

"It's not your fault. It's war."

"Well, war begets war."

Kelly looked away, thinking about what that really meant.

"What if that were our family? What if someone killed grandma or me?"

He took in his last puff and stood up. "I'll tell you what I would do. An eye for an eye. I would have no qualm about burning down their home with everyone in it."

"Exactly. So how could I blame Ali if he grew up to be a radical or a terrorist? How could I persecute him for the sake of righteousness?"

Kelly raised a brow.

"Forgiveness is a virtue that comes with time. At that age, I'm afraid some are just not privy to it, especially when there's no one there to teach it to them. A man at thirty might forgive, but a boy at twelve is ready to fight, kill and eat!"

Kelly awkwardly began tapping his feet, as if I was killing his high.

"People can call them terrorists if it settles their mind, but the three things we have in common, is that we've both bled for something we believe in, we've both buried a body before its time, and we're both a casualty of a bigger, emotional war."

Kelly seemed confounded by my words. He looked at me like I was stranded on a planet all by myself, with no hope of rescue.

After that conversation he always found a way to keep himself out of my path. I don't think it was because he was afraid of me; I think it was because he knew that he could never truly understand my pain. Sometimes weeks would go by before I saw Kelly, and even that was usually on his way in or on his way out. It was all too reminiscent of my childhood. It was exactly how I would act around my father. I never knew what was going to trigger his anger: a word or even a simple gesture. He was always waiting for me to say something, anything. I could see why people never wanted to be around him, and I could understand Kelly's hesitation to now be around me. He wasn't the only one either.

As people slowly ejected themselves out of my life, days became long and nights stretched beyond the point of sanity. They say the older you get, the faster you perceive time to be, but I don't think age has anything to do with it. I think it has something to do with anticipation. When you're not anticipating anything, your days seem endless. I remember how it took forever before winter finally slipped away and spring came rolling in. Everything around me changed, except for me. I was a snow globe on a shelf: a silent, calm nativity scene, encapsulated behind a glass, drowning in fake snow.

I had been back for months and I hadn't even settled into my room. My duffle bag sat, untouched, by the foot of my bed, collecting dust and smelling up the room. During spring cleaning, my grandmother begged for me to put it away. Looking back, I now know why it took so long. I was afraid of finding something that I wasn't emotionally ready for.

The second I opened the bag that's exactly what I found, in the form of Rev's camera (the one he had lent me). It powered up the second I turned it on. Still half a battery left. It contained the last thirty-six shots he ever took. A man's final moments captured in glimpses. Maybe there was something on it that was of importance, maybe something his family could take comfort in: the last image of him smiling, the last glimmer of hope in his eyes, his final salute, his final message, anything at all. Then again, secretly I was hoping there was a picture of the orphanage, the children, Ali or even Nadeel.

And there it was...the very last image. I had completely forgotten about it: the picture that I had taken of Ali and me. His dark brown eyes pierced the screen and lit up my face. Although it was a still picture, it *moved* me. I couldn't help but wonder how he was getting by. I tried to remember, tried to summon back the moment in question, to picture it exactly as it happened, or didn't happen. I remembered his smile and the hope in his eyes, fleeting at times, but still resolute. It was now the last remaining connection I had to him.

I saved the picture to my computer and then deleted it off the camera. As for the remaining pictures, Rev's family deserved to see them. I decided to deliver them, personally. It was one of those situations where late was better than never.

CHAPTER 17

I put a good nine hundred miles on Kelly's odometer and travelled over thirteen hours to Washington D.C to see Rev's family. I pulled up in front of his house, the kind of home you find on just about any quiet, suburban street. It had a small gated fence that even an eleven-year-old could've scaled, and a flimsy front door which could barely take a boot, before popping off the hinges. For some reason I expected Rev's house to be better fortified than that, given the way he was: always the protector, the strategist, always in charge, always on point. The one glaring thing that stood out to me was the house address: 515 (the tattoo on Rev's arm). That's what he meant by his saving grace: his family. It was the reason he was over there, to protect *their* future.

Before ringing the doorbell, I stood there for a whole ten minutes practicing how to introduce myself. "I'm his friend. No, I'm his brother." I didn't know what to say. Neither of them felt quite right.

I drew a big breath, straightened myself up and knocked twice for assurance. I could hear shuffling steps from inside. The way the door opened slowly and carefully I could tell the person behind it was sick and tired of seeing strangers at the door.

I met a pair of eyes and said, "Hello."

The door opened to reveal a woman. I recognized her face from the camera. It was Rev's wife, Mary. She hesitated then opened the door a little more. There was a little boy by her feet.

"My name is Santoli, ma'am. I served with your husband, Rev...uh... Ernie."

"Rev is fine," she said. "Please, come in."

Standing in the doorway, I could see dishes of food prepared for the new widow: casseroles, pies, roasts, and salads.

Mary led me into the living room, where I took a seat on the couch. She took a seat beside me, album in hand, showing me three by five photos of her two beautiful children: Jonathan, and a baby girl named Kate, who never even met Rev. She was born eight months ago, just after Rev's last leave. Jonathan, on the other hand, was a mirror image of his father. He had the same eyes and the same look on his face that Rev had when I first met him, that look of curiosity.

As I looked around the room, it was a reflection of the man. Military pennants lay on the coffee table, ships in bottles rested on the shelves, along with small statues of Christian saints. Not to mention the family photographs that decorated the walls: shots of Rev in happier times with a pregnant Mary and little Jonathan; Rev as a young cadet in his blue dress uniform; a framed headline from the local newspaper, announcing: MARINE LAID TO REST, and one very emotional picture on the mantle: Rev frozen in his salute. He was very much in the room.

I reached into my pocket and pulled out the small digital camera and put it into Mary's hand. She didn't turn it on; she just stared at it, feeling his fingerprints, absorbing his touch.

"Rev was a good man," I said.

She already knew it, and she hurt like hell because of it.

"It was my honor to serve with him. I still can't believe he's gone."

On her finger, Mary had two rings, one clearly larger than the other. She removed the first one—the larger one—and began reading the inscription inside the band. "Ad infinitum. It means 'to infinity without end'." She looked around the room. "Ernie will always be here, in this house, with his children, with me." She placed the ring back on her ring finger pressing it up against the first. She could no longer hold back the tears. She tried to hold it together, but it was too much for her to bear.

I watched her fall apart, yet I made no attempt to save the pieces. As much as I wanted to comfort her, I was not emotionally equipped. I never quite knew what to say in moments like that. *I'm sorry* seemed so obvious. Too obvious. How many times had she heard that already? What do sorries really do anyway? What am I apologizing for? I never understood that. My eyes retreated to the floor.

Feeling embarrassed, Mary got up and excused herself.

As she left the room, in walked little Jonathan, a plastic revolver at his hip and a cowboy hat on his head. Although his eyes paled in comparison to Ali's, they still reminded me so much of him: the eyes of a boy who had lost his family, angry eyes, angry at the world, angry at me. He tried to speak but he couldn't. He clenched the plastic revolver at his hip, perhaps hoping it was real. This was Rev's legacy.

Mary's voice murmured from behind me. "This is Santoli. He was a friend of your father's."

Just like Ali, hearing the past tense *was,* brought tears to Jonathan's eyes and he began rubbing them over and over. His sadness brought on a pang of guilt, like I had just been convicted of third-degree murder.

"I should get going," I said, getting up from the couch.

Mary turned, looked directly into my eyes and said, "Thank you for returning the camera."

"No problem ma'am. It was my pleasure and duty."

Outside, in the front yard, was a blaze of white roses, which were painfully reminiscent of Nadeel's garden.

I looked over my shoulder and there, staring at me from the living room window, incredulous, was little Jonathan. Another child of war, forced to grow up not fully knowing the truth, and secretly hating Rev for choosing war over him. It's not the ones who choose war that suffer, it's the ones who didn't choose it at all.

I got back into Kelly's car and drove through the night, drowning my sorrows in a bottle of Jack. Not a single roadblock or a highway patrolman stopped me, even though I was averaging a speed of a hundred miles an hour in that deathtrap on wheels that Kelly called a car. By the time the sun was rising, I had polished off the entire bottle, and when I say polished off, I mean every drop, licking even the cap clean.

It wasn't exactly smart driving drunk, but I desperately wanted to go home and take my medicine. I don't know how I left it behind. I could feel the pain coming on, just behind my left eye. I needed the numbness more than ever in that moment. I felt like I didn't have a purpose, and I didn't fit into the normal mold of society. My edges were too sharp—enough to cut someone if they walked by too close. The more the despair grew, the more I felt like I didn't belong here.

Lost in thought, my car slowly began to trail into the next lane. The car beside me swerved, honked, sped up and passed me by. If it had ended there it would've been fine, but there are people who want more, the same people who want war, and I've already told you the thing about war: you can't just pour yourself a cup of it and think that'll be that.

The driver in front of me wanted more. His arm came out of the driver side window and a middle finger shouted obscenities at me.

Today was the wrong day, and that finger was all it took to trigger an explosion inside of me. My reaction was violent. *I mean who the fuck does he think he is? Who the fuck does he think he's dealing with, some soccer mom, some nine to five asshole? I am a Marine, motherfucker,* something he was about to find out the hard way.

I put my foot on the gas, heavy. After catching up to him, I pulled up to his rear bumper and fishtailed his car, nearly causing it to barrel role. We came to a stop on a quiet, empty road. It was just me, him and the morning sun. There were two paths I could've taken in that moment: the sane path or the psychopath. Giving into my anger, I became the psycho, the man I never wanted to become, the one who reminded me all too much of my father. Now looking back, it was hard to blame him; he was just a product of the institution after all.

I reacted with violence. I opened up the glove compartment and felt around the car trying to get my hands on any weapon I could find. Under the passenger seat was a revolver. That's right; my stupid cousin had a handgun. I can't say I was all that surprised that Kelly was driving around with a gun even though he had prior convictions. He wasn't exactly the sharpest knife in the drawer.

I grabbed it and piled out of the car. The driver of the other vehicle saw the weapon in my hand and panic shot across his face. He let out a high-pitch scream, transmitting verbal frequencies that only he could understand. He had clearly never seen a gun before, not in real life.

I walked right up to his window and put the gun to the glass. I was losing it, like a man on a ship headed straight for an iceberg. I shouted and aimed between his eyes, "Lower the window, you piece of shit!"

He trembled. "Please, don't shoot me." He was just some Joe Schmoe, heading to his sad, little processing job at eight in the morning. Safe little man, with his safe little life. He probably didn't even know how to throw a proper punch. His delicate, little hands would shatter to pieces if he even tried.

"Lower the window, asshole!"

He shook his head. "Please…no."

"I'm not gonna say it again."

He covered his face with his hands.

"You think your window's gonna stop this bullet? Lower it before I let you have it!"

He reluctantly lowered his window. "Please don't shoot."

"Why?" I asked him "Why shouldn't I shoot you?"

"Please. I got a family. I got kids."

There was a cold smirk on my face. I could feel it beneath the numbness. "You think having a family or kids exempts you from harm? I have made many women widows and many children orphans. What's one more?"

"Please," he begged.

I reached into the car, took a hold of the man's collar, pressed the revolver to his forehead and pulled back the hammer.

Why are you making all that noise? I heard from the far recesses of my mind.

The sounds around me suddenly disappeared and Nadeel's voice became the voice in my head, replacing my own. Hearing it forced me to pull my psyche apart, until all versions of me were looking at one another: my mother's son, my father's legacy, the Marine, the death dealer, the hero, and the scared, little boy.

Who are you so angry at that you're willing to ruin your life over? Let it go.

I could feel the weight of her hand on my shoulder. I came to my senses and immediately sobered up. My fingers unleashed the tight grip around the man's collar, and I slowly lowered the gun. Feeling the past weighing heavily on my shoulders, I quickly got back into Kelly's car and drove off. Looking through the rear-view mirror, I watched the other car getting smaller and smaller, before disappearing completely.

In the mirror, another image soon replaced it. I imagined Ali sitting in the backseat and Nadeel in the front—a sort of make-believe family made up of spare parts. Nadeel's window was half down, her hair blowing in the wind. A breeze or two hit Ali and he opened his mouth to taste the wind. But just as quickly as it came, the image of our family dissolved in the headlights of an oncoming semi. I had to swerve just to miss it. It was clear that I was losing touch with reality.

I drove around all day, trying to calm myself down. It was close to midnight by the time I got back home. I walked up the cracked sidewalk to the sagging wooden porch and stood there, looking for any signs of life: a kitchen light, the sound of a TV, the humming of speakers, something, anything. Inside, Kelly was sitting on the couch, smoking a cigarette in silence. "Where were you?"

"What?" It was one of those questions that registers a second too late. I heard it, but not before Kelly could repeat it.

"I said, where were you?"

"I had a few too many drinks last night, and then today I got lost."

"How'd you get lost? You should know this place like the back of your hand by now."

As I looked down at the back of my hands, I could feel the dull pain in my fingertips, that pins and needles feeling you get, except this was constant.

"Hey, you alright?"

I shook my head. "Not really."

Kelly didn't say anything. I don't think he knew what to say at all. It wasn't one of those moments when you want to hear advice. It was one of those moments you just want to stew in your heartache.

My grandmother's fragile voice followed me into my room. "Are you alright, son?"

"I'll be fine, Grandma."

She picked up a frame off the dresser, which contained a high school picture of me in my awkward batting stance. "You were a good baseball player," she said.

"You're thinking of Uncle Richie's son, Brandon. He was the all-star, grandma."

She took a seat beside me. Even though she could smell the booze on my lips, she never mentioned it. "No. I'm talking about you."

I shook my head. "I think only *you* thought that"

"Hardly. You might not have been the greatest player on the field, but you had something the others didn't."

"What's that?"

"Optimism…I remember how you'd say, 'Wait grandma…wait until the ninth inning. The game's not over yet'."

I smirked. "A lot good it did. In three years, we never went to the finals once."

"But you kept trying. That's what made you a good player."

"Everyone was trying just as hard."

"No. Not like you, not with that kind of optimism. You played like there was an angel on your shoulder. I don't see much of that boy anymore. I see your outer reflection, but I don't see that bright-eyed optimist who believed in bottom of the ninth miracles."

"I'm afraid there are no miracles in the real world. None that I've seen anyway."

"Then you're not looking hard enough, boy."

I looked up at the mirror on the dresser. I looked like an exhausted old man.

"You've been given another chance," she continued, "to put the wrong things right. Not too many men get a second chance. You've been through hell and back, barefoot. Your feet might be blistering but they're still moving. If you ask me...that's a miracle." She brushed my cheek like one would expect a grandmother to do and said, "God Bless you."

I leaned my head back and conjured Nadeel up in my mind. With my sporadic sleep schedule and the time difference between us, she slept while I was awake, and awoke as I slept. It's as if we were never really in the same world at the same time. I began to wonder if I really even met her or just resurrected an image from my dreams. I always felt there was something unreal about her. As much as I wanted to set her aside, I knew she was too deep rooted in my mind. And even more prominent was Ali. I still wondered about that little man's future, surrounded in daily Iraq, desperately searching for meaning. His picture was the only thing keeping me company. I had printed it up and kept it in my wallet. I would take it out and look at his eyes, which were the very definition of unrest. I knew that Ali and Nadeel would be more than just a couple of lines in my memoirs.

The whole time I was over there I was thinking about coming home, but now being here, and seeing all this bullshit, I couldn't help but want to escape it. It wasn't that I hungered for war, it was that my idea of peace had changed. I was no good here. I couldn't put on an ill-fitting suit, slap on a tie, sit at a desk and do a nine to five. Not after what I had been through. Over there I felt like I was making a difference. Here, I felt like I was rotting away, like my potential was dissipating. This world moved too fast for me. I felt out of place. People seemed more disconnected than ever, and their sincerity was wearing away. Every smile felt like a parody. This place no longer felt like home. The road to Iraq was a long time coming. I knew I had to go back. Not as a Marine (not in that capacity); I had to go back as *me*.

CHAPTER 18

Baghdad, Iraq, 2007

It wasn't easy getting back into a war-torn country. I flew to Jordan, which at the time was offering a flight to Baghdad. I still remember the blur of city lights as the plane passed over that hopeless place. People always speak of the good old days, and I couldn't help but wonder if that place had ever truly seen good old days. One dictator after another had left that country raped and in shambles.

It felt strange to be back without an army or any weapons at all to protect myself. I was just a civilian: alone and benign. Well, maybe not alone. Raheem had sent a car to pick me up from the airport. He wanted to come pick me up himself, but I didn't want to rouse any suspicions. I told him to keep it a secret from Nadeel and Ali. I didn't want them rejecting the idea before I had an opportunity to speak.

My driver traveled through the torn streets of Baghdad, maneuvering the craters in the road. Anytime the headlights of an oncoming car flashed at us, we were on edge. Who would be out here this late, on this lonely road, other than a restless spirit? *A description tailor-fitted for me.*

Our car pulled up to a checkpoint manned by Iraqi police, who were not exactly the friendliest people. Half of them were giving intel to the insurgency about every move the military was making. They would've loved to get their hands on an American. I could see their fatigues and automatic rifles, peering through the tinted windows. I never realized how frightening fatigues could be in the night, when you're not wearing any.

One of the policemen motioned for the driver to roll down his window.

He glanced nervously at me through the rearview mirror.

The Policeman looked at the driver, the car, the plates, and then opened up the trunk. They pulled out my luggage, which they thoroughly searched as I sat quietly in the car, trying to remain as inconspicuous as possible. They walked around the car and stopped at my window. Pulling out their flashlights, they shined it right into my eyes. One of them yelled in Arabic, motioning me to pull down the window.

I did so, fighting to remain calm under the man's granite gaze.

He snapped his fingers, asking me to present my passport, which I did with calm hands.

The man looked at it then back at me. He told me to get out of the car so they could check the inside.

I looked to the driver, who was sweating profusely, his eyes shouting *don't get out!* But I had no choice. I knew he wasn't able to do anything to help me. He wouldn't even speak on my behalf in fear of being arrested and tortured.

I was hoping they would check the car, then give a nod to the man tending the lift-gate and send us on our way. But something told me that it wasn't going to be that easy. As I got out, the policeman looked to his partner, and as a Marine, I understood the conversation they were having with their eyes. They were assessing me, discussing if I was of any importance, if they could use me in any way.

The conversation concluded—all of which took place in a four second glance—the policeman raised his rifle to my head, spat in my face, then drove the butt of his rifle right into my gut.

He knocked the wind right out of me. My mind was racing, my hands sweating, and my eyes beginning to water from the pain. I tried to remember my SERE training (Survival, Evasion, Resistance, Escape). I had been subjected to many scenarios involving abduction and kidnapping, but as stated earlier: real life is eighty percent unpredictable and unorganized.

They were shouting for me to get down on my knees. "Enzel! Enzel!" I recognized the words. The fact they were in uniform, meant that they were just middle men. If they wanted me dead, I would've been by now. No, they were clearly under strict orders to keep me alive until a professional interrogation could take place.

They shouted again, "Enzel! Enzel!"

I put my hands behind my head, but I didn't kneel. I needed my legs to run. It's better to take a bullet in the back then to be tortured and eventually beheaded.

Before I could take a step, another rifle butt to the gut had me kissing dirt. I turned, blinking painfully into the head lights of the police truck.

One of the men kept me between his crosshairs, while another pulled my hands behind my back and slapped handcuffs on my wrists. Now I had nothing to defend myself, no legs or arms. Nothing short of projectile vomiting was going to distract these men.

The second they pulled a burlap bag from the truck, I knew where this was going. They put the bag over my face and the first thought that went through my head was *I'm already dead*. I had traveled this far to have my life end here. Like that news reporter who got his head cut off, you'd see me on one of those grainy videos, passed around on the internet or a picture of my face splattered on the front page of the New York Times. You'd feel some split-second remorse for me, and then move on to the video of the cat playing a piano to cheer yourself up. It was only a matter of time now. The countdown had begun.

Another truck approached and a voice shouted in Arabic, "Nahno nbhath an Amrecie." (We're looking for an American.)

The men began shouting back and forth in Arabic. I could hear the fear in their voices. This new party was definitely not a friend of theirs. But perhaps, by process of elimination, they could be a friend to me.

I heard guns being fired and the policemen trying to take cover. I could hear rounds perforating the sheet metal of the car. The windows shattered and my driver screamed for his life.

Through the veil of the burlap bag, I could see muzzle flashes and ricocheting bullets. It was like some suicidal Fourth of July.

This was my chance. I crawled under the car, hoping the driver wouldn't hit the gas and run me over. Before I could get completely out of sight, I felt a pair of hands around my ankles, pulling me back out from under the car.

"Fuck!"

The anonymous man grabbed me by the neck and slammed me against the hood of the car. He threw me in the back of another vehicle with the burlap bag still on my head.

I could hear my driver shouting, "American! American!"
Thanks a lot pal.

As the situation developed, so did my thoughts about death. I think you can only excrete so much adrenaline, before you no longer care about dying. I was pretty close to reaching that level. I slowed down my breathing and began counting the seconds between the stops and feeling the turns of car (a left, a right, another left then a long straight away). After what I presume was a twenty-minute drive (but felt more like an hour with a burlap bag over my head), we arrived outside a building. The men pulled me out and dragged me inside. I walked down a hall with two armed men—one on either side. They unlocked a heavy door and pushed me into a small back room, planting me on a wooden chair. They then pulled the bag off my head and shined a bright light into my unadjusted pupils. They were trying to maintain authority and control, using text book tactics.

I looked around, taking in as much as I could, trying to decipher my location. Cigarette smoke hung in the air, of what I could tell was an interrogation room. I tried to suppress even the slightest signs of fear. Never show them your true emotions or they'll use it against you. That's the name of the game.

A shadowy figure sat across from me. He tossed an evidence bag onto the table, which contained my passport and ID. Leaning in closer, he stubbed out his cigarette on the table and asked the same question my mind was repeatedly asking for the past two hours. "What are you doing here?"

I didn't speak. I wanted to see how far he was willing to take this.

He didn't disappoint. He put a gun on the table and pointed it toward me like a cruel spin the bottle. "You do not have the right to remain silent here. You will speak, or we will make you speak."

I looked closer, regarding the insignia on his jacket. He was Iraqi police. His face was concrete, expressionless. You could've cut the tension with a knife, and with the ten-inch blade he had holstered on his leg, I thought he was going to—maybe more than just the tension, maybe a finger or two.

Two other policemen stood in the back of the room observing the interrogation.

I kept my head down and my eyes straight so he couldn't extract anything from my face. "I'm on a humanitarian mission," I told him.

He stood up, gun in hand, vest strapped tight, reeking of ego. Then again, it's easy to be tough when you have an army backing you. He swaggered around the room, pointing the gun at me, muzzle end, playing his mind games.

My face was a study in strained composure. Although the analytical part of my mind had already acknowledged the inevitable (that it was all over), the creative part of my mind was still looking for ways to escape. But I can honestly say that not a single rational thought entered my mind in that moment. I believe the closest I came was *What would Jason Bourne do in a situation like this?*

The policeman slapped me so hard he knocked all rational and irrational thoughts out of my head. He kept at it, accusing me of being a military spy.

I didn't take the bait. I looked him right in the eyes, so there was no doubt. "I am not military! I am here for humanitarian purposes."

The policeman pulled back the hammer of his gun. He could scarcely contain his excitement. "Bullshit! Everything you say is bullshit! You have five seconds to tell me the truth."

"I told you the truth."

"Four...." The infamous count down—another tactic I was familiar with.

"You know everything there is to know," I told him.

"Three...."

I put my head down. "You're wasting your time."

"Two...."

I could tell he wanted me to beg for my life, but I wouldn't give him the satisfaction. There was nothing left to say.

"One...."

Suddenly, there was a knock at the door. The policeman looked over his shoulder and the guard at the door opened it. Once he saw who it was, the guard turned back with a look that said *the show's over*. And with that, the policeman got up and disappeared into the darkness of the room. He became stone quiet, and even though I couldn't hear what the man at the door was saying, his tone was resolute. The conversation took exactly ten seconds, followed by twenty seconds of silence.

I sat there, inert, trying to comprehend the severity of the situation.

The policeman came back toward me, picked his gun up off the table and moved soundlessly toward the door. He took one last look at me before exiting. Just like that, the interrogation was over. The new man came in. His uniform was covered with a lot more credentials than the last man—possibly a captain. He had certain features that reminded me of someone. I couldn't quite put my finger on who it was. Then again, it might have just been a coincidence.

Without pause or consideration, he said, "Get up."

Which I did.

A guard walked over, uncuffed my hands and escorted me out the rear entrance of the police station. We exited out a large, iron gate, to the back alley, where a lone car was parked in the shadows. I couldn't see who was inside, but I could tell this was the *pass off*. I was sure of it. They were handing me over to the insurgency. There were too many guns for me to make a move. I had no choice but to wait it out until an opportunity presented itself.

A long moment passed as I stood there, watching the car, my pulse racing. Suddenly there was movement. The door opened and out of the darkness stepped a familiar face. It was Raheem.

I looked over my shoulder at the captain. He had a malevolence in his eyes that froze me to the spot.

Raheem nodded at the man, and the second their eyes met, I finally realized who he reminded me of. It was obvious these two came from the same gene pool.

Raheem gave me a confident look that let me know it was alright to move.

I carefully did so, to the passenger side of Raheem's truck. As I opened the door and climbed in, Raheem did the same. Before saying a word, he slowly pulled away from the curb and began driving.

"Are you alright," he asked, once we had cleared the police station.

"I will be now, Raheem, thank you."

"I immediately called my brother, Waahid, after your driver told me what happened. Thank God, he was able to get to you before anything worse could happen."

"I've only been in Iraq for three hours now and I'm off to a good start."

"I'm sorry to tell you, it's only been three."

I burst out laughing. "Even better."

Raheem looked different now than what I remembered, more somber, with the broken eyes of a man who had suffered a hard year. He was clearly tired of this place and its politics. It didn't take much for the two of us to slip back into our old familiar banter. "It's good to see you, my friend," he said.

"That's an understatement, Raheem."

With that raspy voice of his, he began telling me about the past year and how the orphanage was getting by. He told me how storeowners were pitching in, providing food and supplies. People from all around Iraq were helping out the best they could. Raheem even briefly talked about seeing Saddam hang for all his crimes against humanity.

"It didn't make me feel the way I thought it would," he said. "So much has happened since his name was last mentioned that it seems almost irrelevant."

As always, Raheem was very careful about the words he chose. He didn't want to sound like it wasn't a huge victory for Iraq and its people. I suppose Raheem just didn't want to take gratification in the death of a man, regardless of who that man was. Saddam had taken a lot from his family. He didn't want to give him any more emotion or thought. That was fine by me. Saddam was the last name I ever wanted to hear.

We got so wrapped up in our conversation that I didn't even recognize the street we were on. We had arrived outside the orphanage. I looked down at my watch. It was two in the morning. I had barely gotten out of Raheem's truck when I saw Yusuf staring at me. He didn't look the slightest bit happy to see me. He gave me a condescending smile and headed inside.

Raheem looked at me a moment and his eyes drifted toward the field of white roses. Sadly, there were more now. I swallowed a breath. The garden had reached the end of the courtyard, filling it with the cries and colors of pain. More roses than anyone could count. I was instantly hit by a wave of sadness.

Raheem saw the pure, raw emotion on my face and my hands clenching into fists. "Anger begins with madness," he said, "and ends in regret. In order to change the current situation, we must not fall victim to despair."

"It's not always that easy, Raheem."

"I never said it was easy, but it is necessary."

He was right. I offered up a weak nod, all the while wishing that someone had said that to me before I went off to war.

"Let us go inside."

We entered the dark foyer, where lit candles sat on nearly every table; it reminded me of a church on Christmas Eve.

"Iraq's electrical grid is still in terrible shape," Raheem said. "The lights go out often."

A lone candle came down the stairs. For a moment I thought *Nadeel*. Although it was a pretty woman, it wasn't her. The difference was that of fresh orange juice when compared to concentrate: both are sweet, but deep down inside, you know that one is just better for you.

The pretty girl smiled, propped her head up on her elbows and introduced herself as Sahar.

Raheem requested, "Can you please make up the spare room upstairs for our friend?"

Sahar took a second look at me and smiled. "Yes, of course."

"Come," Raheem said, "the children will be happy to see you."

Some of the children were excited to see me again, clamoring for my attention, while others were scared from all the stories they had heard about me.

I was just excited to see some old faces, to see them in high-spirits, after everything that had happened to them. I moved around the room, hugging them all…all but one. A slow smile crept across my face. "So, where is he?" I asked Raheem, wandering through the crowd of children, looking for Ali.

"Let's have a seat," Raheem replied. "You've had a long journey."

"No…I'm fine. I just wanna see…."

Suddenly, a foot appeared in the doorway and a sudden hush fell over the children. My eyes turned to see who it was. The foot quickly withdrew out of sight, and the children all pushed their way past each other and jumped into their beds.

Nadeel emerged from the shadows. She saw me, and a small smile crossed her face, large enough to feel invited, yet small enough to wonder what I was doing back here. It was the last thing I expected to see after our final conversation. In a place like Iraq, where things change day to day, she was still the same young lady she was the day I met her. And her impression of me remained the same: a lost soul, searching for answers, yet finding only questions. She drew closer, touched to see me, touched by the inner struggle that drew me back. Reaching out, she wrapped her arms around me. I hugged her back. This time, she let herself be hugged.

"So, where is he?" I asked again. "Where's Ali?"

I got the sense that something was missing, like looking into a mirror and finding no reflection. It was written all over her face. Before she even said it, I knew. "He's gone, isn't he?"

Her eyes stood me up and ran to the lonely plant sitting on the table. It was the only thing that remained of Ali.

"Come…we'll talk downstairs."

I followed her downstairs into the kitchen, where a few candles were the only source of light. "Come, sit. You must be hungry." She took a seat at the table, which was set with an appetizing spread of Arabic food. "We're celebrating Eid-al-Fitr. It's the first day of the Islamic month of Shawwal. It marks the end of Ramadan. During this time, we give zakat al-fitr: charity in the form of food."

I took a seat at the table and had a few bites then looked up at Nadeel, waiting for the answer to my earlier question.

She got comfortable in her seat and let out a long breath. "He wet the bed almost every night," she said. "He would have these horrible nightmares. The only sounds I ever heard from him were the moans and muffled screams he would let out in his dreams, seeing the faces of his family in their last moments. His hand would reach out sometimes, and even though he never said it, I knew it was for his mother. Who else would a twelve-year-old reach for if not his mother? Who else would a thirty-five-year-old reach for if not his mother? Outside, the sounds of war filled his ears. He would crawl into the fetal position as if it would protect him from the bombs at his doorstep."

Her words evoked an image of a lost child, with his umbilical cord still dragging by his feet. "Where did he go?"

"The occupation has planted the culture of revenge, the culture of hatred. They have torn the tissue of our society." She shook her head. "There are men waiting in the streets, waiting for boys like him, who are looking to trade in their hate for revenge—a fair trade as far as they're concerned. They recruit them under false pretenses, for a cause they know nothing about, making them targets for cruelty, both physical and mental."

Nadeel was worried, but strong. This was nothing new to her. He wasn't the first boy to be led astray. Her field of roses told the story of the countless children who were either killed or died in a similar struggle. She looked down at her sullen hands—the dirt still under her fingernails—and let out another long breath. "You call it the American dream, but you're not the only ones who have had that dream. You are, however, one of the few countries who can acquire it. But it is not your dream alone. It doesn't belong to you any more than it belongs to me or every other person in this world. We all want freedom. We all want our potential realized. And that's what they're selling these boys: potential. They're willing to set themselves on fire, just so the world can see their light."

I was disheartened by the news. *What if he's dead?* That's all I could think about—fueled by the last words I said to him. I had never killed anyone with words before. I had never constructed a word-box beneath someone's feet, laced their neck with a noose made of consonants and vowels, and left them dangling—from the metaphorical beam—just like a participle, while they counted out the syllables they had left before committing su-i-cide. I'm sure he was still spiraling somewhere, replaying our last conversation, hating me a little more every time he thought about it.

"He left because of me, didn't he?"

Nadeel didn't quite know what to say, and luckily, she didn't have to. The sounds of a crying baby from the hallway paused our conversation.

In came Sahar, with the infant. She smiled as she handed the child to Nadeel.

Nadeel lit up and took the baby graciously. "There, there," she said to the baby. "All is well child."

The infant lay smiling in Nadeel's arms. Her lips coddled the baby's forehead as she hushed her cries away.

"Would you mind?" She said, handing over the baby to me. "I have to get her milk."

"Sure," I said, awkwardly taking the child.

"Her name is Kalif."

Two boys watched from the doorway, giggling. Nadeel was uncomfortably aware of the kissy faces they were making and what they were implying. "What are you doing up?"

Before they could run away, Nadeel called one of them over. "Hakim, come here."

Hakim entered the room and Nadeel took a hold of his arm. "What happened to you?"

Hakim had lost his cherub smile and gained some bruises. His stuttering lips tried to catch up with his thoughts. "I-I-I fell down," he replied.

"Always hurting yourself," Nadeel said, "you have to be more careful."

He nodded and slowly slunk out of the room.

Just then, Kalif let out a happy squeal safely in my arms. She was so vulnerable and fragile.

"I've never seen her take to anyone like that," Nadeel said. "She likes you."

"Well, she aint so bad herself."

Nadeel smiled. "I believe everything happens for a reason. You came back when you didn't have to. That means you're ready to receive forgiveness. There are many boys here, looking for peace. Perhaps you can help them."

I quietly nodded and then reached a hand for the baby, who took a hold of my finger. Staring at her, my mind began racing, thinking about another vulnerable child: Ali, now in the hands of insurgents, or on the streets alone by himself. As my thoughts built, somewhere not too far, something exploded, and plaster powder fell from the ceiling, into my eyes. I handed the baby back to Nadeel and rushed to the window. All havoc ceased, and I had to remind myself that I wasn't a Marine anymore. In the distance, all I could see was smoke rising into the air.

Sahar came running back into the room and Nadeel gestured that everything was alright.

Nadeel draped Kalif in her little blanket. "Are you alright," she asked me.

"I'm fine. You?"

"Sadly, I'm used to it by now."

We checked on the boys, together, making sure they were safe. They had doubled up in each bed, holding onto each other tightly. "It's going to be alright," Nadeel told them. She healed their wounded hearts, lifted up their battered spirits and gave birth to their self-esteem. She did more than most mothers do for their children. And she did it all for them, taking nothing for herself, other than pride in their strength. It inspired me to do the same. Maybe Nadeel was right. Maybe I could be of some use here, helping these boys with their hurt, and them, helping me with mine.

Once the boys had calmed down, Nadeel and I continued our conversation out in the hall. "How long have you come to stay?" She asked.

I shrugged my shoulders. I didn't yet know myself. "Maybe...forever."

"Forever?"

"Maybe. I haven't thought it through."

"Is that what you're going to promise these children? Or me?"

I was taken aback by the cadence of her voice. *I thought this is what you wanted.* "What's wrong with forever?"

She shook her head. "Don't promise people forever. It's a cruel promise. One that has no place in this world. Not that I've ever seen, and definitely not anything these children have ever witnessed." She then turned and headed to her room.

She was right. I was the last person in the world who should promise anyone forever. I wasn't exactly the kind of person who finished everything he started. So, I kept words like forever to myself, in fear someone would hold me to my promise. It wasn't fare to anyone saying those words, and especially not to anyone hearing them.

CHAPTER 19

Raheem woke me up the next morning, still trying to fix that old junker of a bus. "Give it up," I told him, "you're wasting your time. The last time it started was a fluke."

He smiled at me and said, "If a man remains patient, beautiful things await him." He had the characteristics of a Buddhist Monk: always calm, always patient. Not to mention, he spoke the truth, whenever he did speak. Never a wasted word with Raheem. That's why anytime he opened his mouth, I knew something important was coming. He would've made a great mentor and a horrible politician, on account of his truth.

After two hours of poking and prodding, the bus finally started.

"Alright," I said, "let me have it. Say I told you so."

Raheem smiled. He never gloated. Not once. He simply patted the hood of the old, rust bucket like it was just one of the kids at the orphanage.

"You're a better man than me, Raheem. I'm not sure I could keep working on a lost cause."

"There are no lost causes, my friend, only limitations to a man's patience."

I smirked. "You are definitely the Yoda of this place, Raheem."

"Yoda? I'm not familiar with that reference."

"You never heard of Yoda? Star Wars?"

He shook his head.

"It's a reference to a wise man."

He smiled. "Then I will take it."

As I wiped my hands, I heard a familiar voice just outside the cement wall. Through one of the shell holes, I glimpsed a boy on the other side. A boy who looked an awful lot like.... "Ali!"

There was no movement on the other side. *Perhaps he didn't hear me.* Raheem looked confused.

"I'll be right back," I said, quickly running to the gate, trying to get to the other side of the wall.

From the distance I couldn't really make out the boy's face. I called out again, "Ali!"

After seeing me, he made a run for it, ducking down and nipping through an opening in a fence.

I went sprinting out across the road, right on his heels. I had to speak to him. I had to let him know that I came back because of him.

He made his way across a patch of wasteland, with me trailing a few yards behind. "Ali! Wait!"

He definitely heard me that time. But he didn't stop. He kept on going, with the speed of a sprinter.

I moved on impulse, as did the boy. He ran through houses, and I followed, shouting at the top of my lungs, "Ali!"

He was small, fast and maneuverable. He went dipping down through another fence, through an alley and then a courtyard, creating a few meters gap between us.

Suddenly, I had a flashback of playing cops and robbers with Kelly as a kid. Kelly was always the robber, which made a lot of sense now. He was always lightning quick, leaving me in his dust. I never quite caught him. I grazed him, I poked him, but no matter how fast I ran, I never caught him once. But this time it was the robber chasing the cop. The thief who had stolen a life, chasing the honest individual who wanted justice. Who deserved justice.

"Ali!" I shouted. "Stop! Please!"

He sprinted across the road, took a corner, and then, suddenly, disappeared out of sight.

For a frantic moment I searched. "Ali!"

He was gone.

A pain started in my head and ran down my spine, touching my toes before shooting back up into my retinas. I pinched the space between my eyes and took a moment to gather my thoughts.

Suddenly, a blur appeared in my peripheral and Ali surfaced again. "Ali!"

Again, he didn't stop.

I chased after him through a narrow corridor between two buildings, before bursting out of a door into the streets. Grabbing him by the arm, I finally turned him around. "Ali...."

But it wasn't Ali.

The boy was terrified, yelling in Arabic.

I quickly let him go and he ran off back the way he came.

I had a feeling of blankness. No real emotion. Only disappointment. I had come this far to heal and move on, yet everything around me was a reminder of a failed past. Just then, at my lowest, I was once again reminded of a life that I thought I had laid to rest. A military truck full of Marines roared past me. It was just a memory now. *Not my life anymore*, or so I thought. I then made the mistake of making eye contact with a young boot. He looked wide-eyed and oblivious, with no idea of what awaited him. He was a reflection of a younger me. I felt like I was stuck in a time loop, living out the worst days of my life.

I cast my mind back to the first day I arrived in Iraq. It started like a war movie in high-definition, except you couldn't turn it off, or lower the volume. There were men at my feet, with neither a pulse or breath, and still others were telling me that victory was ours. But what victory was there? Clearly none for me, if I'm still living through the streams of trauma, looking for any excuse to unleash my demons. The thought *not my life anymore* played again, and this time, I tried my hardest to believe it.

I stared at the boot, until the truck careened around the corner and it was gone. I stood there in the street for at least an hour before returning to the orphanage. For the next week, I kept my mind preoccupied with odd jobs, all the while, my heart was still with Ali, wherever he was—jack hammers tearing up the road to his dreams.

As days went by, I would stare down at the streets below, in hopes of figuring out Ali's whereabouts. Sometimes my mind would drift and I would forget where I was. I would wake up in the middle of the night in my small, bare room, illuminated only by the moonlight. Outside, instead of coyote's howling, Beretta's barked and I was instantly reminded of where I was.

One night, I lay in bed, wide awake, staring at the ceiling, listening to the soft and sordid sounds of Iraq. As I turned to my side, a crisp line of light cut through the center of the darkness and the silhouette of a boy stood in the doorway. *Am I dreaming?*

I sat up in bed and waved my arms stiffly at the apparition. "Ali?"

He stepped forward, into the light. It was Hakim.

"What are you doing up so late?"

"I heard guns outside," he said.

"I know. I heard them too. Don't worry; they're further away than they sound."

"Are you sure?"

I got up out of bed and put a hand on his shoulder. "As a Marine it was my job to know exactly where bullets were coming from."

The truth is, the shots were only three hundred meters away, but I could tell they were getting further, so why scare the boy?

He slinked out of the room and I noticed sweet, poignant music coming from the hallway. I walked across the hall toward the source of the sound: Nadeel's room. Through the crack in the doorway, I saw her sitting in her small room, which was just a little bigger than a service elevator. It was filled with books on philosophy, two and three deep, in the corners of the floor, on tables, on chairs and stacked on the shelves like trophies.

She was reading one of them: a first edition, worn from many readings. As a matter of fact, she was very much like the books she read: with a strong spine, soft skin, hard edges, and filled with deep, intellectual words that were chosen very carefully. It was what drew me to her in the first place and kept on drawing me to her after all this time—a connection, I feared, only went one way.

Two more steps into the room and I knew she could see me out of the peripheral of her eye. She didn't move or say a word, however; she didn't even acknowledge that I had entered the room. She was in a kind of reverie, her fingers dancing down the page, dervish-like.

"What are you readi...."

She held up a hand without looking at me, "Shhh."

She finished the last paragraph and then closed up her book. "It's Moby Dick. My father gave it to me when I was a child. It was his favorite book." She held it up and recited. "'He piled upon the whale's white hump, the sum of all the general rage and hate felt by his whole race from Adam down; and then, as if his chest had been a mortar, he burst his hot heart's shell upon it.' Perfect example of man's obsession in my opinion."

I got the feeling she was drawing a parallel between Ahab and myself (our inability to let things go and make peace with ourselves).

It was just her way: to imply rather than force feed it to me. Needless to say, I got the point. I threw her a small smile, just to let her know that I heard her, and I wasn't beyond the turn of a key. There was still some hope for me, as long as she kept on believing.

"Can't sleep?" She asked, changing the subject.

"No, not really."

"I guess that makes two of us."

She got up from her bed and laid the book down on her dresser. In front of her, were pictures of every child that had ever come through the orphanage. They were all there, stuck in the corners of her mirror.

As I scanned her floating album, there he was, smiling back at me: Ali. My fingers tranced the outline of his face. "I thought if I came back here things would be different, but so much has changed, and the second I get used to the changes, it changes again, unexpectedly."

She looked down at my chest as if it were made of cellophane. "Are you ready for change?"

"I don't know. I mean I look at you and I have no idea how you adapt so well. You've seen more death and destruction than most Marines, and yet you're still out there every day, planting your roses and watering your garden. How do you keep your peace, when all hell is breaking loose around you?"

She took in a deep breath as if the answer were long and draining. "A lot of things have changed, but colors are still the same, morals are still the same, ethics are still the same. We're all striving for the same things in life, while trying to avoid the same pitfalls. We all want happiness and joy, and we all want to put rest to hate. The knowledge of that, keeps me grounded and hopeful." Her gaze was warm and intelligent, and her voice rich with emotion.

"Why roses by the way?"

She raised a brow.

"The garden? Why roses?"

She smiled. "There were roses in The Hanging Gardens of Babylon. The rose is from here. It is a child of Iraq. I could think of no better symbol."

As she spoke, a long, soft expanse of leg appeared from under her blanket, unintentionally, of course. I had forgotten how inaccessible she truly was. Not the kind of girl to give into temptation. You don't seduce a woman like that; you praise her, you respect her, you listen to her—which I did, for two hours.

Suddenly becoming very aware that it was inappropriate for a now engaged woman to be alone in her room with a man, she said, "I think I should turn in. It's late."

The last thing I wanted to do was leave, but I respectfully nodded and went back to my room.

The following afternoon, I saw Nadeel sitting between the rose beds, pruning stems. The mid-day sun held her face and planted a light kiss on her forehead. As I watched her, a kind of nourishing peace instilled me. Just a pinch of all that brightness and beauty that she kept to herself could've calmed me for a lifetime.

She looked at me and smiled. "Are you up for a trip?"

"To where?"

"Somewhere special."

One of the boys was by her side, dressed in a clean, white shirt and a pair of dress pants, like he was off to Sunday school. "We've located Cassem's great uncle. He is very excited to see his nephew. Will you come with us?"

"Of course," I said, "if it's alright with Cassem."

Cassem gave me a little nod, but he looked scared, unaware of what to expect. This place had become his home, and the last thing he wanted to do was leave it. But an orphanage is no place for any child. If there was a chance of reuniting him with family, any family at all, he would be a fool to pass it up.

Cassem ran back up to his room to make sure he hadn't left anything behind, and to hand out a few more farewells.

Raheem loaded a small bag filled with food and water into an old Jeep that he had borrowed for the day. "Mr. Santoli, I'm glad to see that you'll be joining us."

"I haven't really had the opportunity to see the real Iraq."

"Then you'll really enjoy where we are going today. It is a place most people do not get a chance to see. Iraq has a lot of beauty to it."

I looked back at Nadeel. "I don't doubt that."

Raheem caught me looking and smiled. I could tell it was his way of saying *you persistent fool.* I couldn't help it, and Raheem knew it. That's why he didn't say anything. He let me indulge in my fantasy for the time being.

As we left the orphanage, Raheem drove, I rode shotgun, and Nadeel sat in the back with Cassem—his head on her lap. We drove miles across the sun-scorched desert, west of Baghdad to a small

Bedouin village on the outskirts of Al Anbar. It was a small oasis in the desert, where, according to Nadeel, her grandfather grew up. The Bedouins were nomadic tribesmen, who moved into the desert during the rainy, winter seasons and back to the desert's edge during the hot, dry summers.

On the way there, Nadeel recounted her times visiting as a child and watching the old women of the tribe sun-dry fruits and flowers for home remedies. She told us about the meals that were cooked from morning till night on an open fire. She told us about the handmade bread that she would make with her grandmother, and the colorful head scarfs she would sew to be sold in the market square. Her face lit-up as she told her stories, which reminded me of all the old Arabian tales that I had heard as a child.

When we arrived in the small village, I felt like I had gone back in time. There was nothing to remind us of where we were. No sounds of gunfire or mortars, no cries or wails, just silence.

I stepped out of the Jeep and onto the sand, which was like molten bronze. From the desert mirage, two men materialized off in the distance. They wore head scarfs and light, loose-fitting clothes and spoke in Bedouin Arabic, in a language called Badawi.

They pointed just over the hill and Nadeel translated their request. "They want us to follow them."

The two men led us by foot, over the hill, where several large tents made from woven, goat hair were erected. It was a scene right out of Arabian Nights. We entered the largest of the tents, where women weaved cloth on ancient looms, and four old men sat in a semi-circle—coils of hookah smoke, rising from their dry, tinder lips. Their voices were as silent as the sand, yet their eyes uttered their life stories with each blink.

The eldest of them, who was also the head tribesman, welcomed us. His old hands, which were weathered and cracked could no longer comfort anyone anymore, but his lips displaced advice to his eldest grandson, who carved a piece of desert palm into a beautiful horse figure. The old man smiled and patted the boy on the head, satisfied with his legacy.

Nadeel crossed her legs and took a seat on the sands below. I watched her every move, mimicking her the best I could. There was a lot of excitement in the air. I could hear women laughing somewhere nearby.

Nadeel turned to me and smiled. "Today is a special day. A son is born."

It was a celebration. Women laid out food: bowls of milk, yogurt, rice, round loaves of unleavened bread, figs, raisins and apricots. Ripe delicious dates, which could only be found in the desert oasis, where laid before us. They were sun-dried for two whole days and sifted by hand to remove the ends. Goat meat was brought out, which Nadeel said was only served on special occasions such as a birth, ceremonial events, or when guests were present—all of which applied on that day.

I was poured tea in a small, skinny, plastic glass, then handed a cup of dirty, white sugar cubes. I remember how the best places to eat in Iraq were in small dives and half-constructed mud-brick rooms that had flies buzzing about. Maybe I was expecting everything to taste bad based on the conditions, that I found even the smallest bit of flavor surprising. Either way, everything tasted delicious, and it was all made from scratch, from recipes as old as the sand itself. I remember how beautiful the small village seemed, how beautiful the culture was: derived by people who were driven by nightly steps, people who crossed the desert by moonlight, turning one of the harshest terrains into their home.

Just as we finished eating, the tribesmen began singing in tune with the sun as it travelled over their heads. When I asked Nadeel what they were singing about, she said, "They speak of the invisible winds of chance that rule us all. According to them, they push our fate in directions we cannot control, but in directions that are necessary."

I pulled the Polaroid of Ali from my wallet—his sweet innocent face, looking back at me. "I hope the winds know what they're doing."

Nadeel gazed at the photo. "They always do."

I smiled at her, and she smiled back. There was an unspoken moment between us, which I soon ruined by speaking. "You have a beautiful smile."

The moment was spoiled. She simply nudged me with her finger and said, "Thank you."

Why did I even open my mouth? But seriously? Thank you? What am I supposed to do with that? Nothing. That's why she said it.

With the moment now ruined, I stood up and took a seat next to Cassem, saying my goodbyes and giving him some last minute advice that I wish someone would have given me at that age. Advice about girls and bullies, letting him know that the two aren't necessarily mutually exclusive. I told him to chase after something meaningful and let go of the things that would weigh him down. I used myself as an example of who not to be, and instead pointed to Raheem, saying, "Remember what he taught you. It's going to come in handy someday." I finally finished with a hug and said, "Be good." A request that might've sounded hypocritical coming from me, but nevertheless, it was the one that I made.

We all said our goodbyes and watched little Cassem close a tragic chapter in his life, while ushering in a new one—one filled with family and friends.

It was hard for Nadeel to walk away from one of her boys, but this is what she had wished for all of them: to find their family and reclaim a piece of themselves. Cassem was better off here than that dingy orphanage and she knew it. She took her time getting back into the Jeep. She wiped her cheeks half a dozen times or so and blew Cassem a kiss, even though he wasn't looking.

On the way back, she sat quietly staring out the window at the setting sun, looking somber, most likely recollecting the first day Cassem appeared on her doorstep nearly three years ago.

By the time we arrived back at the orphanage, Nadeel was a touch worn from the evening, but she was still composed, not a single bead of sweat on her forehead, not a single hair out of place. *How do you do it?* I desperately wanted to ask her, but I didn't.

She soon retreated back inside along with Raheem, while I stepped outside to gather my thoughts. There wasn't a single functioning streetlamp in the neighborhood, providing a kind of dark serenity, which permeated the streets. It was easy to forget that there was literally war to be found in every direction that you looked. As usual, I made the mistake of looking a little too hard.

From the darkness, the tip of a cigarette burned in the alleyway, across the street. It was in the mouth of a man standing in silhouette, his face obscured in shadow and his legs illuminated only by a shaft of pale, blue moonlight. He looked suspicious, and suspicious in Iraq usually leads to a firefight.

As much as I wanted to believe that it was just my imagination and that it was probably nothing, I knew better. Here, paranoia keeps you alive. The more I stared at him, the more my mind entertained terrible images every bit as real as the stories on the news: Marines and Soldiers ambushed, children massacred, innocent people left by the wayside, a ground littered with bullets, an orphanage smoldering and decimated by a bomb, and women and children crying. I tried to shake the thoughts, but I couldn't, not when the streets were full of anarchy, and the city itself was a stewing-pot of fear.

Although I couldn't see the whites of his eyes, the man seemed to look right at me, with his featureless face.

His hand dropped the cigarette butt and crushed it out beneath his boot. He slowly moved toward me, his face slipping in and out of the shadows.

I knew a thing or two about intimidation. For the most part, men who rely on intimidation alone are usually cowards. They wouldn't know the first thing to do if someone were to challenge them, and that's exactly what I did.

I started across the street, and the second I did, the anonymous man turned down the alleyway, where I lost sight of him, briefly.

I called out to him, "Hay! Enta!" (Hey! You!)

As I took a turn down the alley, Nadeel's voice drifted up through the dark. "Is everything alright?" I could hear the nervous tension in her voice.

When I turned back, I had lost sight of the man completely. He had disappeared down a labyrinth of twisted allies. To follow after him would be suicide. I turned back toward the orphanage. "Yeah," I replied. "Everything's fine."

She exhaled a profound sigh of relief. "I was afraid."

"What are you doing out here? It's not safe."

"I was looking for Hakim; he's not in his bed. I swear that boy will never learn."

I instantly turned back toward the alley. There were predators lurking everywhere. "It's late," I said to Nadeel. "You should go inside. I'll look for him."

"I can't sleep, not while he's missing."

"You check inside. I'll look out here."

Nadeel agreed and headed back inside, while I checked the gate to make sure it was locked. I took a look inside the small tool shed off in the far side of the courtyard, and then walked the perimeter to make sure there were no exit points. Scared for Hakim, I checked every possible hiding spot, like the old school bus and the back of Raheem's truck-bed. But he wasn't there. The boy had vanished without a trace.

A warm glow from the kitchen lights, invited me back inside the orphanage. I couldn't sleep without finding Hakim first. *Where the hell did he go?*

While in the process of searching the interior of the orphanage, I noticed a light crawling out from under the closet door next to the kitchen. I quietly walked toward it, putting an ear against the door. The sound of a moan came from inside. I swung the door open, and there was Hakim, his naked torso trembling. Standing in front of him, was Yusuf, with a sudden look of panic on his face and an unzipped fly.

He quickly shrunk back into the closet.

I looked at him with disgust, and he stared back at me as if I wasn't privy to the entire truth. Like there was any explanation that I would've accepted in that moment.

He quickly zipped up his fly.

Faster than I could have even considered the action, I punched him, sending him back into the wall. "You piece of shit!" I pulled him out of the closet and began beating him senseless.

This whole time Yusuf was a spider, spinning his web in indiscernible places, trying to catch the boys in his invisible web. He repeatedly shouted in Arabic, "Twaqafo!" (Stop!)

But there's no stopping an avalanche, hell, there's no surviving it either.

He cried and put his hands up, trying to take a hold of my wrists, but he wasn't strong enough. His skin turned red at the attack upon him, and he continued to shout for help. "Musaeada! Musaeada!" He winced at the pain of broken ribs. Each one, I could hear cracking under my fists. I was blinded by rage at the sight of Hakim, his little fingers scraping against the door, until his nails bled.

I jabbed my elbow into Yusuf's larynx, I could feel it crushing under my weight. I kept digging deeper and deeper, while staring into his corrupted eyes. He was just as weak and helpless as the children were in his treacherous arms. I didn't want to talk or ask questions, I just wanted retribution on behalf of the boys who couldn't seek it themselves.

Still half conscious, Yusuf kept struggling. "Musaeada!" (Help!)

I heard footsteps racing down the hall. It was Nadeel. She looked on shocked by the sudden violence in me. "What are you doing?" She tried to restrain my arm.

In the flurry of confusion and rage I accidentally pushed her. She fell back and hit her head on the corner of the kitchen table. She was terrified of me.

As I reached out for her, to make sure she was ok, Raheem appeared out of nowhere and tackled me off of Yusuf. My hands were covered in Yusuf's blood. He was now cowering before us—a pathetic excuse for a human being.

I tried to get out of Raheem's hold. "No!" I shouted. "Don't let him go!"

Yusuf quickly scurried out of the room like the rat he was and disappeared through a squeaky door at the back of the orphanage.

The room was swirling in front of me. My blood pressure was sky-high.

Two six-year-old boys stared at me from the doorway, scared. Seeing the look on their faces, forced me to settle my emotions and calm down.

Nadeel didn't hide her disappointment. "Why were you hitting him?"

I turned to Hakim as he stood in the corner of the room, shirtless and shivering. His little hands tried to cover as much of his torso as they could, and his wide-set brown eyes were brimming with emotion.

Nadeel looked at him and then back at me and I saw her eyes putting it all together. She was in complete shock that something as heinous as this could've gone unnoticed by her, only a few feet away from where she rested her head. She let out a strained breath. "God help us."

Raheem took his hands off of me and went running out the back door in search of Yusuf.

Concerned for Hakim's wellbeing, Nadeel moved toward him. But he edged away, too embarrassed to speak, too afraid to be touched.

"It's going to be alright," Nadeel said. "He's gone now."

Hakim burst out into a passion of tears. Who knows how long this had been going on, or more frighteningly, how much longer it would have persisted if I hadn't caught him when I did. How many boys had fallen victim to that disgusting piece of shit? Hakim had gone from yelling, 'stop', to thinking this was normal. He had been completely broken by that rat.

Raheem came back inside. "He ran out the gate, into the back alley."

That's why the suspicious man was most likely waiting out there: for Yusuf.

"It's too dangerous to go after him now," I told Raheem.

And just like that, it was over. We would probably never see him again.

Nadeel took Hakim upstairs and helped him into bed, where he curled up with his pillow. She was clearly distraught. For the first time ever, I saw her damp with sweat, as she tried to console Hakim, hugging his little frame in her arms. She tucked him in and sat at the foot of his bed, watching him until he finally drifted off to sleep.

I went to the bathroom to wash the blood from my hands, when Nadeel came in and gently touched my arm. There was tenderness to it, a reassurance that she cared and was grateful for my help. And that for all my hot-blooded anger, there was still a sensitive and sincere man in me.

As she headed to bed, I walked by the boy's room and saw Hakim asleep now. He was twitching in a dream, his little face still showing the faintest remnants of bruises at the hands of Yusuf. I could feel the curses starting under my breath. *What kind of human being would do something like this? Hadn't these kids suffered enough? How much more can you take from a dry well?* I hoped that Hakim was strong enough to come back from this. Having to deal with one problem is hard enough, but when they start stacking up that's when you feel like you're going to break. I wasn't just referring to Hakim; I could feel myself breaking under the weight of this place. I thought it was bad before, but now bad became worse, and I could feel the Devil digging ditches in my valley.

CHAPTER 20

Raheem and I motored into the city bazaar to get groceries for the orphanage. The street was a hive of activity, with merchants selling produce, clothes and cheap DVDs. Raheem greeted the store clerks, who were all familiar with him. They smiled and went to the back and gathered what they had: dates, fruits, nuts, chicken and lamb. They packed a small bag along with sweets for the children. Even though their money and supplies were running low, they still found a place in their hearts to give us as much as we needed.

They refused to take any money from Raheem. I could tell he was overwhelmed by their generosity. It wasn't uncommon for practically everyone to know a family member or friend that had been lost in the war. This was their way of helping out. These children belonged to everyone, and most everyone took responsibility for them. Their help was greatly appreciated, after all, we had many mouths to feed.

As I watched Raheem thank the storeowners, a shadow moved behind me. There was a man standing in the door, awkwardly looking about the shop. Suddenly my military training kicked in and I could feel his eyes on me, like I was the subject of his surveillance. His hands were shifty and his demeanor that of a pick-pocket.

I looked over his shoulder, where a black Mercedes was parked on the other side of the road. A hand came out and dropped a cigarette butt from the driver side window, which was tinted black. The vehicle seemed out of place. It was clean. Too clean for these dusty roads. I hadn't seen a clean car in a while.

I tapped Raheem on the shoulder and said, "We have to go."

He gathered what rations the clerk donated and lurched behind me. "What is it?"

On the street corner, another man studied us with interest. I shot Raheem a quick glance. "I think we're being watched."

Raheem quickly understood the situation and dropped the groceries in the back of the truck and got in.

The man appeared again, close in the mirror's reflection.

As we pulled away from the curb, the Mercedes waited a minute, and then, keeping six car lengths behind, followed us.

"I think I saw the same man outside the orphanage last night," I said to Raheem.

"Are you sure?"

"I couldn't see his face last night, but his body language looks familiar."

"I hope for our sake, it was just a coincidence." Raheem said, reaching in under his seat and pulling out an old, dusty revolver.

"What the hell does that thing even fire, muskets?"

"It is not the size of the gun that kills a man; it's the accuracy of the eye."

Damn.

Raheem always had his one-liners loaded up and ready to go. He could've given Schwarzenegger a run for the chopper.

We crossed an intersection, taking a right.

The Mercedes matched our turn, pulling in thirty meters behind us.

Even though all my instincts were telling me we had to punch the gas, I looked over at Raheem and said, "Slow down."

"What?"

"Relax, I'm playing a hunch."

"It might be the last one you play, my friend."

"Let's hope not."

Raheem lurched to a stop in the middle of the road and waited for the Mercedes.

As the car approached, I took a hold of the revolver. I wasn't really mentally ready to handle a weapon yet. The idea scared me. I was being brought back to another life. If Marines kill, and that's what they're programmed to do, then call me defective. My warrantee had expired.

With shaky hands, I brought the gun up, just under the window, out of view.

Raheem looked scared. "I'm not sure what you are doing."

"Just keep your hands on the steering wheel and your foot ready on the gas."

"Allah help us."

"Here they come."

I'm not afraid of anything! The voice in my head shouted. I can't tell you how much I wished that lie was true.

The car approached, and I took in a final breath to steady my hands. *Don't you dare shake on me.*

The Mercedes swerved around us. I craned my neck for a quick view of the driver: a young man, who glanced back at me and then, unexpectedly, continued on past us.

Suddenly, another black Mercedes appeared heading in the opposite direction. They were everywhere.

Shit.

Raheem looked at me concerned. "A misunderstanding?"

I checked the rear-view mirror as the second Mercedes continued on. "Maybe."

Raheem reached for the gun and slowly pried it out of my shaky hands. "It's OK, my friend. You can't be too careful here."

I looked away, feeling a little ashamed. *How could every instinct I have be wrong?*

"Perhaps we should head back to the orphanage," Raheem said in a sympathetic tone.

I kept my eyes glued to the rear-view mirror. Something still didn't feel right. I had been in too many similar situations that ended in a firefight or even worse. "No," I told Raheem. "There's someone I need to talk to first."

Raheem raised a brow. "Who?"

It was a good question to ask, I suppose. After all, who would I know out here?

"Just take a left," I said, looking just as unsure as I felt.

Raheem gave me the benefit of the doubt and didn't ask me where we were going. It wasn't his way. He either trusted you or he didn't. And he clearly trusted me. Why? I don't really know. I wasn't even quite sure we were going to the right person. I just had no other options left.

Forty-five minutes later, we approached Al-Mahdi's compound, which was now the scene of great activity. An army of security guards scoured the place—their guns bulging through their coats.

Al-Mahdi was clearly not a man you see without an appointment. Lucky for me, he was by the gate, preparing to leave. A Suburban was loaded with luggage and Al-Mahdi and his aide, Samir, were standing just outside of it.

I stood in the street in clear view of his eyes.

The man who was so suspicious last time I saw him was even more suspicious now. He didn't recognize me at first. I guess in the uniform we all looked the same to him.

I waved, and he ordered his guards to bring me to him.

I told Raheem to wait in the truck. He had his reservations, but he never shared them with me. He simply nodded and quietly waited.

Al-Mahdi narrowed his eyes, straining for recognition. "Ah, my American friend, what are you doing here? It would seem that you have lost your uniform."

"My tour of duty is over, I'm here as a civilian. I'm over at an orphanage now, helping out."

"Going the humanitarian route, I see. That is good."

I looked around at the heightened security. "And you? You look like you're going to war."

Al-Mahdi smirked. "Yes. Security is tight. Everyone is on edge. There's been a lot of activity in the area. It's dangerous for you to be here." He took a long, deep puff of his cigar and eyed me harder. "What are you doing here?"

"As you know, there are little resources made available for these independent orphanages. I guess more people care about keeping their car looking pristine than feeding starving children. We could use some money for food and supplies."

Al-Mahdi smiled. "Of course. Anything I can do to help, I will." He could tell there was a bigger reason why I had come to see him. "Is there anything else?"

"We've had problems with insurgent members recruiting children. The military has bigger fish to fry, and I know that you're a man of influence. Perhaps there's something you can do, or even security you can assign to watch the orphanage."

Suddenly there was a strained tension between us. Al-Mahdi and Samir shared a glance and then Samir got into the Suburban. "Food and supplies, I can provide, but there are too many of these low-level recruiters with a tremendous amount of resources. Even half a dozen security guards won't stop them."

"So what can we do?"

Al-Mahdi shook his head, as if there were things to be said that he couldn't say, or rather, shouldn't say. "I cannot promise anything, but I will see what I can do."

I suppose that was better than nothing. "Thank you."

Al-Mahdi gave me a nod and slapped my shoulder. "Be safe."

Be safe? That's like asking a two-year-old to share his toys; it's not going to happen.

Raheem sat in the truck, watching Al-Mahdi's entourage drive off. "There are rumors of Al-Mahdi and how he acquired his fortune."

"I'm sure there are many men who made their money selling out their people."

"Some men had a choice," Raheem said, in a tone I had never heard him take.

"Not many, from what I hear."

"Do you trust him?" Raheem asked, without looking at me.

"I don't know him that well, but I do know that the enemy of my enemy is my friend. We're fighting for the same cause, and for the time being, our interests are aligned. Let's hope that works in our favor."

For once, Raheem let me have the last word. No quick-witted lines, no Confucius-like advice, no mantras, no parables, just silence. He didn't speak at all on our drive back, which didn't sit well with me. Like I said before, never a wasted word with Raheem. The fact he didn't have anything to say, showed me that there was nothing left to say at all. For better or worse, I had invited a man (a powerful and possibly dangerous man), into our lives, and into the lives of the children. It was a decision that I would have to live with.

When Raheem did finally open his mouth, it wasn't really a word that came out, but more a groan. A similar sound was reciprocated by me. We had just arrived back at the orphanage, when a white van suddenly screeched to a halt in front of our truck, blocking us in.

The man in the passenger seat pulled out a gun. His heartless eyes and chainsaw-safe smile disclosed his intent.

I followed Raheem's eyes to his lap, where his revolver still sat.

We didn't need to speak, we both understood the situation. I quickly took a hold of the gun and tucked it into my pants, covering it over with my jacket.

Three men climbed out of the van. One of them paused—not twenty feet from Raheem's truck—shouting in Arabic, "Okhroj mn hona!" (Get out!)

We climbed out slowly.

My eyes widened in recognition of the driver of the van. It was Yusuf. He sat there with one hand on the steering wheel and the other, adjoined to his prosthetic courage: a pistol, which hung out of the driver-side window, aimed at the ground.

…*This asshole!*

As I looked into the whites of his eyes, I felt anger spreading within.

Two men stood watch over me and Raheem, while the other one approached the gates of the orphanage. BANG! He shot open the lock on the door and stormed in.

One of the gunmen began extracting a burlap bag, intended for my head. After my last ordeal, I promised myself, never again.

As his attention diverted for a second, I pulled the gun from my hip.

The man in front of me immediately became my mirror opposite, following my every move.

Just as I took a shot, he took a shot.

I prayed for God. He prayed for God.

I held my breath. He held his breath.

I missed my shot. He missed his shot.

God heard both prayers and answered neither. You can't ask God to sully His hands with the blood of your enemy; both sides are equally loved by Him, I suppose. That's why He chooses no victor in war.

I fired again this time without God's consent. It turns out that prayers can't solve problems like bullets do. It punched a hole right through my enemy and he keeled over into the dirt.

The second shooter let off a round of uncoordinated shots.

In order to escape the flurry, Raheem dove behind the truck.

I dropped to my knees and fired a quick, second shot, killing him immediately. The first gunman lay in front of me, his weapon still in hand. I pulled the automatic from his grasp and trained it on Yusuf, who was still behind the wheel of the van. Shots pinged off the hood as Yusuf quickly backed up, then powered the van forward, stepping on the gas. Like the coward he was, he tucked tail and made his getaway.

I threw Raheem's pistol back to him, and ran through the gates of the orphanage, after the last remaining gunman.

Beyond the gate, it was surprisingly silent. The man stood in the courtyard, in the middle of the rose field, with a gun to Nadeel's head. She had a four-year-old boy by her feet, who was about to see his first genuine act of violence.

Sahar was inside, scared, crying, holding back the other children.

I saw Nadeel's hands, which were soiled from the garden. Tightly clasped in her right one, was a small garden spade. She looked frightened, but not for herself, for the child by her side.

The gunman yelled at me in Arabic, "Da'a alslah ala alard!" (Put the gun down!)

Nadeel and I locked eyes. She shook her head, ever so slightly, to indicate *take the shot and save the child*.

My face was a mask of rage. My finger slowly tightened around the trigger. But I couldn't do it. I didn't have a clear shot, and I couldn't jeopardize Nadeel's life, regardless of how much she wanted me to.

Then, without warning, Nadeel plunged the spade into the enemy's thigh, and pushed the little boy to safety.

The gunman discharged his weapon.

I pulled my trigger and caught him right in the sternum, bringing him down to one knee.

The little boy stumbled back toward Sahar.

The gunman hoisted himself up. He coughed and spluttered blood, barely able to keep his footing.

Without thinking, I put a bullet in his head and he slumped down dead.

I turned back to Nadeel, who now lay amidst her field of shimmering white roses—their petal tips streaked with drops of her blood. All around her, stems seemed to break in half as waves of agony pulsed through the field. She'd been shot in the stomach.

I ran to her side and checked her vital signs, which were fading fast.

Sahar and the children came running out of the orphanage. Slowly, the boys gathered around Nadeel, craning their necks for a view of their fallen angel. She was in great pain. Her flickering eyes peered at me from a hopeless place. Then her eyes lost focus and her head went slack in my arms. All reason was gone. The only thing that remained was an unbridled, animal fury. I turned to Raheem. "Get the truck!"

I quickly lifted Nadeel's body and carried her in my arms, moving through the crowd of silent witnesses.

Raheem had the truck started and ready. I got into the passenger seat, and Raheem dropped his foot on the gas, hard and heavy.

"Hold on," I said to Nadeel, putting pressure on her wound. "Hold on for the kids." I wanted to say hold on for me, but something told me that wasn't going to be as effective.

She was now barely breathing. I applied even more pressure on her abdomen. "Come on, Nadeel."

Raheem reached over and put a hand on her forehead. "Nadeel, you have to stay awake."

She opened her eyes halfway, but she couldn't hold them there. I could tell it was taking a lot out of her.

"Drive faster, Raheem."

Raheem looked at the speedometer, which was shaking so bad I thought it was going to snap off. "I don't think that's possible."

There was no other person I would want behind the wheel than Raheem. He maneuvered the crowded Iraqi streets with Grand Prix type precision, finding the fastest and safest way to the nearest hospital.

My hand was wrapped around Nadeel's wrist, monitoring her pulse, which felt like footsteps, going deeper and deeper down into a dungeon. My own heartrate went from the mid hundreds down to what felt like thirty. I don't know if it was shock or delirium, but I was there with Nadeel, in the darkness, sharing a single pulse, our realities and illusions melting together.

The crushed lavender scent of her hair was enough to pull me out of the truck and back in time to see echoes of my mother. Her hair always smelled of lavender. That scent was ingrained deep inside my mind. Although I would never hear my mother's voice again, every time I smelled lavender, I knew it was time to slow down. She would always tell me to be patient—something I had never quite mastered. Slowly, that smell replaced her voice, and ironically or by design, it would find me at times when my patience was disintegrating.

I let out a breath, like waking up from a long lost dream and brushed the hair out of Nadeel's face. I turned to Raheem, hoping he would tell me that everything was going to be alright, in that believable tone that only *he* had. But he didn't say a thing. He was too busy concentrating on the road.

As soon as we arrived at the hospital, Raheem jumped out and yelled for help at the top of his lungs. Paramedics came running out and quickly took Nadeel out of my hands and laid her down on a gurney. They rushed her into the operating room. I was so distraught that I went in after them. It took Raheem and two paramedics to pull me out of the O.R. and into the hall.

Raheem pushed me up against a wall and said, "Get a hold of yourself!"

It took me a good three minutes to calm down enough to even speak. "I'll be alright, Raheem. I just need some time alone to process this."

Raheem released me, but not before shaking me one more time. "You have to be strong now."

I wiped my face and gave him a nod. "I'm trying."

"I'll be right here if you need me."

As I wandered away from him, I was once again reminded that I am *Jin*. I floated through the corridors of the hospital like a ghost for hours, with that sense of being pushed beyond all reason, to a level of complete and utter madness. All I could think about was how Nadeel's efforts had been in vain. There was no stopping this death-engine that had been let loose by the insurgency. Her children were never going to be safe.

I tried pushing all the violent thoughts to the back of my mind. The longer they stayed in the forefront, the more I could feel my sanity slipping away. Before I could lose it completely, the smell of lavender brought me back to reality. It was all over my hands, which I had put through Nadeel's hair. Again, my speeding heart came back down to a respectful rate. *Patience*. I wiped the sweat off my forehead and took a seat in the waiting room.

By the time Nadeel came out of surgery, the sun was rising. Miraculously, she was still alive. They rolled her into a recovery room, with IV lines hooked up to her arms, re-infusing her with plasma.

The doctor emerged from the operating room and approached me. He sat me down and went over Nadeel's condition. "There was tissue damage and internal bleeding, but no projectile fragmentation. The bullet went through her, just missing her vital organs. She's going to be alright. We'll be monitoring her vital signs closely."

I got up and breathed a sigh of relief. "Thank you."

The doctor left, and a nurse came in and dimmed the lights and pulled the curtains, obscuring my view of Nadeel.

I stood there, listening to her heart monitor beeping. The darkness just seemed to swallow me. I took a seat by her bedside, thinking about her words: about dropping my anger. But when right and left stopped being directions, I found that turning around was not an option. I think every person reaches a point in their life when they realize there's no turning back. There's nothing waiting for them back there but regrets. The only logical course of action is to pile forward, regardless of the uncertainty that awaits. How oddly reassuring it was, when all the choices dropped away and I was left with only one.

I stood up, and with every step that I took toward the exit, I entered deeper and deeper into an unstable place. The voice inside my head cried *revenge*—a word I thought I had buried away. But once again it was dug up by the dogs of war, and I couldn't shut it off no matter how hard I tried. It became my anthem and my hands instinctually went into the pose of an M16.

Out in the hall, I saw Raheem pacing the floor. He was a nervous wreck. We both were. I motioned for him to follow me, and he did, off into a quiet area of the hospital.

"These men won't stop," I told him. "They're going to keep coming back."

Raheem stared at me blankly, unsure of where I was going with my comment.

"If we find Yusuf, we'll find the rest of them."

Raheem looked troubled. "These are not the kind of people you want to find."

"I have to try. I'm not giving up, Raheem. You'll see my tombstone long before you see me waving a white flag."

"I don't know what to tell you, other than Nadeel would've advised against it."

"Well, she can't exactly speak for herself right now, can she?"

"You're not thinking clearly, my friend."

"I'm thinking clearer than ever. These people won't see us coming."

Raheem looked deep into my eyes, where a revolution was waging. He could tell that I had crossed over into dangerous territory. "Are you sure this is what you want?"

"They're going to keep coming back for the kids. And if not these kids, then the ones out on the streets, the ones looking for a home, looking for someone to take them in. They'll recruit them all. They'll fill their minds with false hope and turn them into weapons. I've seen it."

Raheem took a step back from me, as if my madness were catching.

"Before I left for America you said, you didn't know what I was doing here. And I didn't know either. But I do now. This is why I'm here. This is why I came back. So I can do something about this. I left my uniform back home, so you know the words I'm saying are coming from me, and not some command center."

Raheem and I shared an instant look of understanding. This was the final straw.

There was a long silent moment from Raheem, like one would expect from a jury before a major verdict. This was either going to be the end of the subject or just the beginning of it.

Raheem nodded, his weathered voice sounding very firm. "I may know someone who can help us."

CHAPTER 21

When Raheem pulled up in front of the police station—the very same place my kidnappers had taken me—I looked at him with skepticism. "What are we doing here?"

"You must trust me, my friend," he said, with the same inflection as when I had asked him something similar less than twenty-four hours ago. I remember how quickly he handed me his trust. Raheem was many things, but untrustworthy wasn't one of them.

"I trust you, Raheem," I said, trying to sound as confident as possible.

"And one more thing," he added. "Please, let me do the talking in there."

"Of course."

As we stepped into the office of the same man who escorted me out of the interrogation room after my abduction attempt, I saw pictures on his desk of him and Raheem. They were clearly brothers.

Raheem saw the nervous look on my face and tried to put my mind at rest. "We can trust Waahid, he's a good man."

It turns out Raheem's brother was a captain in the Iraqi police. He walked into the office, looked at me and then turned to Raheem. "What are you doing here with this American?"

Before I could open my mouth, Raheem shook his head, and then spoke on our behalf. "We had no choice, Waahid."

"You have three dead insurgents and a fourth one somewhere out there. What were you thinking?"

"We were only trying to protect the boys. Their lives are in danger."

"What do you expect me to do? The whole country is at war. There aren't even enough men to patrol the city."

"We're looking for the man who got away. We think if we can find him, we can find their safe house."

"Even the military, with all its resources, still has trouble finding these men. What makes you think the two of you will have better luck?"

I couldn't sit quietly anymore. "The military leaves a big footprint. The insurgency has eyes on them; I know from experience. The fact that it's only two of us, means we'll be able to get into places the military can't."

Waahid looked to Raheem. "You're willing to jeopardize your life for this?"

"What good is winning this war if we lose our children? These boys are no older than Nasser."

Waahid looked down at his desk, where a picture of his son, Nasser, sat. He touched it gently and sighed, not looking altogether certain that something could be done.

"We need to find this man," Raheem said, putting a picture of that rat on the desk. "His name is Yusuf."

Waahid picked it up and stared at it. "I have seen this man before, but Yusuf is not his name. It's Faaz Al-Qurashi. He has no insurgent ties as far as we know."

"How do you know him?" I asked.

"He was brought in a few times for small crimes, then he became an informant for a while. I haven't seen him in a couple of years."

Raheem turned to me. "That's around the time he came to the orphanage."

"Do you have his last known whereabouts?" I asked.

Just as Waahid nodded, two of his own men burst into his office, rifles raised.

Waahid shouted, "Maza thfaal?" (What are you doing?)

In an affirmative voice, one of the officers replied, "We've been asked to bring these men in for questioning."

"By who?" Waahid asked.

The men had no response. They simply gave him a look as if to say *you know who*.

Waahid remained undeterred. He raised his voice and let the men know who was in charge. "I'm conducting my own line of questions right now. So leave us."

The men eyed me for a long, hard second, before slowly retreating out the same door they burst in through, closing it behind them.

"The insurgency has eyes and ears everywhere," Waahid continued. "Their money has lined many pockets. Even here." He moved to a table covered with maps of Iraq and an area marked off in red. "Fazz was picked up here," he said, pointing to one particular building on the map. "It's located within Anbar Province, in a hostile neighborhood. There are many safe houses here and many insurgent sympathizers."

A long silence passed, then Waahid went to a steel cabinet. He opened it up, extracted something, turned around and dropped two 9mm pistols and four clips on his desk. "This area is considered a tier one insurgency stronghold, where civilians aren't allowed. You will need these. They are the only weapons I can give you without arousing suspicion."

"These will do," Raheem said. "Thank you, Waahid."

"I can make sure you get out of here safely, but you will have to leave now."

I stood up and reached out my hand for Waahid to shake.

He looked me in the eyes a beat and finally reached out his hand, which was swollen and stitched up—clearly a hand that had been fighting for justice.

"May peace be with you," I said.

"And you as well."

Waahid, quietly escorted us out the back exit, and before heading back inside, he pulled Raheem in for a hug—one of those hugs that looked as if it would be their last. Raheem then reached into the back of his truck, took out a black thawb (ankle length dress shirt) and threw it to me. "Put this on," he said, "you'll blend in."

It smelled like goat-cheese. "This smells horrible, Raheem."

He shrugged his shoulders. "I'm sorry, it's been sitting there for months."

I quickly unbuttoned my shirt and threw it on. Even though it smelled rank, after being around Marines on patrol for days on end, it was far from the worst thing I had ever smelled. As I opened the door of the truck, Raheem gave me a glare across the roof. A final plea: *Is this what you want?*

I nodded without hesitation. There was no going back now. My brakes were snapped off, my reason wearing thin. If we didn't do this, the men would keep coming back, and eventually take everything. I remember my original decision to join the army was so that women and children back home could have a better life, but what about the women and children over here? They deserved a better life as well, at any cost. The problems back home were nothing like the problems here. It would be like comparing the *cost* of living to the *price* of freedom. One is clearly worth more.

My confirmation was all Raheem needed to see. Even though he relied heavily on his words, he could read a face better than a professional poker player, and he could see that mine was resolute.

Raheem raced down the narrow dirt roads, driving with total focus. The intensity in his eyes was obvious. He knew this was most likely a suicide mission—one that he had already given his word to. To Raheem, loyalty was everything.

He negotiated every twist and turn with the simplest of ease, pushing his old truck to a near breaking point—gears grinding, dash shaking and axel rocking all the way. When we crossed over into Anbar Province, near Fallujah, Raheem kept an eye on the rearview mirror. His forehead was slick with sweat. He knew that this was no man's land, or at the very least, a suicidal man's land.

Raheem slowed down and took a turn down an alleyway, at the end of which, sat a deserted and foreboding two story building.

Raheem jerked to a stop and said, "We have to go by foot from here."

We piled out of the truck, stuffing the guns and clips into our pockets. As soon as I slung my gear over my shoulder and wrapped my fingers around the 9mm, I felt very much in my element. "I never thought I'd be in this situation again," I said to Raheem. "This time, with no fire team or snipers watching my back."

"Let's hope all your training pays off, my friend."

Yeah, let's hope so.

We moved carefully, searching for threats. The area had been hit hard by war. Abandoned store-fronts and beaten buildings loomed in the distance of the deserted slums.

"By looking at this place, you'd swear the world was coming to an end," I said to Raheem.

He patted his chest pocket, where he kept the picture of his deceased son and wife. "For some of us, the world has already ended. It's about what we do now in the aftermath." He pointed to the ground, where, through the concrete sidewalk, azaleas had begun to grow. It brought to mind Nadeel's line about how children were like weeds, capable of growing even through the harshest of conditions. "The last glimmer of hope has not yet fallen."

I smiled. "Thank you for being here, Raheem. I'm not sure I could've done this alone."

"For better or worse, I am with you, my friend."

"Let's hope it's for the better."

We quickly climbed over a grimy concrete wall into an old-style building, standing on its last leg. After entering it, we immediately made our way up to the second floor, which gave us a view of the suspected safe house.

I quickly spied the entire area through a pair of binoculars. "The security perimeter looks weak."

"Because no one would dare enter this place," Raheem replied.

"Well, lucky us."

"How do we get in?" he asked.

"No one's guarding the window on the basement floor, that'll be our access point."

Raheem took the binoculars from me; his eyes strained to get a better look at the perimeter. His face quickly became remorseful and he dropped the binoculars, which dangled around his neck.

"What is it?" I asked him.

He removed the binoculars and handed them back to me.

I took a second look and saw two boys, fourteen and sixteen, standing on the side of the building, both holding Russian rifles.

Raheem's head fell down to his shoulders. "I know the older boy. His name is Baasim. He was at the orphanage for a little while, until he ran away. These are not fanatical terrorists; they are teenagers. They are not bad people. If you have to shoot, aim for their legs. No one has to die."

No one has to die. That's what he said to me. That's what he believed: that war could be won without casualties. It was a misguided hope. Raheem had been through this before. Ali wasn't the first boy he had tried to save. That's why he was so reluctant to come this far again, to put all his hopes down on a single gamble, when he had lost so many times before.

"I know how hard it is to refrain yourself when someone is shooting at you. I know how hard it is to look a child or a woman in their eyes and know that a decision has to be made. That it's either their life or yours. The ideal situation would be where you both come out of it alive, but that rarely happens. And if you are the one that survives, you have to carry that knowledge with you for the rest of your life."

I instantly thought of the boy in the alleyway: the one that had the misfortune of meeting Alvarez. I remember the look in his eyes. That look of fear. He didn't want to shoot. He was more scared than any of us. Regardless of how much you brainwash a child, you cannot take away a child's fears. Deep down inside, they're still afraid of thunderstorms and monsters under the bed. We could use that to our advantage.

I looked at Raheem confidently and agreed that no one had to die.

As we carefully made our way toward the safe house, the streets were quiet. "This is clearly not a training facility," I told Raheem.

"Why do you say that?"

"Listen."

Raheem pricked an ear. "I don't hear anything."

"Exactly. If this were a training facility, we'd be hearing AK's right now. No. This is something a lot more important. They want absolutely no attention diverted here. That's why it's lightly guarded with minimal surveillance."

But there was surveillance, nonetheless, and as Raheem deviated off course, he crossed in front of a video camera inconspicuously placed in a tree. I pulled him back and pointed between the branches, bringing his attention to it. "Go around."

He took in a deep breath and wiped the sweat from his brow. We carefully went around the surveillance line, while trying to stay covered.

Then suddenly, between two buildings a cluster of pigeons took flight, startled by our footsteps. They flapped noisily out of the alley, attracting the attention of the boys. The older one, Bassim, came to check the source of the noise with his rifle in the crook of his arm.

Raheem looked clueless, his hands moving about his body, unsure of where to position themselves. He began taking long, deep breaths like he was bracing himself for combat.

I pulled Raheem into the niche of a doorway and said, "Don't move."

We could hear the boy coming, his size seven shoes softly sweeping up the alleyway. He had been trained well. He kept his gun high and close, and his eyes moving from side to side. But in the end, he was still a boy, and a soldier with the attention span of a boy doesn't stand a chance. He couldn't see us from his vantage point. He was too distracted by the flock of pigeons, who were now perched on the edge of the building.

The second I saw the toe of his shoe appear past the niche of the door, I swung the butt of my 9mm around the corner, waste high, and caught him right in the sternum. He fell to the floor, his gun peeling out of his hands. He was out cold.

Raheem was shaking, which made me wonder if he could even handle the situation. "You sure you can do this?"

"I am sure of nothing," he said checking the boy to see if he was alright. "But I know this is something I must do."

"You're a good man, Raheem. Stick close to me. We'll get through this together."

Raheem wiped the sweat from his brow again. "Sorry...I can't stop sweating."

"That's ok," I said, "just make sure your hands are dry, you don't want your fingers slipping over the trigger."

He wiped his hands on his shirt and gave me a little nod.

Just then, a voice came bouncing into the alley. "Bassim?"

It was the second boy looking for the first. This one was not so trained. He came running around the corner—his rifle down by his side—and walked right into my muzzle. His face reflected all the inner-fears of a child, and his hands were trembling, caught somewhere between his chest and the rifle.

I put the gun right between his eyes and shook my head. "Don't be stupid, kid."

He swallowed. Wide-eyed. A deer in the headlights.

I turned to Raheem. "Take his weapon and tie him up."

Raheem's hands were still trembling, yet not so much that he couldn't use them.

"Take some breaths. You'll be alright."

He did so, trying to focus on the bigger picture.

"Don't worry; we'll be back for them."

Raheem was reluctant to get up.
"Come on Raheem, we have to go. They'll be safe here."
After a minute or so, he finally got up and followed after me.

CHAPTER 22

Raheem and I slipped in through a window on the basement floor and entered the safe house. We quickly moved up two flights of stairs, to a grim corridor on the top floor. It was long, with several rooms on each side. I told Raheem to secure the hallway, while I moved through the rooms, checking each one carefully. To my surprise, they were all empty.

"What is this place?" Raheem said. "There's nothing here. Why would they need guns to protect it?"

"Shhh…" I said to Raheem. "You hear that?" I could hear voices—barely audible—from somewhere else in the building. "This way." I moved cautiously, 9mm in hand, while Raheem followed behind me.

"There are no more rooms to search. So where are the voices coming from?"

I felt a breeze on the back of my neck. I turned to find a poster on the wall, which moved just slightly. I lifted it up and found a crude square cut out of the wall, leading into a claustrophobic room. Inside, the windows were boarded up, the walls were sweating from the moisture, and the florescent lights were humming and flickering.

Raheem softly whispered, "Over there."

The voices were coming from a small radio that was sitting on a rusty, metal table. To the right of that, a heavy, iron door led into a much larger room that contained recording equipment, four blocks of C-4, a blasting cap and a coil of unspooling detonation wire. I took a second look at the iron door and I knew it was being used as a bomb shield.

Up against the wall was a familiar backdrop. The dried blood on the floor immediately conjured up a quick flash of the grainy beheading video of the American reporter who had his head chopped off. This was definitely where it was shot.

Through the large mirror on the wall, I suddenly saw something behind me. I gripped my gun like a security blanket and whirled around, ready to shoot.

Lying on the floor, stripped to the waist was a little boy. I rolled him over and found a filthy syringe imbedded in his arm. His jaw was slack and his eyes were wide and vacant.

"They've drugged him," Raheem said.

"A horse rides better once it's been broken. They need these boys ready to sacrifice their lives." I sat him up. He was limp, but alive. "We have to get him out of here."

I picked up the boy and we began to exit the room, when my eyes glanced down at a table cluttered with Polaroids. A faded surveillance photo of myself stared back at me. It was taken only a week ago, near the orphanage.

"What is it?" Raheem said, turning around.

I passed the boy over to him. "Get him out of here."

"What about you?"

I stared at the picture again. "I'll be fine."

Raheem hesitated. "I can't leave you here by yourself."

"The boy's going to die, unless we get him some help."

Raheem had no choice. He carried the boy back out the way we came.

I pulled the surveillance photo of myself, slowly putting the pieces together. *The men who attacked the orphanage weren't after the kids, they were after me.*

I was startled by the sudden silence in the room. I could tell someone had just cut the air-conditioning. With the creaky old floorboards, even the slightest movement could be heard.

Without warning, someone jumped me from behind, putting me into a rear-naked choke. Like a snake, he coiled his legs around me.

I tried fighting back, but it was useless, he had me. I pushed his frame around, slamming into the wall, but he held on tight.

I could feel the blood rushing to my head. My face quickly became a red hotplate. I was running out of air. It was the moment where most men panic and end up dead. Then again, why wouldn't they? It's hard to *think* when you're running out of air and the enemy has the drop on you. Somehow, I managed to collect myself. I rationed my air, I calmed my mind and I looked around the room for any means to get him off of me.

On the table in front of me was loose detonation wire. I grabbed it. Then reaching behind my head, I wrapped it, first around the nape of my assailant's neck, then across his anterior jugular vein, and squeezed as hard as I could.

One of us was going to pass out before the other. It was just a matter of who had the tighter squeeze.

He began to panic, loosening the hold he had around me. He sputtered a low moan, and in one swift motion, I pulled him around and pushed him to the floor, pinning his limbs.

For the first time I could see the face of my assailant. To my surprise, it was Yusuf. The position of power was now reversed, and *his* life now rested in my hands. *What will I do with this power?* I instantly saw the face of little Hakim, and all the other boys that Yusuf had defiled. Why would a person like that deserve to live?

He lay there, watching me, his eyes begging for mercy, while mine screamed death! I had no more mercy left in me. Not that day. I could feel his pulse slowing through my hands, as I squeezed the life out of him. The whites of his eyes burned and his breath became shallow, until, finally, he was dead.

Before I could catch my bearings, I heard someone else coming down the corridor. Using a piece of broken mirror, I put it low in the doorway and saw a body at the end of the corridor, only in silhouette. He took out a gun and slowly made his way toward my location.

I got ready to take a shot. As the man got closer, I shot low, hitting him in the leg.

"Hold your fire!" The man cried out.

I recognized the inflection in his voice. It was all too familiar.

"Hold your fire," he said again.

The second time I heard him I knew exactly who it was. But his presence there didn't make any sense.

He approached me slowly and carefully.

I looked at his face: the unmistakable face of Samir, Al-Mahdi's assistant.

What the hell is going on? My gun remained aimed at his chest.

He could tell I was ready to kill. "Don't shoot."

I was desperately searching for answers. "What are you doing here? You better talk quick."

"Al-Mahdi sent me. He thought you could use some help. We've been following you."

Al Mahdi? Of course. Leave it to him to keep everything a secret. "How many men do you have with you?"

He looked at the gun, nervously. "Five."

I slowly lowered it and assessed the situation. "There's another man with me, Raheem, he should be outside with a little boy."

Samir nodded.

"There might be more children here, get your men to sweep the area."

"I'll have them check it out right now."

I gave him a once over. "Are you shot? Did I get you?"

Samir confidently shook his head. "No. I'm alright."

How can that be? "I shot you in the leg...."

I noticed the movement of his hands, subtle yet sharp. And as my eyes drifted lower, I saw the hole in his pants with the absence of blood.

Almost instantly, drops of sweat began accumulating at the base of his hairline. I was in awe, unable to speak. *It can't be, can it?*

That's when all the little details suddenly became clear: all the whispers, the bad intel, the enemy always one step ahead of us, and even the security he had surrounding Al-Mahdi around the clock. He had spent countless hours practicing his walk, to make sure he didn't limp even the slightest, but it was still there. As microscopic as it was, it was still visible. He used the guards to cover any tiny discrepancy, by keeping them close. One big blur of dark suits to keep all the eyes away from his secret. The one thing he was trying so hard to hide: his prosthetic leg.

I quickly raised my gun again and took aim at Samir's head, and the thing that went unspoken was finally said. "You're Abdul-Razzaq."

In Samir's eyes was a glint of darkness that wasn't there a second ago—perhaps surfacing with the truth. He made no attempt to hide the obvious. "It's more complicated than that, I'm afraid. Razzaq is just a fall man, the alter-ego."

"You were right in front of our eyes the whole time, hiding in plain sight, using us as your personal chaperone."

A cold smirk came out of him. "I knew that the game could not be won, unless played from both ends. A change of clothes, a few handshakes, some hair dye and minor surgery had you looking for a ghost."

I brought his attention to the table with the bomb equipment. "So, is this your legacy?"

"*My* legacy?" He began laughing. "That's amusing coming from you. You're the ones out here selling oppression masked in democracy, and you wonder why people resist you?"

I took a step back and steadied my aim. "What was it that Al-Mahdi said about villains? 'Not a single one born who looks in the mirror and sees a villain; he only sees his own version of the truth'."

He shook his head. "And what version is it that you think you're privy to? You only *think* you know what happens here. You simply receive orders. You don't know what goes on behind the scenes at the Pentagon, or the Oval Office. You don't know the true intentions."

The look of disdain was all over my face. "I'm done with your ivory tower bullshit. You've been lying from the beginning. You're the one who manufactured all those false reports."

"They weren't as falsified as you think. Even I have enemies. Better the military sacrifice soldiers than me."

"Soldiers? You call these soldiers? These boys who you kidnap and brainwash? These are your soldiers?"

"How are we any different than you Americans selling a dream to the next generation? Even you came over here fighting a war that wasn't yours, one that you inherited, one that you didn't even understand. And now you want to be righteous? Well, your boys maybe older than ours, but not by much. At least ours aren't as misguided as yours. Most of them came to us, wanting revenge on you Americans. We merely gave them the tools they needed. We gave them peace with dignity, peace with commitment. After all, it's better they die for a purpose than to fight for a lie like you."

Sadly, there was some truth in his words. "You're right. It is a lie. It was all a lie. They lied to me, just like they lied to my father and all the countless others. We're the victims, and men like you, are the liars, waiting to take advantage of us. But no more…."

I got ready to pull the trigger, when suddenly; a loyal boy ran into the room and covered Samir with his body.

Samir pulled out a gun and put it to the boy's head, using him as a human shield. His exterior reflected exactly what he was on the inside: dangerous.

The boy didn't struggle; he was glad to be his sacrificial lamb.

"Don't move!" Samir shouted, training his gun on me, while keeping the boy close to him. Samir's finger slowly coiled around the trigger and the words *I'm done for* shot through my mind, along with a million emotions: fear, anxiety, anger, sadness. My eyes remained on Samir, watching him weigh the decision of his life, of *two* lives. To him, this was the greatest cause of all, one worth dying for, one worth killing for.

The silence between us grew as Samir came closer. This was obviously the end for one of us, and no more words would help either of our causes.

Now, only ten feet away from me, he hugged the boy to his chest. I knew he would kill him if he had to. I had neither a clear shot nor a clear conscience for what was about to follow.

I heard the hammer of Samir's gun being pulled back…and then…a barrage of shots being fired.

My eyes widened and that placebo effect, that subliminal sense of pain rode through my body, tightening up every muscle along the way. *So, this is what it feels like to get shot.*

I stepped back taking a breath, while Samir did the same. I looked down at my chest, and saw nothing. Then I looked at his, and the red blossom that was growing, slowly spreading outward, staining his white shirt, crimson. He'd been shot. I could tell he was thinking the same thing: *how?*

I turned around and my eyes carried to the smoking gun. It was Raheem; he stood in the doorway. his hands were now steady, and his back was straighter than a ship's mast. The adrenaline had transformed him from timid to brave in a matter of seconds.

Samir dropped to the floor and the little boy ran out the door.

Raheem and I looked at each other solemnly. "God damn it Raheem, that's the best shot I've ever seen anybody take."

"Are you alright?" he asked.

I checked again just for good measure. "Yeah. I'm fine." But I was the furthest thing from fine. My body was aching and my mind was reeling, trying to put it all together.

I looked down at Samir; even though he was dead, I knew the game was far from over. Here, new insurgent leaders pop up every day.

Just like a hydra, you cut off one head and two more spring up in its place. Who was going to take up his mantle next? Perhaps the boy who would've gladly died for him, or the boys tied up outside, or the one name I feared the most in that moment, but couldn't bring myself to even entertain.

"We should get out of here," I said to Raheem.

But Raheem didn't move. He was frozen, staring straight ahead, his hands quivering once again.

I followed his gaze only to find something I didn't expect to. *I swear I never entertained his name. I never actually thought it.* But nevertheless, it was him. It was Ali. He was standing in front of me, aiming a gun right at my chest. His hate-filled eyes were shooting rays of chaos and confusion, while his jaw was clenched tight enough to shatter all his baby teeth. His bruised face moved through the shadows, and with trembling hands he raised the gun higher, taking aim at my head.

As his arms lifted up, I could see wires emerging from his chest. There was ten pounds of C-4 strapped to his torso.

I remember talking to Kelly about how children retaliate. It was as if my words had somehow foreshadowed his future. His final fragments of innocence were gone; his transformation was complete. Sweet, little Ali had now become an instrument of destruction.

I watched him with a mixture of mounting horror and morbid curiosity, both excited to see him and fearful of his retribution.

His once tranquil features were made hard, and his eyes were now lit with a kind of hellish fire that no amount of words could put out. His mind was speeding. He was going a hundred miles per hour with blown-out brake lights; I couldn't even tell if he wanted to stop. Then again, I don't think he could've stopped even if he wanted to. This wasn't a question of should I or shouldn't I, this was an opportunity for payback. Ali was already at death's door, knocking with the palms of his hands, shouting for someone to let him in.

I stared at his small, fragile face, trying to comprehend that which could not be comprehended: all the whys and hows. But *Ali* knew, and that's all that mattered. Hate had drifted up in all the cracks of his heart like spring snow, freezing, expanding and cracking along the way, making a home for itself.

I walked toward him with soft steps.

He nervously edged back, his gun shaking. He steadied himself and thrust the gun forward as a warning. "Don't move!"

"It's OK," I said, lifting up my hands.

Raheem stood over my shoulder watching the scene unfold. He held his gun awkwardly, somewhere between Ali and the ground, not quite knowing what to do and not having the courage to take an affirmative aim.

I let him off the hook. "Lower your gun, Raheem."

I turned back to Ali. "It's OK."

But it wasn't OK, and Ali knew it. This is what Nadeel saw when she looked at me: all the past hate that I couldn't let go of. In that moment, Ali became my mirror image, and I could see a lifetime of hurt rising up out of me through *his* eyes. It was as if my mother herself were looking down at me, disappointed by all the choices I had ever made.

I tried to reason with him. "Hate is a shackle, and at the end of it a hundred-pound ball that slows you down throughout life. You get sick and tired of dragging it around. I know, trust me. It blinds you from seeing anything else. Don't fall victim to it."

Ali remained unconvinced.

"I know you hate me, and I'm ready to bear the burden of your hatred. I'm sorry for everything that's happened to you. But it's not worth your life. Mine maybe, but not yours." I took a knee in front of him and slowly put my forehead to the muzzle of his gun.

Raheem was dumbfounded. His eyes shouted *what are you doing?*

I spoke to Ali as a doomed father would to a son who still had a chance for survival. "You deserve better than this, than what I've brought into your life. If this is what you need to heal, then do it. Take it. I won't blame you for it. But then let that be the end of it."

With dithering eyes, he began searching around the room, desperately trying to make sense of it all. I could tell he didn't want to do it. I had seen that look before, in the eyes of the boy in the alleyway, and many others like him.

"Look at me," I said. "There is war all around us, but you and I can make our own peace, right here, right now. Just you and me. Too much has already been lost. No more. Please."

A moment of silence passed, like the one you call for when remembering a loved one. Ali then pulled the hammer of the gun back. His eyes—very much like the finger he had placed on the trigger—were trembling severely. I was close enough to feel the air sprinting out of his mouth.

His rage had quickly turned into a quiet, unsettling focus.

Raheem hung back at a respectful distance. He knew this whole thing began with *us* and would inevitably end with us.

The moment seemed endless, and then Ali slowly lowered the gun, his eyes now glazed with tears.

At first, I hesitated, not sure what to make of this. Then I extended my hand, calmly, eagerly, pulling him in toward me, hugging him tight.

I remember smiling. I remember it because it had felt like forever since I had smiled last—truly smiled. As I gave into the moment, a ragged gasp came from the corner.

Samir wasn't dead. His eyes shot open and he raised his hand, which rushed to his inside coat pocket, taking a hold of something.

I had no weapon to defend myself.

Raheem and I locked eyes, then quickly and clumsily lifting his gun, Raheem let loose the entire clip into Samir's chest.

He laid out flat on the ground, dead.

Without warning, the timer on the bomb that was strapped to Ali's chest activated.

As Samir's hand peeled out of his pocket and hit the concrete, out rolled, not a gun, but a remote detonator.

I grabbed it off the ground, desperately looking for an off switch. But there wasn't one. *No, there wouldn't be.*

"We have to cut it off," I shouted to Raheem.

There were no metal cutters in the room. Raheem managed to find a rusted screw driver, which he attempted to pry open one of the locks with. As he foolishly scraped against the metal, I reached out and studied the dangling wires hanging from the crude battery pack, which was strapped into place using duct tape. As crude as it was, this was not your ordinary homemade bomb. This was designed to elicit as much damage as possible.

"Wait," I told Raheem. "Be careful. Make sure you don't touch the battery pack."

"I can't get these locks off," he said, frantically. "The metal is too thick."

I grabbed the screwdriver and worked it deep into the groove of the metal. But Raheem was right; it was too thick. It just scraped futilely against the metal, over and over.

"Come on!" I shouted.

We doubled our efforts. The blade bit the lock, but it didn't give.

I squeezed with all my might. My eyes bulged and the vein in my temple nearly exploded. But nothing. My arms felt like they were going to fall off, and still I kept at it. Somewhere in the back of my mind I knew there wasn't enough time. But deciding when to quit, when a boy's life is resting in your hands, is an agonizing choice. How do you make that decision and still live with yourself? How do you go about the rest of your life, pushing that thought further and further into the back of your mind, until it finally breaks you? Then I realized...*you don't*.

I looked up into Ali's eyes; he was terrified, calculating what time he had left. I had abandoned him once before, but I didn't have the heart to do it again. So I held onto him. "I'm here, Ali. I'm here with you. I won't let go. I promise." I turned to Raheem. "We don't have much time left, get out of here. Save yourself."

Raheem wasn't going to budge.

"Get out of here!"

He shook his head.

"There's no time, Raheem."

He took in a deep breath. "Then let's not waste it arguing."

For a second, I had forgotten about Raheem's loyalty. He wasn't the kind of man to abandon someone, even in a life or death situation.

I nodded back, knowing there wasn't a single thing I could say to make him change his mind.

He closed his eyes; if this was truly the end, he didn't want me to see the dread in them.

I looked to Ali and said, "Hold onto the sound of my voice."

With each tick of the hand, oblivion drew near. Then, for a brief moment, all time shuddered to a stop, reaping all that time had sewn. And there, within Ali's pained and overwrought eyes, was a reflection of a cruel world. A world where a child could lose his entire family, his limbs, his hope, and even his life, yet no universal force would come to the rescue. A world where innocence accounted for nothing, and love could easily be diffused by a trigger. That was the world that Ali lived in...for now.

But time waits for no one. It is perhaps the most unbiased thing of all. It doesn't distinguish between man or child, innocent or guilty, just or unjust. It's inevitable. Time is the greatest judge of the highest court in which there is no second appeal. But even with all that righteous power it wields, it doesn't mean that you can always count on time. And I was sick and tired of counting all the times where time had let me down. Like the last thirty-five minutes of my mother's life, being raced to the hospital, where I could've told her how much I loved her, or the twenty minutes the EMTs say my father struggled on the floor before the overdose, where I could've said I understand, or the seconds right before the blast that claimed Rev's life, where I could've thanked him for all his advice, and even the five minutes before Sophia went under the knife, where I could've stopped it, and kept our baby. I can't get those minutes back. They're gone forever. So, I gave into *time* and admitted defeat. Ali and I stood idly by as it deliberated our fate. We were now seven seconds, six moves, five feet, four heartbeats, three breaths, two blinks and a prayer away from death.

Expecting a suicidal blast at any moment, Raheem began saying prayers in Arabic. "Allaahu akbar!" (Allah is the greatest!) "Rabbanaa lakal Hamd." (Our Lord, all praise is to you.)

With precious seconds slipping away, Ali and I locked into a stare—the molecules around us vibrating with emotion. Suddenly, a kind of inner peace spread throughout Ali, and he offered up a sweet, quiet expression. He touched a hand to my cheek and spoke to me in a voice that I could only describe as God-like: a powerful whisper. There was only enough moisture in his mouth and on his lips to conjure up two words and no more. He then pushed me away as hard as he could, his small child hands summoning up a man's strength.

As I fell back, he ran off into the next room and slammed the big, iron door so hard that it rattled the plywood sheets covering the windows. They fell to the ground, bringing the full wrath of the sun's light into the room.

Before I could give chase, Raheem grabbed me and held me to the ground. "No! No! It's too late!"

I shouted and reached a hand for Ali, begging for one last second with him, perhaps to see his face, his smile, his innocent eyes. But like I said: time waits for no one.

Now they say a supernova occurs when the inside of a star can no longer support itself. This happens when the star is running out of the fuel that keeps it shining. There was no more love left inside Ali's heart. He had pillaged his soul for every ounce of it and came up empty. There was nothing left to fuel his imagination or his dreams, and that sweet thing that was supposed to bring him life, now fostered only death. His spark had burned out. His body, on the other hand, like the supernova, erupted with a blinding, deafening light. Every window shattered outward in a hailstorm of glass, the concrete walls cracked in every direction and the floorboards flew out of the ground. The iron door buffeted the blast, which shook the bones in my body, forcing my cells to absorb every last bit of the shockwave.

Usually, where there's a supernova, there's a black hole, bringing all reality to a closure. A pinpoint in space where nothing can escape—not even a child's screams. Ironically enough, the gravity of a black hole distorts even *time*, causing it to finally slowdown. And in those still moments fished out from a sea of passing events, I witnessed ghostly images of my youth, running parallel to Ali's. I could hear the distinct sounds of our parents' voices becoming one. I felt the suffocating weight of nostalgia setting in. I could smell the sweet scent of dripping honey and the fragrances of scented oils and palm trees, encased by ferns and coral hibiscus. I could see visions of timeless streets and sun-ravaged limbs and faded Polaroids of faces once brightened by love—long forgotten reminders that smiles weren't just a myth. I witnessed all the cherished memories torn from hands no bigger than rosebuds, and held tight the lifetime of laughter, which I plucked from the wells and kept out of the defiant hands of despair for as long as I could.

Suddenly, the initial shock began to wear off, shifting the atmosphere around me and I could no longer hold onto anything at all. When the truth finally did come into focus it was brutally painful. Just as my eyes shook off the blurry, brain-shattering aura of the explosion, a stream of blood rolled underneath the door and across the slanted floor, lapping about my feet. The peripheral ringing of the ears finally died away, and I looked at the tattered remains of Ali's body through the blown off door and found myself in a waking nightmare. There weren't enough solid pieces left of him to stitch him together. His little limbs had become shrapnel, and his blood splattered on the walls like some cruel inkblot test, where the image could not be mistaken for anything other than death.

No sounds or words were shared between Raheem and I, only a look of utter despair.

As my tiny, insignificant mind tried to understand the extreme enormity of the event, my emotions shut down. Like blowing out a fuse in the fuse box, it was all just too much. I had seen death before, many times, and in many forms, but this transcended anything I had witnessed in my life. The word *impossible* shot through my mind and I tried to hold onto it for as long as I could, in fear that if I let it go, all possibilities would have to be entertained. As long as I could hold onto *impossible*, I thought maybe reality would alter somehow, change, implode, explode, evaporate.

Eventually I had no choice but to accept it. Although I can't say it was total acceptance. I suppose it's the same quality of the brain, which accepts the idea of God, until further evidence is brought to light. It's that part that wants to desperately believe in something, even if that something seems bleak.

I sat there still and silent, bathing in the wisps of smoke that escaped the cinders of Ali's broken body. That's when it dawned on me: Ali was buried underneath the rubble of his family home. We never saved him. Not his spirit anyway. That died with his family at the point of impact. We just carried out his empty shell.

I remember how muted the colors seemed immediately afterward. The city seemed quiet for once. Barren. Lifeless. I felt like I was the only one left on the planet, yet the last one who wanted to be there. The sole-survivor of a race doomed to oblivion.

I turned to Raheem, trying to decipher Ali's last words. "He said, 'Ana emsamhak'. What does that mean?"

Raheem was still in shock.

"Raheem?"

He looked up at me, slowly.

I grabbed him by his collar. "What does it mean?"

His head fell; he was without words.

"Please...tell me, Raheem. Ana emsamhak. What does it mean? I have to know."

He looked up, slowly trying to find the words, his languid eyes finding no rest. Then from his lips, softly fell the words, "I forgive you."

In that moment, there was no soul sadder than me, not in this universe or any other that's ever existed or will ever exist. Although he was just a boy, Ali learned something in his final hour, which takes some people a lifetime to learn. Something I am still trying to learn: forgiveness.

It was once again silent, the kind of silence that comes only after forgiveness: a true silence of the mind. I will always remember it as my quiet, little hell. Then, just like everything else, came the death of silence with the distant sound of shelling, which reminded me that the city was still surrounded by war.

"We must go, quickly." Raheem said, helping me up to my feet. With an arm draped over his shoulder, he assisted me back down the stairs and out of the safe house. "We should be lucky to walk away with our lives."

"I don't feel lucky," I told him, "and this doesn't feel like a victory. We came here as two men and now we're leaving as two. What did we gain?"

Raheem—always the optimist—pointed to his truck, off in the distance, where the little boy that he had brought down, now lay in the passenger seat. "We're leaving with hope."

Even though I would have gladly chosen to face death one more time just to see Ali again, I had been given a second chance to live. I knew there would be others ready and willing to take up Razzaq's mantle, many others in fact, but it wouldn't be Ali, and it wouldn't be this boy either. People like Nadeel and Raheem would make sure of it.

As I got into the truck, Raheem went back and untied the two boys we had left out in the alley. He gave them a chance to change their lives and come back with us. But as I had come to learn over the course of my life, forgiveness isn't for everyone. They ran off before Raheem could even finish his plea.

"They're not ready," Raheem said, getting back into the truck. "Not yet. But hopefully one day."

As we left that hostile place behind, I sat in the passenger seat, literally on the edge of sanity. In my arms, was the nameless boy, unconscious, but alive, breathing his warm breath across the small hairs on my forearm.

Raheem looked at the boy then up at me and said, "You look right at home. Fatherhood would suit you well."

I didn't dispute the comment. It was the first time anyone had ever called me a father, or thought I was worthy of such a title.

We travelled down the deserted road, heading toward the hospital. Through the rear-view mirror, I could see grey plumes of smoke still rising from the safe house. The unruly sun was setting, weaving a tapestry of colors—reds and oranges—mimicking the the cries of the fallen.

I sat there, thinking of broken hearts and mended fences, both of which Ali's last words imbued upon me. *How strong we are, yet how easily we break.* I thought about the rooftop where Ali talked about his life. How he wanted to walk along the earth, across all the great shores, feel the sand under his feet and sing with the waves. He wanted to carry his father's stories and his mother's lullabies to every corner of the earth, every city and small town, and God willing, back home again. But like dust, we had both been swept away; me under the rug, and him into the air, to finally be free.

As he embarked on his new journey, one in which I could not follow, I remembered his eyes and how they were like the moon: always shining in times of darkness. My tense brows finally relaxed and let my tired eyes close. I thought of Ali and how magnificent and brave he was, hoping that I could be half as brave in the face of fear. As the call for prayer rang throughout the city once more, for the first time since I arrived in Iraq, I prayed along with it.

CHAPTER 23

Four days later, Nadeel came out of her coma. She was in bed, hooked up to monitors, tubes and IVs, but the doctor said she was going to be fine. She was in the middle of a conversation with an anonymous man when I came to visit. From the way the man held her hand, I could tell it was *him*: the man she had defended on many occasions, the man that I envied, the one who was better than me, the one she was promised to. He had come in from Jordan to take her back home.

She looked up to see me entering from the hallway, limbs weakened, spirit broken, slowly moving toward her. She lay in bed, sharing her attention between him and me. He got most of it, of course, but I was happy with just a glance here and there, an acknowledgement of my existence.

She made a request, and the man eyed me over his shoulder, then kissed her on the forehead and walked right past me without a word. His eyes said it all though: *This is my woman. Respect that.*

It was an unnecessary request, given the fact that Nadeel had already chosen him over me. But still I honored it. Not for his sake, but for hers.

As I approached her bed, she could feel the weight on my shoulders. Relieving me of some of it, she asked, "What happened?"

But this weight was heavy, and I remember how long it took to lift up. "We found Ali...."

Before allowing any emotions to rush to her face, she waited for me to tell her the specifics.

"He's...he's..." My lips slammed to a halt, not wanting to repeat the horror I had seen, not wanting to relive it. I just shook my head.

She recognized the look on my face. She had seen it before on the faces of mothers, fathers, brothers, sisters. Her eyes quickly filled up with tears. Even though she had seen it before, she couldn't process the reality of it any more than I could.

Taking a hold of my hand, she said, "Ya rab aateny alqwa. Allahuma alhemna assabr." (God give me strength. God grant me patience.)

My legs felt weak. I wanted to collapse, but I stayed strong for her. I looked over my shoulder at the man. "So, he's come to take you back?"

Nadeel rubbed her eyes, not liking where the conversation was going. She composed herself and said, "It's time to meet some of my other obligations: to get married, to start a family."

"What about the orphanage?"

"Raheem said he will take care of things now. And there is Sahar, who's taken a shine to you I might add."

I gave her a wry smile. "She's very beautiful...." I then paused as if to say *not nearly as beautiful as you*. "But...she's a little young."

"You're not that old yourself."

I smirked. "I suppose."

"So what will you do now, go back to America?"

"I don't know."

She looked into my eyes. "I think you do."

I raised a brow. "You can read minds now?"

"I don't have to." She threw a glance toward the door, where the children—all of them—stood in silence, not enough smiles to fill all their dimples. They looked at me with sincerity.

"Love is the only real answer if you ask me," Nadeel said, smiling at them. "Show someone love and they'll discover their vocation, show someone hate and they'll wish they were never born. You have a lot of love inside of you...they'll need it."

As I walked toward the boys, the crowd parted, solemn and silent, nodding and whispering in Arabic.

Nadeel and I shared a reassuring smile. The look on her face was wonderfully sweet; the look of somebody, who regardless of all that had happened, knew that there was a God. Her belief somehow ignited my own, and the strangest thing happened. A reaction, no one, including myself, would have suspected. The answer popped into my mind unexpectedly and I remember letting out a breath and cleansing myself of all the hate, all at once, in one long burst of air. It was like a balloon deflating, releasing all the oxygen, to be filled now with helium. Lighter. Less convoluted. More ambitious. Like someone who had at long last found a home.

I buried my hate, like Nadeel had told me. As a matter of fact, I let it all go: the hate, the neglect, the spiritual bruises, the regrets, everything. And when I left the old me behind, all I kept was the humility. It was the only thing I needed in this new life.

Little Hakim reached out for me and took a hold of my hand. In that moment, it was more than just *his* hand; it represented every hand that needed to be held, to be comforted, to be cared for, to be guided, to be understood. It was every child's hand. It was Ali's hand as well.

That same afternoon, we brought the boy we had saved from Razzaq's safe house to the orphanage, filling the void left by Ali. He limped out of the car and stood in the doorway observing everything. The way he looked at me, anxious yet optimistic, reminded me so much of Ali. He didn't speak, but maybe with time, he would tell me his name.

I approached him slowly. "You're safe here."

He looked about the grounds, his eyes turning, scanning over the boys.

I made the mistake of touching his shoulder and his entire body trembled in fear. I realized my mistake all too late. I pulled away, giving him his space.

He had come to fear men's hands. He had come to know them only as weapons to be used to break, bruise and hurt. With time, hopefully we could earn his trust, and show him that there was in fact good, honest people here, trying to make a difference.

With a simple gesture of the hand, Raheem escorted him up to the boy's room. As he showed him his new bed, I couldn't help but notice Ali's plant lying on the floor, dying of thirst. That plant had gone through the same journey as Ali from beginning to end. It deserved more than to just be left to die under the bed.

I took it out to the courtyard, where Nadeel had planted her roses—a flower for every child that had passed away. She feared that she'd run out of space in the field long before the war was over.

I walked across the field, where Nadeel's roses lay trampled. But a rose is a rose even when trampled; its beauty is still just as evident. As I took a knee and dug a hole for Ali's plant, a cloud moved across the sun, unevenly rationing the light in the courtyard, just out of the plant's reach. In that moment, I swear it moved, as if blown by some invisible wind. Not a single other thing on the ground moved in that moment, not a blade of grass, not a single leaf took to the air, yet that plant swayed into the light, as if choosing light over darkness. I knew it was Ali. He was still there, still watching over me, guiding me, finally giving me some of that innocence that I so badly needed.

They say that everyone perceives time differently, and that the past, present and future are all happening at the same time. Although it hurts to think about, a part of me will forever be there, with Ali, holding him seconds before the blast. The best of him still lives within me, showing me that the world is beautiful just as much as it is terrible, and that the background noise can only drown out the symphony of joy if you let it. I hear his voice through the voices of the other children, always reminding me that hate is for the weak hearted, and that forgiveness will save my soul.

AFTER THOUGHT

Iraq has turned into one of the worst places for children in the Middle East and North Africa with around 3.5 million living in poverty. Since the invasion in 2003, the American occupation forces and the Iraqi government grossly failed to fulfill their most basic duties towards the children of Iraq in accordance with the UN Convention on the Rights of the Child.

About 20% of households surveyed had lost at least one member. According to the Iraqi government, around 4.5 million children have lost one or both parents (almost 1 in 3) and approximately 600,000 children are living on the streets. Each year, around 35,000 infants die before reaching their first birthday. Over 1.5 million children under the age of five are undernourished. Around 700,000 children are not enrolled in primary school, while hundreds of thousands more drop out before graduating. 2.5 million children do not have access to safe water, and 3.5 million lack adequate sanitation facilities.

America has deliberately changed the social fabric of the country, used ethnic cleansing to break up the unity, destroyed water purification systems, health and educational facilities and indiscriminately bombed dense populated areas, leaving the children extremely vulnerable on all levels.

Kentane, Bie. "The Children of Iraq: Was the Price Worth It?"
Global Research, February 19, 2013
BRussells Tribunal and Global Research 7 May 2012